ACTON
PUBLIC LIBRARY
60 OLD BOSTON POST RD.
OLD SAYBROOK
CT 06475
860/395-3184

P9-DFY-093

3 3520 00112498 9

9/15

DATE DUE

BRODART, CO.

Cat. No. 23-221

VIVIAN APPLE NEEDS A MIRACLE

VIVIAN APPLE NEEDS A MIRACLE

by Katie Coyle

Houghton Mifflin Harcourt

BOSTON | NEW YORK

Copyright © 2015 by Katie Coyle

All rights reserved. For information about permission to reproduce selections from
this book, write to Permissions, Houghton Mifflin Harcourt Publishing Company,
215 Park Avenue South, New York, New York 10003.

www.hmhco.com

The text was set in Berling LT Std.

Library of Congress Cataloging-in-Publication Data
Coyle, Katie.
Vivian Apple needs a miracle / Katie Coyle.
p. cm.
Sequel to: Vivian Apple at the end of the world.
Summary: The predicted Rapture was faked by Pastor Frick's Church
of America and 3,000 Believers are now missing or dead. Seventeen-
year-old Vivian Apple and her best friend, Harpreet, are revolutionaries,
determined to expose the Church's diabolical power grab ... and to
locate Viv's missing heartthrob, Peter Ivey. —Provided by publisher
ISBN 978-0-544-39042-3
[1. End of the world—Fiction. 2. Fundamentalism—Fiction.
3. Religion—Fiction. 4. Revolutionaries—Fiction. 5. Missing
persons—Fiction. 6. Coming of age—Fiction.] I. Title.
PZ7.C839492Vl 2015
[Fic]—dc23
2014046783

Manufactured in the United States of America
DOC 10 9 8 7 6 5 4 3 2 1
4500543891

VIVIAN APPLE NEEDS A MIRACLE

PROLOGUE

The Book of Frick 9:1–15

And thus I, the Prophet Beaton Frick, speak to the depraved among you, those evil multitudes whom God will forsake when He brings his chosen Americans into heaven—I address the loose women, sodomites, criminal doctors, malicious socialists, and you who do not strive with all your might to condemn them:

Thou canst be ransomed from thy wicked ways; thou can embrace thy Savior as thy Founding Fathers would have wanted. Never forget this: the island of heaven lies across a deep ocean, but the boat to heaven makes more than one trip.

But fail Him a second time, and you deny yourself the eternal splendor of His kingdom—you condemn yourself to witnessing the apocalypse. You will stand on this earth as it tumbles helplessly into oblivion, and you will hardly notice the planet's dying gasps, because your body will be set upon by beasts of all shapes and sizes. Hellhounds will tear the flesh from your limbs with teeth sharp as razors; vultures will pluck out your eyes should you be fool enough to open them; locusts will fill your every orifice, and you shall feel their dreadful hungry buzzing inside yourself; and you shall know only regret for every heedless moment of earthly pleasure.

In these moments, your painful last, you will try to believe in such a thing as a Savior. But do not let your desperation fool you into clinging to such a story.

For you, there is no such thing.

CHAPTER ONE

I t was right here," Harp says.

We're standing a couple of blocks uphill from my half sister Winnie's apartment in San Francisco, staring at an empty space of curb. A space with no car parked in it. It's early afternoon, and the sky is an unsettling red, like the inside of a blood orange. Harp steps off the sidewalk, moving her hands carefully around the general area where the roof of the car should be. Like it's simply invisible. Like it's still a tangible object in front of us.

"Viv." My best friend turns to me. "I swear—this is where I left it."

A year ago, before Harp and I were friends, when we were just girls who lived in the same neighborhood, one of us timid and aggressively well-behaved (me), the other a whirling dervish of schemes and creative combinations of expletives (her), I might have suspected Harp to be playing an unnecessarily cruel prank on me. But we're coming off the longest night of our lives. We haven't showered, we're tired and frightened, and anyway, Harp has a wild look in her eye, so sharp I can't look directly at it.

"Maybe it's another block up." I scan the stretch of road leading up the hill, looking for the little black sedan that has carried us so far. If I believed in some kind of god right now, I'd pray for Harp to be mistaken. "All these buildings look the same to me."

Harp shakes her head and points to the house behind me. There's a handmade sign propped up in the first-floor window: FRICK IS A PRICK.

"I remember seeing that when I got out of the car," she says. "I laughed for a solid five minutes. Why did we never think of it before? The rhyme. So simple, so powerful."

I try to stay calm. But the car is all we have. With it, we're revolutionaries. If it were here, we'd drive back over the Golden Gate Bridge into the forests of Point Reyes, where Prophet Beaton Frick's secret Church of America compound lies, to find two things: (1) Peter Ivey, the bluest-eyed boy I've ever met, whom we left behind when we escaped; and (2) evidence of the thing we now know to be true: there was no Rapture. The world is not ending, at least not in September, as predicted. The disappearances, the fear and panic, the families torn apart—all of it was engineered by the Church of America Corporation. Because they could do it. Because they could make money off it. Once we had evidence, we'd expose them. And then? There'd be no Church. My life wouldn't go back to normal—it's changed too much— but it isn't hard to believe the lives of others would. With the car, we are the most dangerous teenage girls in America.

But the car's not here. If we've lost it, we've lost everything: suitcases, clothes, most of our money, my diary, Harp's Xanax. My only pictures of my parents—I want them badly now; I want the picture of my dad. It's taken three thousand miles to get to this point, and along the way I've lost everything I've ever owned, and most of the people I've loved. The adrenaline I've been running on since last night fades, and with it, the pain in my hand—the hand I might've broken on the face of Frick—throbs harder. I feel the pinprick of a headache forming between my eyebrows.

"You didn't park here," I tell Harp. "You parked somewhere else. You saw the sign while you were walking."

Harp looks confused. "Are you . . . trying to hypnotize me?"

"You didn't park here!" I mean to sound confident, but my voice comes out shrill. "We'll do a loop around the block. You just thought you parked here. You didn't park here."

She nods uncertainly, and the two of us spring back in the direction of Winnie's apartment. Harp chews the inside of her cheek. I try to calm myself with rationality—what are the odds our car could have been stolen? What are the odds that since this time yesterday, I could have learned the truth about the Rapture, confirmed that my parents were dead, abandoned in the woods the closest thing I've ever had to a boyfriend, learned that actually my mother is *not* dead and has just been chilling in the Bay Area with the half sister I only recently found out about, decided to leave said alive mother in favor of taking down the Church of America alongside my equally pissed and confused best friend, *and* had my car stolen? What kind of vengeful Old Testament shit is this?

"Viv?"

Harp is several paces ahead, but she stops to gape at me. I don't understand why until I hear myself—I'm rooted where I stand, laughing in a gasping, hysterical way, tears streaming down my face. I taste the salt in them. It's not funny, the way Harp looks at me, but for some reason that makes me laugh harder. She takes a tentative step toward me.

"Oh shit, dude," she whispers. "Is this it? Have you finally gone bonkers on me?"

I shake my head. I can't breathe. I want to say, *My dad.* I want to say, *Peter.* But I can't calm down, and if I say their names, it will only get worse. Harp's expression softens, and I can't look at her, because I know she understands. If Harp understands, it's real—I'm not imagining this pain—and if it's real, I'm never going to stop feeling this way. I'm going to hurt this much forever. I tip my head back. I start to feel dizzy, like I've taken a half step outside my body. I have a brief, delirious moment of understanding: This is how I die. Not proudly, not fighting for the things I believe in, but of a panic attack in an unfamiliar city while Harp looks on helplessly.

"I'm really, really sorry about this," I hear her say from somewhere far away.

Then—screaming pain. Everything goes white. I open my eyes. I'm on my knees on the sidewalk, and Harp has my injured hand in hers. She barely touches it now, but I know a second ago she squeezed it. She has a fierce look in her eyes, like she's ready to do it again.

"No, no, no," I gasp. I pull my hand from hers. "I'm okay. I'm okay."

Harp leans down and hugs me. Even in my post-hysterics state, I'm surprised and weirdly touched by her willingness to publicly display affection for me.

"I know how it feels, Viv." Her voice is rough in my ear, and I hold tighter to her. It's only been a few months since Harp's brother, Raj, was murdered by Believers, and if Harp's Raptured parents escaped the fate of my father, we have no idea where they might be. "If we're going to survive it, we have to feel it. Even when we think it'll wreck us. We'll lean on each other. You won't let it wreck me and I won't let it wreck you. I'll be right here, and I'll pull you out of it when you need to be pulled out. Okay?"

I nod. My eyes still stream tears, but I can breathe easier. "Harp?"

"I'm here."

"Next time, please don't literally pull me out by my broken fucking hand, okay?"

Harp pulls back so I can see her grin. "No guarantees, Apple. When I have to pull you out, I'm just going to grab whatever's closest."

| | | | |

The park across from Winnie's apartment is sloping and green; it spans three city blocks. Harp and I climb to its topmost point, where a bench faces the wide expanse of grass. Beyond are rooftops and, in the foggy distance, the spires of the city. We take a moment to breathe. The car is gone. We got tricked somehow, driving through San Francisco this morning—everything was so vibrant, so unlike the huge swaths of Church-dominated country we'd been traveling through. We convinced ourselves we were safe. But of course even a city apparently free of the Church of America contains its own dangers: flaky mothers, startling tidal waves of grief, and—hidden in plain sight—your average everyday run-of-the-mill car thieves.

"What's up with the sky?" Harp asks.

I tip back my head. It looks like sunset, but I don't think it can be that late. We have no way of knowing the exact time, though. We've been relying on the car's clock and Peter's phone, which was still in his pocket when we left him.

"I have no idea. Pollution, maybe? It doesn't look natural. Like

7

you said before"—I remember what Harp told me, not an hour ago—"the apocalypse is coming. Maybe not anytime soon, but it's definitely coming."

We sit that way a while, staring up, trying not to feel discouraged by the magnitude of the task ahead of us. Afternoon fades into evening, and even as the crimson sky looms more ominously overhead, a powerful, winter-cold wind bears down on us. Still dressed for summer, Harp and I get up to walk and warm ourselves.

"On the bright side," Harp notes, observing the neighborhood around us, "this seems like a popular city to be homeless in!"

Now that we're actually seeing San Francisco up close, it's less of a Non-Believer utopia than I initially believed. Winnie's neighborhood seems active and trendy—the blocks Harp and I walk are lined with antique stores, restaurants with puns for names, cheese shops, quaint bakeries. Young men and women bustle past, wearing casual clothes that seem secretly expensive: pre-ripped jeans and thick-framed glasses, tweed blazers. They smoke electronic cigarettes and all seem vaguely tipsy. But the sidewalks are also jammed with a miserable, huddled mass, wrapped in sleeping bags to ward off the evening chill; they're unwashed, unshaven. Adults, children, dogs. There are so many—it feels like there are two for every hip young San Franciscan we see. It's not like I've never seen homeless people before—Pittsburgh had them, of course, and New York, too—but there's something wrenching about these people. Maybe it's just the disparity between these hungry masses and the happy hipsters we see wandering in and out of upscale taco joints.

A furious gust of cold wind makes Harp shudder, and she nods at the coffee shop we're about to pass. "Let's check this out."

Inside are high ceilings and white walls covered in ugly oil paintings of naked women, overlaid with text from the Book of Frick: SHE SHALL BE BURNT WITH FIRE. I think the art's meant to be ironic, but remembering the foreboding statues outside Frick's compound—Peter's father, Adam Taggart, burning a group of women alive—I can't find much humor in it. Everyone here is hunched over a laptop. According to a chalkboard hanging from the ceiling, the cheapest option is plain black coffee for eight dollars.

"There's no way we can afford this!" I catch the eye of the bespectacled barista and see her skeptical assessment of my torn jeans, my messy hair, the broken hand I'm cradling.

"I know," Harp says, guiltily fishing a ten-dollar bill from her pocket. "But I was freezing out there—and it's not like we have anywhere to go."

She orders a drink and we wedge ourselves at a table next to an older man reading the news on his laptop. We pass the coffee back and forth, taking tiny sips. I've never liked the taste, and it seems especially bitter right now.

"The first thing we need to do is get to Peter," I say. "Hopefully he managed to get his dad and"—I hesitate to say the name *Frick*, aware of the man at the next table—"his dad's boss to safety. Once we have them, making the truth public will be easy."

Harp stares deep into the coffee and doesn't speak the reservations I can tell she has.

"At the very least," I continue, "we need to figure out what the corporation has planned for the next Rapture, and what they have planned for the apocalypse. They're clearly willing to kill to make their myths seem true."

"We should figure out who the Three Angels actually are,"

Harp notes. "If we knew, we might understand better what they want to accomplish."

I nod, remembering the people who appeared on the screen in Frick's compound, dressed as angels, ordering him to do their bidding. Two men: one bald and a little pudgy, the other thin with light-gray eyes. One severe-looking blond woman. We assume they work for the corporation, but we don't know their names or positions. Harp clears her throat.

"I know this isn't an ideal solution—" she begins.

But I shake my head. "I'm not going to Winnie's."

"Viv, I get it, I do. You did a big dramatic walkout on your mom and you don't want to come crawling back three hours later. But we don't have a ton of options here. If we're going to do this, we'll need a car. We'll need a place to sleep tonight."

"No, Harp. I made a choice." She sighs in exasperation and looks away, but I continue. "I won't be the person I used to be, and I don't trust myself not to revert back to her when my mother's around. I want to move forward, okay? There has to be somewhere else. A shelter, maybe. Somewhere we can rest without getting caught in the ongoing implosion of my family."

Harp doesn't reply. Her attention has wandered to the screen of the man beside us. I'm about to make a crack about her undiagnosed attention deficit disorder when I realize her expression has gone twisted and scared.

"Harp?"

She glances at me. "That's a great deal they have right now." Her voice is broad and loud. "Buy one caramel macchiato, get a thousand Twitter followers free. What a bargain!"

A group of girls to our left goes quiet, then they leap to their feet. On our right, the man abandons his laptop to storm the counter, along with the occupants of nearby tables. Others, sensing a trend, get up and form a line, much to the alarm of the barista.

"Harp, what—"

"Shhh!" She grabs the abandoned laptop, spinning it so I can see the screen.

The Church of America's news feed is dominated by an enormous headline written in blood-red type, surrounded by animations of enraged-looking angels tossing 3-D thunderbolts at the viewer to underscore the seriousness of the situation:

Enemies to salvation: Immoral and dangerous

Church offers reward of $1 million plus guaranteed salvation to anyone with information on whereabouts

Those found aiding or abetting these felons will face severe judgment when the apocalypse comes

WANTED ALIVE

I've never seen the Church target anyone this aggressively; all the enemies of their early days—liberal politicians, gay pop stars, feminist scholars—they'd simply undermine on the feed and sue into oblivion when the targets fought back. But this sounds like they want someone captured, like they want someone handed over. This headline makes the Church seem like the law. I feel an uneasy prickling at the nape of my neck, because I'm beginning to understand what I'll see when Harp scrolls down.

The picture is grainy black-and-white, magnified from the security feed in Beaton Frick's compound, but you can recognize us easily: a short Indian girl with messy dark hair, a taller white one with bangs in her eyes. Harp and me. Our faces. We're unmistakable.

And we're everywhere.

CHAPTER TWO

The coffee shop is too bright, too crowded. I feel heat emanating from my cheeks, like my face is glowing, a beacon. My brain sends some urgent message to my legs, and before I fully realize it, I'm up and through the door. I hear Harp scrambling to her feet, but I don't wait. Every second we hesitate we become more visible.

Outside, the wind picks up, scattering dust, stinging my eyes with cold. I try to tuck into myself, to shrink. I don't know where I'm going—my instinct is just to get away from that screen. But I must be on thousands of them by now. Walking past these buildings, I glance into open windows and see the ghostly bluish glow of screens inside; it seems impossible they could show anything but my face, spreading like a virus through links on Twitter and Facebook, until every person in America has it memorized.

I've reached the end of the block before Harp catches up. I notice a laptop under her arm that she did not have when we walked into the coffee shop.

"I know, *I know*," she mutters. "I'm aware that petty larceny is not the most inconspicuous way to handle this development, but I panicked, okay?"

I pick up my pace, steering us down a side street—darker, uphill, lined by trees. I don't want the laptop's owner to catch up. My hand throbs. The posting of our faces means no hospital for me. No motels, no stopping at a gas station to ask directions. No food. I didn't realize until this moment how good we'd had it, being anonymous. I didn't realize how much we'd been able to get done. Realistically, I think, we have a small window—maybe until the evening news. After that, our best hope will be to split up. The Church's reach is wider than anyone's—there's no way the two of us together are getting out of this city alive.

"Look, Apple." Harp pauses to catch her breath. "We're in deep shit here. I know you're Vivian 2.0 now; I know you want to move forward. But we need to hide, quickly, before we bump into someone who's seen the feed. Do you think your sister would keep us safe?"

I press my palms to my face—partly to think, partly to feel less exposed. "I don't know. I barely spoke to her. I didn't exactly get a fugitive-abetting vibe from her. She seemed like kind of a goody-goody. She quoted the Bible at me. But I guess I don't think she's actually a Believer. And anyway, my mom will vouch for us. She'll want to keep me safe. But it might only be a temporary solution."

"A temporary solution is better than nothing," Harp says.

"I know. But if Winnie can't be trusted, we'll need a backup plan." I finally lower my hands to look at Harp's worried face. "We'll borrow money from my mom—she's got to have something, right? Then we'll make our way back to Wambaugh's parents' house."

It seems hard to believe that the last time we saw my old history teacher was just yesterday morning, in Sacramento. So much has happened since. But Wambaugh will know we're not actually dangerous; Wambaugh will keep us safe. My head runs through other possibilities—we could return to Keystone and again seek shelter with the New Orphans, among them our old friend Edie; we could move east, searching for anyone who knows us well enough to trust us. But that number is far fewer now. Raj is dead. Dylan Marx, his old boyfriend, is missing. Even if my grandparents survived the hurricane that devastated New York in May, it's highly doubtful they want to see me. If Winnie's apartment doesn't work out, Sacramento is the best option we have.

"Okay." Harp touches my elbow. "Let's move."

I lead us to the top of the hill. I recognize the park ahead, gray-blue in the gathering dusk—we're on Winnie's block again. This morning I walked up to her building, hopeful at the prospect of a sister. But then Mom was there. I still feel a flicker of distrust toward them both, jealous of the bond they've shared these last months, while I mourned a mother I thought was gone forever. But I'm too afraid to let that hold me back. Cars zoom between the park and us, and as their drivers switch on their headlights, we're illuminated in the glow. We keep our chins tucked in to our chests and sprint to Winnie's building. I try the door—locked—and then I press the buzzer for apartment 3.

Silence for a long moment, then a crackle of static. My mother's uneasy voice hits me like a blow. "Hello?"

"Mom," I say. "It's Viv. I'm out here with Harp and we need your help."

Immediately, the buzzer sounds. I push open the door and we burst into the lobby; we retrace my footsteps from this morning. A few hours ago I left my mother here without telling her where I was going, but now she stands at the top of the steps, waiting for

15

us in Winnie's doorway. She wears a blouse buttoned to the collar, and her long red-blond hair hangs loose around her shoulders. It's still a shock to see her alive, after months of trying to get used to her being gone, but I let out a breath I've been holding—we're safe. It's not until I'm eye to eye with her that I notice the expression of intense anxiety on my mother's face.

"What did you do?"

She seems paralyzed with fear, and I stop short. The hair on the back of my neck stands up, the way it did once a few months before the Rapture, when she caught me sneaking in after a tipsy night with Harp—the anticipation of imminent punishment.

"Your face," my mother continues. "Your face is on the Church of America news feed."

"I know. It's a big misunderstanding," I assure her, hoping I sound convincing. "We need to lie low a day or two. I swear we'll get it sorted out."

"What kind of a misunderstanding?" My mother seems at the point of tears. "They're offering a reward, Vivian! A million dollars! This is serious!"

I hesitate. I know I should tell her the truth. But a small part of me fears she's not strong enough to hear it—I fear the news that the Church of America helped kill my father will destroy her. And a bigger part imagines that even if I tell her the truth, she won't believe me. She won't want to believe me. I'm trying to think of another way to dodge the question, but then my mother's face softens. She steps forward and lays her palm against my cheek.

"Listen. You don't have to tell me now. Come inside and settle down. When Winnie gets home, I'll come up with something to tell her—but I know she'll want to help protect you. We'll figure something out, okay? We'll figure this out together."

16

I nod and move into the apartment, but I quickly realize my mother has not moved with me. She stays in the doorway, blocking Harp's entrance. Over her shoulder, I see Harp's eyes grow wide.

"Mom," I say. "Let her in."

"I don't know if that's a good idea, Vivian."

Her voice is quiet, but firm. I move forward and put my hand on her arm. I try to pull her away so Harp can pass through, but my mother doesn't budge. My best friend takes a step back, the fear draining from her expression. A cold resentment takes its place.

"It's not Harp's fault," I say. "What we did was my idea. Okay? If you're going to protect me, you have to protect her, too."

I watch my mother struggle with this. She's never been Harp's biggest fan—"a little too much," she called her just this morning—and I know she's got some lingering Believer in her. *"Honor the Church above all earthly things,"* the Book of Frick says, *"and beyond it your own flesh and blood only. Man has no obligation to fight the wolves scratching at his neighbor's door."* It's not a guarantee my mother would let Harp in even if Harp were an upstanding young citizen, a badge-earning Girl Scout.

"I can't!" Mom practically whispers now. "Vivian, what if they find out I took her in? I could still make it onto the second boat. I could see Ned again. I can't risk that!"

"It's fine!" Harp interjects before I can argue. She tightens her grip on the laptop. "I'll figure something out. I really hope you make it to heaven, Mrs. Apple."

I watch her turn on her heel and stalk down the steps, and though I call her name, I hear the front door slam behind her. I push past my mother to follow, but she grabs my arm.

"Sweetheart, please! Stay. Let me help you work this out.

We'll call the Church of America hotline. I'm sure we can convince them you're no threat to them."

I'm still, disbelieving. "Harp's my best friend."

"I know, honey." Her eyebrows pinch together—she looks, more than anything else, like she pities me. "But she's more trouble than she's worth."

"How can you say that? You don't even know her!"

"I used to be just like her!" Mom practically shouts this; her voice trembles. "And so I know firsthand the kind of destruction she can cause. The kind she already has! I don't want her to take you down with her, Vivian. I love you and you're better than that! I know you don't want to abandon your best friend, but—"

"No, I don't." My heart pounds painfully. "That's the kind of thing *you* do, remember?"

She doesn't get it at first. But then her concerned expression turns to stone and she jerks back, like I've slapped her. I wait for her to slam the apartment door in my face, but she seems too stunned to move. Before I can say anything else, before I can think to apologize, I turn and race down the stairs.

Pushing open the front door, I'm hit with an icy blast of air. The sun has set, and this night in San Francisco feels as cold as Pittsburgh winter. I'm so surprised that at first I don't notice her in front of me, surrounded by three young men. But then I see the whites of Harp's eyes. One man holds her lightly by the shoulder. I wonder if it's an attempt to Magdalene her: a popular custom among good-looking male Believers, to seduce unmarried girls and women and guilt them into converting. But these men don't look like Believers, and anyway, Harp would never fall for such a thing.

The door slams behind me and the men look up. With a lurch,

I realize the man holding Harp has a smartphone in his other hand. He glances at the screen, smirks.

"Is this you?"

He holds the screen out to me and I approach cautiously. I peer at my own face, magnified and pixelated on the phone, as though I'm really curious. My pulse is so loud I'm sure they can hear it. How did they find us so quickly?

"No?" I say, sounding far too uncertain.

Another man laughs and grabs my injured hand. When I cry out, Harp moves, shoving the edge of the laptop hard into the teeth of the man holding her. He reels back, howling, and she goes running down the hill. I wrench myself from the other's grasp, feeling the pain shoot up my arm, feeling it behind my eyes. I run after Harp, catching as I go a brief glimpse of the awful bloody grin of the man Harp attacked.

I hear their shoes slap the pavement behind me, a tug at my hair as one attempts to grab me. I'm dimly aware of a black car halfway up the block screeching and swerving to trace my path. At the curb, Harp slows to see where I am. "Keep going!" I scream. But then the black car zips in front of her, blocking her, and I push myself to reach her just as the passenger throws the back door open. Harp moves to dart around it, but I grab her, because I recognize the woman inside the car, waiting.

"Get in!" Winnie shouts.

We climb in quickly and Harp slams the door shut. The car peels off. I hear a bang on the window as we drive and turn to see one of the men standing in the street with his fist raised.

Winnie watches us catch our breath. She wears a leather jacket and bright red lipstick I'm sure she didn't have on when she left her apartment this morning. I glance beside her. The driver is small and curly-haired—in the rearview mirror I see her blue-framed glasses and freckled nose.

"And to think for a moment I honestly thought," Winnie finally says, unable to keep the amusement out of her voice, "that my long-lost baby sister had come all the way to San Francisco just to pay me a visit. I'm Winnie," she tells Harp, sticking out a hand.

"Harp." My best friend shakes it, startled.

"Where are you taking us?" I ask once I can breathe.

"Somewhere you'll be safe," Winnie replies. "Listen, maybe we can circle back to the pleasantries in a bit, because right now I'm dying to know—how *exactly* did you manage to get yourself on the Church of America's shit list?"

Another shock of cold fear—Winnie has seen the feed too. Is there anyone in this city who hasn't? When I look at my half sister, I see she has a wry look in her eye. This morning in my haze of grief and envy, I'd taken her to be prim and a little precious, like a hipster kindergarten teacher. But now her personality seems like a different beast entirely: bold and playful and a tiny bit reckless. I'm confused. Was she playing a part this morning, or is she playing one now?

"I'm . . . not sure what you're talking about."

Winnie smiles. "Vivian, I appreciate that you're in a situation here. You probably don't feel inclined to trust a relative stranger—no pun intended—but really, I'm here to help. I *can* help. It's just nice to know *why* I'm helping."

"I didn't ask for your help."

The driver laughs. "Little sis is *feisty*, Win. But I'd guess you'd have to be to piss off the Church as much as she has."

"Yeah, Birdie, let's definitely go with 'feisty.'" Winnie's voice is still light with sarcasm. "That sounds a lot nicer than 'a real pain in the ass.'"

I feel a retort on the tip of my tongue but stay silent. I *am* being a pain in the ass—I know it. I feel a fierce urge to punish Winnie for the mistakes our mother has made. It isn't fair, and I can't afford to indulge in these newfound bratty little sister instincts. We've only been driving a few minutes, but when I glance out of the window, I see we're far from the affluence of Winnie's neighborhood. Outside is a park, bigger and wilder than the tame patch of green across from her apartment. On the other side of the street are houses abandoned or in disrepair, and the sidewalks in front of them appear to have become a mini civilization— dirty nylon tents set up in small circles, dark figures surrounding meager bonfires. San Francisco is in a desperate state. Harp and I are not safe wandering around it blind with a million-dollar reward on our heads.

"How do you know we'll be safe where you're taking us?" I ask, trying to keep it from sounding like a challenge.

"Fair question," Winnie replies with a nod. "I'll give it to you straight—Birdie and I are part of an organization dedicated to the destruction of the Church of America. A kind of volunteer militia."

I feel Harp glance sharply at me, but I'm too shocked to look back at her. For months, the only resistance movement I've been aware of has been the hapless New Orphans. The discovery of another, and the fact that Winnie is a part of it, plants a seed of hopeful energy in me. But the word *militia* makes me pause—is she saying she actually means to do battle?

"We have a wealthy benefactor funding our efforts," my half sister continues. "She works hard to keep our operation hidden.

I always monitor the Church's feed. Luckily, I saw the picture of you the second it posted. I left for home the second I did."

"We appreciate it," Harp says. "Right, Viv?"

I nod, overwhelmed. Winnie waves a dismissive hand. "Truly our pleasure. Anyone the Church is looking for, I'm happy to help hide. But still . . . do you mind telling us what happened? We could protect you better if we know what we're up against."

I feel as though my head is spinning. I want to trust Winnie— I'm working hard to trust her—but something holds me back. Right now our information is our only currency, and I'm afraid to give it all away at once. Especially since I don't yet understand who Winnie is working for, or what kind of work she does. I take a breath.

"Last night, Harp and I broke into a secret Church compound outside the city. I guess it must be very secret, because they sent people to capture us. We barely made it out alive."

"Where's the compound?" Birdie's voice is eager.

"Not sure, exactly. North of here, in a forest—maybe an hour away?"

"That's . . . interesting." Even in the dark, I can see Winnie's suspicious expression. She already knows me well enough to know I'm not telling her everything. "Can you tell me what you saw there?"

I pause like I'm trying to remember, then shake my head. "I don't know. I'm really tired. It's all fuzzy right now."

"I ask because I imagine it'd be the same compound to which Mara and your dad were summoned—the place they were going to receive Frick's blessing, pre-Rapture."

I look up at Winnie, surprised. Somehow I forgot she was standing in the room this morning as my mother told me her whole sorry ordeal.

"I'd never heard Mara's story until today," she explains. "She showed up about a week after the Rapture, no explanation. She led me to believe she'd hopped a plane to San Francisco after being left behind. But I had a feeling there was more to the story—I wonder if she even realizes how much."

"So the last known location of the Raptured was this compound? No wonder the Church wants you dead." Birdie laughs gloomily. "How'd you find it? How'd you even know it existed?"

I open my mouth to answer, but my throat goes dry. I don't want to tell them about Peter. Somehow he feels like the most valuable piece of information I have. *There's a boy, and his name is Peter, and he likes me, and we don't know where he is.* I touch the pendant of my sledgehammer necklace and feel relief when Harp answers for me.

"We got a tip from the New Orphans in South Dakota," she says, not exactly lying.

"The New Orphans gave you that info?" Birdie sounds shocked. "Shit."

"I've heard about that chapter," says Winnie. "Goliath, right? He's supposed to be a visionary. Built a powerful anti-Church sanctuary in the middle of one of the sacred sites. I wonder if we could recruit him . . ."

"Depends on the quality of your coke supply, I'd guess," Harp mutters.

I don't want to answer any more questions about Frick's compound—I'm not sure how long I can feign ignorance. "So what more can you tell us about this 'militia' of yours? Or is it too top secret for our tender civilian ears?"

Birdie laughs again. In the glow of a passing streetlamp, I see Winnie grin.

"I can give you the basics," she says. "Our benefactor, Amanda

Yee, recruited us over the last year, based on a shared commitment to taking down the Church. Amanda funds the operation, keeps us hidden from the community at large, and plans future attacks."

"When you say 'attacks' . . ." I trail off, not sure how to proceed.

"Am I saying that we kill people?" Winnie supplies. I notice a tartness in her tone—some annoyance or defensiveness I can't quite decipher. "That's not outside the realm of possibility. But our scope is pretty broad."

She pauses. I realize she doesn't intend to elaborate further. I glance out my window at the tent cities lining the block. "I guess your benefactor's pretty rich?"

"Very. But not as rich as she could be. Amanda's a genius; she'd founded half a dozen tech startups by the time she was twenty-one. Two years ago, the Church tried to buy her most successful venture. Surveillance software—very powerful, dangerous in the wrong hands. They offered billions. But Amanda said no. She knew what the Church would use it for. She sold it to another company for slightly less; then the Church turned around and bought them."

The road ends, and Birdie turns right; now beyond my window lies the Pacific Ocean, vast and dark, the full moon's reflection sparkling. Harp presses closer to stare across me.

"But that wasn't enough for them—they were angry she turned them down. I imagine it was a slap in the face, to have been spurned by a successful young female." Winnie hesitates; then her voice goes cool. "About a week after the company Amanda sold to was folded into the Church, she and her partner were attacked outside their home. Her partner died. Amanda suffered a spinal injury—she doesn't walk anymore. There's no proof the Church arranged it—there never is—but it was enough to convince her to funnel her money into something more powerful than an app."

Listening to Winnie, I feel a flare of righteous understanding. All day I've been trying to bury thoughts of my father, for fear that if I let myself start to grieve him, I'll never be able to stop. But Amanda's story has brought it all to the surface: My father is dead. The Church killed him. Maybe I used to be the sort of person who could work to forgive them, but I know at this moment that I'm not anymore. I have the distinct impression that Amanda's militia is a force far more dangerous than the New Orphans—as violent as they are organized. And right now, with no idea where Peter is or what is being done to him, I can understand the appeal of such a weapon. In the dark, I curl my good hand into a fist.

The car climbs an incline, the road hugging a rocky cliff side on our right. There's an orange barrier, a sign reading ROAD CLOSED, but Birdie blithely swerves around it up the cliff. The other side of the road drops steeply down to a beach and, beyond that, the inky ocean. Before us is a large, bone-gray building, half of which rests on the level of the road, half of which hangs below, built into the cliff this road travels up. On the roof are thin letters spelling out CLIFF HOUSE. Birdie slows and parks.

Harp and I follow Winnie out of the car and down a few yards to the edge of the cliff beyond the building. The cold is even more bitter by the sea, and Winnie grimaces in solidarity when she sees me shiver. "I'll bring you some layers as soon as I can. It's been like this for months now: inexplicable red sky during the day, freezing temperatures at night. Really makes you feel optimistic about the earth's future, doesn't it?"

When we reach the cliff's edge, I stop in my tracks. Beside me, Harp gasps. It's hard to understand exactly what we're looking at. At our feet is a long, green downward slope giving way at last to a flat pool of still water, the moon casting a weird glow on its surface. The pool is separated from the white crash of the Pacific by a low rock wall. Beyond the pool are weird stone structures and, above them, cliffs higher and steeper than the ones on which we stand. Behind us, before she heads into the place called Cliff House, Birdie explains that this used to be the site of a popular old-fashioned bathhouse that burned down long ago—we're looking at the ruins of its largest pool. It's strange and beautiful. I see small figures pacing the rock wall. One turns in our direction and stops, waving up at us. Winnie waves back, then turns to me, a shy smile playing across her features. She looks so much like my mother at this moment, I could cry.

"Hey, little sis—want to meet my boyfriend?"

CHAPTER THREE

Winnie leads us along the cliff's perimeter and down a sloping, sandy path overgrown with wildflowers. The man who waved makes his way to us, pausing periodically to consult in murmurs with one of the shadowy figures.

"Oh, baby," Harp mutters when we can see his face. He's extremely good-looking—tall, graceful, golden-skinned, with dark eyes and black hair cropped close to his head, a disarming smattering of freckles across his nose.

"Vivian, Harp," Winnie says, once he's reached us. "This is Diego, Amanda's second-in-command. Diego, this is Vivian Apple—Mara's daughter—and Harp."

Diego steps forward and stares at me for an uncomfortable moment. "Yeah, I see it. You guys have the same eyes, pretty much. You probably think they're brown, right?"

"Uh . . . yes?"

"So does your sister. They're actually a gorgeous green. Hints of brown, sure, but definitely green. I don't know why either of you insists on calling them brown—false modesty? Genuine stupidity? And *you're* trying to hide them beneath your hair." Diego glances at the bangs falling into my eyes, and, flustered, I push them back.

"Oh, for God's sake, D.," mutters Winnie, but I see her mouth twitch.

"I'm sorry you're colorblind, Win," he says, moving to sling an arm across her shoulders. "I'm sorry you'll never be able to fly a plane, which I know is your lifelong dream."

Winnie laughs. They're so easy and happy together; they're good-looking and dangerous and impressively grown-up. Just being near them makes me feel so alone. I want Peter. I want to know where he is; I want him here. I want to stop the awful loop of possibilities that has played in my brain all day: Peter running scared through the wilds of Point Reyes; Peter beaten and bloody, the Three Angels closing in; Peter dead.

I have to distract myself. I nod at Diego and ask Winnie, "Does Mom know about him?"

She looks amused. "No, Mara doesn't know I'm in a relationship with a man planning a violent coup against the Church of America. Somehow, it hasn't come up. Sorry, love." Winnie turns to Diego, affecting a pitying look. "The fact is, I'm ashamed of you."

Diego smiles. "I've never been good with parents."

"In fact," Winnie continues, glancing back at me, "Mara knows nothing about my involvement with this. As far as she's concerned, I'm only a saintly social worker, finding suitable homes for the poor left-behind babies. Which, in a way, I am! But what she doesn't realize is that I'm finding the kids secular homes, where they'll be safe from the Church. I doubt Mara would be *thrilled* if she knew, so next time you see her, please don't mention it."

I feel something constrict inside me. "Yeah, I don't think that will be an issue."

"No?"

I don't want to talk about it, but Harp explains. "When we saw ourselves on the feed, we went to your apartment. But Mrs. Apple was a real see-you-next-Tuesday to me, and then—"

"We fought. She wouldn't let Harp in." I'm amazed at how cold and controlled my own voice sounds. "I wasn't going to stay there if she wouldn't let Harp in."

The laughter drains from Winnie's face. "I wondered why you were out on the street. Why you weren't inside. I didn't realize— Viv. That sucks. I'm really sorry."

She reaches to touch my hand. But her skin is cold from the wind, and I struggle to feel comforted by it. I know it's like she's throwing me a rope; she's attempting to pull me onto safe, dry land. Maybe she really wants to be my sister. And I want to accept the gesture, to let her in. That would be the nice thing to do, the right thing to do. All I have to do is speak, or smile, and we'll be on track. But I just can't. I think of the hard look in my mother's eyes the moment before I ran. I'll work alongside Winnie; I'll be as friendly as I can be. But I never want anyone who claims to love me to look at me like that again.

After a long moment, Diego clears his throat. "So . . . a million dollars, huh? That's hardly standard practice. What exactly did you do?"

"They found the compound Mara mentioned this morning," Winnie replies when I don't answer. "North of here; they're not sure where. They broke in and the Church chased them out."

Diego's eyebrows rise. "And?"

Winnie looks at me. I can tell she still suspects me to have more information than I'm letting on, but she doesn't seem to want Diego to know it. He gives me an appraising look, then turns it on Harp, who I see bristle. "And *what?*" she snaps.

"The Church has about ten dozen secret compounds," Diego explains, "so why would they be so public about wanting to find a couple of girls who stumbled over one?"

"Who knows?" Harp sounds breezy—she is, I note gratefully, a better liar than I am, even if she doesn't understand why I lied in the first place. "They also worship a text that claims Jesus can travel through space and time in a powder-blue convertible, so I've personally stopped looking for logic in their actions."

Diego's expression gets stony. Like Winnie, he's unconvinced. "You do realize how weak the Church of America looks, hunting you down like this? How fallible? They're willing to let every Believer know that the weakest possible entities—children, *female* children—pose a threat to them. If it means finding you, they're willing to look destructible. They wouldn't take the risk if the only thing they're looking to hide is a compound."

Harp looks at me, and though her expression stays blank, I know the mere fact of her looking has tipped our hand. I continue to keep my mouth shut. Diego moves toward me, taking my right forearm into his hand—when I try to pull away, he holds on tight.

"What happened here, Vivian?"

I look down. The pain hasn't subsided since the man on the street grabbed my hand, but in the excitement it's somehow become just another fact about my otherwise hunted, threatened, dangerous body. I notice how swollen my hand has become. I look up at Diego and see something I didn't notice before—an undercurrent of danger. A silent, reluctant message that he's someone I do not want to cross.

"You know something." He keeps his voice low. "You can tell

me what you know or not, but I don't like lies, Vivian. If you're going to lie, I'm going to have my people fix up your hand and then I'm going to send you on your way. I'll think of you fondly— I'll worry about you—but I won't be lied to."

I shiver. I don't like how quickly Diego has shifted from playful to threatening; I don't like the way he used his strength to overpower me. I didn't like the tone in his voice when he called us *female children*.

"What we know," I tell him, "is all we have at this point. If I tell you, you have to understand that it's part of an exchange. Not a gift."

Diego lets go of my arm. "Hard to understand the terms of the exchange without knowing the information. What if I promise you something big and you give me nothing?"

Harp laughs. "It's not nothing. You better believe it's not nothing."

"They asked for us alive," I say loudly, trying to make myself heard over the crash of the nearby ocean and the blood pounding in my ears. "But if they get their hands on us, we won't stay that way. If you want to know what we know, I need you to swear to me you can keep Harp and me safe. That you'll do everything in your power to keep us hidden from the Church of America. If you can't guarantee that, we're leaving and taking our information with us." I squirm uncomfortably—Diego has fixed me with a wide, unreadable grin. "What? Why the fuck are you smiling?"

"Because you're so like Winnie, it's actually spooky. You both clearly possess the take-no-shit gene." He sizes me up for a long moment. Then he puts out his hand. I force myself to pause before I put out my left hand to take it.

"Vivian Apple," Diego says. "I swear to—not God. What should I swear to?"

"The universe," I supply without hesitation.

"The universe," he echoes seriously. "Vivian Apple, I swear to the universe that I'll keep you safe. I'm going to keep you safe because you're young and innocent"—I scoff at this, but he ignores me—"and you deserve to be safe. I'm going to keep you safe because I think we want the same thing, which is to finish the Church of America once and for all. But do you know the main reason why I'm going to keep you safe?"

"What?"

"Because I love your sister." Diego lets his eyes wander away from mine, over to Winnie's face. He continues to hold tight to my hand. "And I have a feeling she wants me to."

Beside me, Harp snorts. "Oh God, we *get* it," I hear her say. But Diego's words have a potent effect. I've never been someone's sister before, and it seems as though being Winnie Conroy's is a particularly valuable identity if it buys me the protection I need, if I can use it to find Peter, if I can use it to hurt the people who have hurt me. I glance at Winnie and see she's watching me closely. I turn back to Diego.

"Frick wasn't raptured. He's alive," I say. "So is Adam Taggart."

He flinches. Winnie gasps, then looks to Harp as if for confirmation. Harp tosses her messy hair and grins.

"Those dudes are alive as *fuck*," she exclaims. "Breathing, blinking—the whole deal."

"But that's . . ." Winnie shakes her head, letting it sink in. "You actually *saw* them? They were just there, hanging out in the forest?"

"They're being held there," I say. "The corporation is keeping them under surveillance. They're both insane. Frick didn't know what he was saying, but he told us the Rapture was faked. The Church of America summoned a couple hundred Believers

32

to the compound and killed them. They told Frick it was sacrifice. While we were there, he got a message from three people we didn't recognize. He said they were angels, that they had orchestrated the whole thing. We think, basically, that Frick predicted the Rapture, and once people started to believe, the corporation made money. They had to make the Rapture happen to keep people believing. So they did."

Winnie seems speechless. She raises a hand to her mouth. Diego's brow is furrowed.

"There are three thousand people missing," he says, like he's trying to think it through. "If a few hundred went to the compound, where did the rest go?"

"That we don't know," I tell him. "We have no idea where to begin looking for them."

They stare at us for a moment I fear will go on forever, before they finally turn to each other. To my surprise, Winnie laughs.

"I mean, we *knew* it, right?" She runs a hand through her long red-blond hair. Her eyes look a bit wild. "It's not like all those people could just be *gone*. But that it all happened an hour away? Frick's been that close the whole time? That's just unbelievable to me."

Diego rubs his jaw. "Where is the compound?"

"Point Reyes. But we stumbled onto it. I don't know if we'd be able to find it again."

"Don't worry about that. We'll take care of that." Then he grins again. "Not to criticize, Vivian, but you undersold that information. For that information, I would have protected you and your best friend and your dog and basically everybody you've ever met in your entire life. That information, my friend, is everything."

I smile weakly. But I'm beginning to feel a growing ache near the base of my spine, the result of keeping my posture so rigid. The effort of keeping my guard up has worn me down. Diego nods toward Cliff House and says, "Let's get that hand looked at." He leads the three of us up the steps, and I feel a gnawing revulsion, a shuddery feeling deep in my bones, at the thought of anybody touching me for any reason at all.

CHAPTER FOUR

Inside Cliff House, the lights are off.

I think at first there must be some kind of problem—a power outage, or something more sinister—but Diego ushers us forward, explaining that they keep the lights off at night to avoid notice from passing ships. As my eyes adjust, I see the huge windows lining the back wall, overlooking the dark horizon. Amanda's militia has converted what seems like a former restaurant into something between a command center and a home—to our right is a balcony, looking down on a space crowded with beds, and to our left is a section functioning as an office, with desks and laptops. I notice people dressed like soldiers moving around, dark shadows holding flashlights they point at the floor. I don't know what I expected the nucleus of this billion-dollar operation to look like, but this is not it.

Diego leads Harp and me over to a woman with short salt-and-pepper hair and thick horn-rimmed glasses. Her name is Frankie; she was a doctor before she joined Amanda's army. Diego briefly explains the situation—even in the dark, I see her go pale at his quick description of the faked Rapture; he tells her there will be a strategy meeting in ten minutes. Then he wanders away with Winnie, speaking in murmurs I can only just make out: ". . . tonight? Do we have enough intel?" "Research . . . ask Suzy . . . can't be that hard, if they did it."

Frankie leads me behind a bar left over from the building's previous function; the shelves underneath are piled with medical supplies. She lifts my arm and tests my fingers until I inhale sharply through my teeth in pain.

"Well, you certainly did a number on these guys," she says cheerfully. "Luckily, it seems like a sprain rather than a break. What happened? Did you fall on it?"

"She punched Beaton Frick's face last night," Harp bursts out proudly.

Frankie gives me an appreciative look. "Badass." She gets me to relax my fingers, then places a thick wad of gauze beneath them and tapes them together. "Well, I'm sure it hurts, but you were smart not to go to the hospital."

"Why?"

"You don't know about the Church health care initiative?" At my blank look, Frankie groans. "Lucky you. In the last month, the corporation bought most of the major health insurance companies. The premiums are higher than ever, and really, it's just another way to keep Believers in line. You know—no abortions, no birth control, no assisted suicide. It's a pretty genius way to convince your faithful following that their bodies don't belong to them. Anyway, all hospitals do surveillance for the Church now—I imagine they got your picture even before it went up on the feed. There's no way you could have gotten in and out without getting recognized."

Once Frankie has tightly swaddled my hand, she closes the first-aid kit and walks around the bar to the center of the room, joining the circle that gathers around Diego. Harp and I move to follow, but when Diego spots us, he shoots Winnie a look and she comes rushing toward us, a tablet balanced on her forearm. She beckons us to follow her and, a little dazed, we do. She leads us down a staircase and into the sleeping area. Winnie gestures to two empty beds and explains, "Diego has to brief everyone, and we need updates on a few individual projects. Why don't you take this time to get some rest?"

She beams at us and races back up the steps before I can object. I can hear Diego's voice above us, but from this distance I can't make out a word he's saying. Harp sprawls on her stomach on one of the beds, snatching up an old issue of a Church of America magazine someone's left lying around. I recognize the cover—we devoured it months ago back in Pittsburgh, laughing over lists like "100 Reasons Demure Girls Have More Fun!" and "How to Tell If Your Best Friend Is Doomed to Eternal Torments in the Pits of Hell!" Now, staring at the shyly smiling ingénue on the cover, I feel a surge of rage. I reach out and yank the magazine from Harp's hands.

"Uh . . ." Harp watches in bemusement as I throw the magazine across the room. "I *was* about to take a 'Which Biblical Female Are You?' quiz, but that's cool, Viv, you know. Gotta practice your fastball."

"When I think of how many issues we bought *ironically*, that every penny of it went into the corporation's pockets—that they used that money to . . ." I can't finish. I close my eyes, try to make my breaths come out slow and even. "I'm glad we found these people. I hope so hard that when we go back to the compound, the Three Angels are waiting for us. I want to see their faces when they see us coming. I want to watch Diego mow them down. I want to help."

I open my eyes and see Harp staring at me with an inscrutable expression. "He can't mow them down," she says. "Not tonight, anyway. We have to go public. We have to make them tell the world what they did."

"Who cares, as long as we get rid of them?"

"I care, Viv." Harp frowns now. "And you should too. Look, I get that you're angry. We're all angry. But I'll be honest—I don't like this side of you. Seriously, you should have heard yourself out there: 'Swear to me'! 'Why the fuck are you smiling'! It was like an action movie. Not a good one." She pauses. "The goal is not to hold on to this secret. Just because we're the ones who found it out doesn't mean it belongs to us. The only way to take down the corporation is to get the truth into as many heads as we can reach."

"People won't believe us."

"Diego and Winnie just did. And people have believed weirder things."

I know that what Harp's saying makes sense, but still I feel this bloodthirsty itch—new and strangely satisfying. "Since when," I say, "are you about *not* taking action? I thought we weren't going to be meek anymore."

"This isn't meekness. This is caution. We don't really know anything about these people. I like Winnie, but . . . you heard how she avoided answering you when you asked her about their attacks. That shit was shady, man. I don't know. I want a better reason to trust Diego than the fact that he loves the sister you've only known for a day."

"We know them better than we knew Goliath," I reply. "And I don't remember you hesitating to put your faith in *him*."

Harp's mouth twists into an angry knot. She lies back to stare at the ceiling. I feel a rush of remorse, and I'm about to apologize, but she speaks before I'm able, and her tone is odd.

"Viv. We need to talk about something else."

"What?"

"Our faces were the only ones on the feed. You saw it. Peter's not on there. They didn't post his picture; they didn't say anything about there being a boy with us, an accomplice."

"So?"

"So . . ." Harp sits up. "For the picture of us to exist, they watched the security feed. They saw all three of us. There's no way they could have missed Peter. I'm worried that if they're only looking for us, that means they've already got him."

My stomach drops. I lower myself to sit beside Harp. I've been so wrapped up in everything that's happened since we escaped — my mother, Winnie, the danger we're in — that it never occurred to me to wonder about Peter's absence from the feed. The only thing that's kept me from falling apart is the sliver of possibility that he is on the run, just like we are.

"I can't see what else it would mean," Harp whispers. "If they didn't have him, he'd be in the picture. The only other reason he wouldn't be . . ." She shakes her head. I wait for her to continue, but she doesn't.

"What? What's the other reason?"

"I don't think—" Harp falters again. "I mean, there isn't one."

But somehow I realize what she doesn't want to say, and I'm torn between being so angry at her I can hardly see straight and a fear that turns my fingers numb.

39

"The only other reason Peter wouldn't be in the picture," I supply, "is if the Church isn't looking for him. Because they don't need to. Because he stayed behind last night to join them."

"I'm not saying that! Not exactly! I'm only saying we have to prepare ourselves for anything. Maybe Peter escaped; maybe he's got Frick and his dad and he's on his way to the nearest TV station to prove the Rapture was faked, to take down the Church single-handedly. That's what I want, Viv. That's my dream scenario. But the fact that he isn't on the feed like we are makes me think it's not what happened. Either he got caught, or . . . he didn't."

"And if he didn't, he's a traitor," I drawl. "If he didn't, I just spent the last month batting my eyelashes at a psychopath."

"Viv—"

"Harp, I love you. I don't want to fight. But you sound completely paranoid. I know you have your suspicions about Goliath, but this is Peter we're talking about." I shake my head. "Remember Nevada? Remember how he let that crazy Believer beat him senseless just so we could escape? If he's working for the Church, he's not doing a good job of it."

After a moment, Harp gives me a weak smile. "You're probably right. Sorry, Viv—I'm just freaked out by the feed, I guess. I wish so hard we weren't on it."

I wish it too. But at the same time I realize that all we would have had to do to continue going undetected by the Church was nothing. It was our own defiant actions that brought us to this point. And though the consequences are huge and terrifying, I can't regret the actions themselves. I'm about to tell her so when I see movement on the balcony above—Diego.

"Ladies?" he calls down. "Would you mind joining us?"

Harp and I exchange a look, a silent agreement to talk more later. We walk up together. I know she's not totally convinced about Peter, and that her doubts are born out of love for me. I'd do the same for her; I *have* done the same. There's not a single person Harp's made out with this year whom I've not vocally suspected to be a Church of America sleeper agent. But I can't, I *don't* believe Peter lied to us. Even if it means the Church has him, I won't believe he lied to us. I glance down at the necklace he made me—he spent all that time whittling a tiny sledge-hammer out of wood, because he thought it would make me happy, because he thought it would help me be strong. No one can lie as well as that.

Can they?

Diego waits at the center of the room above in a soldier's stance. The militia forms a semicircle around him. I watch them watch us approach. I only recognize Birdie and Frankie. Winnie appears to be gone. Diego nods as he sees me looking for her.

"She went to check on Mara," he explains. "We don't know if the Church realizes your mom escaped the Rapture—if they do, they might be looking for her. Don't worry—Winnie will be back tomorrow for our morning meeting. She'll update you then."

"Great." I wonder if he hears the acid in my voice. I haven't considered the possibility that my mom might be in danger, and I'm glad Winnie's looking out for her, but the thought of their cozy evenings at home together makes me want to run at full speed through Cliff House's windows.

There are over fifty people in Amanda's army, but Diego only introduces us to his core team: Robbie, a boy who can't be more than thirteen, who peers at us from beneath shaggy blond bangs; Elliott, mustachioed and older than our dads, who gives Harp an unnerving wink; Colby, the tallest person in the room, who stands straighter than even Diego; Julian, long-limbed and fidgety, who turns out to be Diego's cousin; Suzy, tall and curvy

41

and pigtailed; Karen, a bubbly woman around Frankie's age who makes a point to say the word *welcome;* and Kimberly, who has a curly black halo of hair and a long, intimidating rifle strapped across her back, who greets us with "What up, ladies?"

When introductions are complete, Diego turns to Harp and me. "A team of us will breach the Point Reyes compound tonight. We don't want to waste time—it's possible the Church has already taken steps to destroy it now that you've seen it. We want to thank you for this info—it's a big step in the right direction for us. Now, I'm sure you're exhausted, so please get some sleep. I'll fill you in as much as I can in the morning."

A handful of soldiers breaks away to head for the front door. Diego has already turned away when I call out, "Wait! I'm not tired. I want to come with you!"

When he faces me again, I see the slightest hint of irritation in Diego's eyes. "That wasn't part of our agreement, Vivian. I'm sorry."

"But . . ." I'm confused; I feel like I've been tricked. There's no way I'm not going into that forest again—I won't let anyone but myself find Peter. "You don't know what you're looking for! How do you plan to find this compound you didn't know about until an hour ago?"

There's a cough beside me, and when I turn, Suzy waves. "I hacked into the tax returns of local Church branches and found a few million set aside for construction—fall, two years ago. Then I matched that with a public works notice about Point Reyes—a *very* specific press release that went out at the same time, claiming an outbreak of rabies-infected rats." She shudders. "They've put out the same notice every month since: still dealing with the rats, here are the coordinates to avoid. That whole area's been closed to the public for the last two years—it's a perfect place to hide a compound, if you've got a compound to hide." Suzy grins. "You have to give them points for creativity."

"Okay. But look, we *want* to go. We want to see this through. We can handle ourselves. Please, Diego, this is important to us!"

He sighs. "Vivian. I appreciate that you and Harp have some real balls between you, but I'm sorry—I'm not going to take a couple of teenage girls along just for the hell of it. This is a dangerous mission, okay? This isn't a trip to the mall."

Harp makes an indignant noise. "You're taking that little boy with you!" she says, pointing at Robbie, who scowls at us as he passes with his gun.

"Robbie is trained in combat," Diego replies.

"You wouldn't have this information without us," I say firmly. "I don't know what this Amanda person had planned before we told you about the faked Rapture, but surely this changes it. We're a part of this now, and we intend to come with you."

He assesses me for a long moment. If he refuses again, I don't know what I'll do. I'll steal one of the cars parked in front of Cliff House; I'll race back to the compound myself. But I will not sit here and kill time while Peter's in trouble. I don't know if Diego's convinced by some fire he sees in me or just cognizant of the pressure of time, but he finally sighs. "You'll do exactly as I say and nothing more. Do you understand?"

Birdie and Frankie lend us dark jeans and black jackets to replace the summery clothes we've been wearing for nearly two days now. We bundle into the back seat of Diego's car alongside Suzy; Julian rides shotgun. Another car carrying Colby, Robbie, Kimberly, Birdie, and Elliott drives behind us. Within moments, the Golden Gate Bridge towers above as we cross to the Point Reyes side. The mood is tense; the only voice speaking is the GPS on Suzy's phone. I shiver against Harp, even though the windows are shut tight against the cold night air. We're headed back to the place my father was killed, back to the place where we last saw Peter. I'm scared as hell, but I can feel my pain transforming with every passing second into angry energy.

After about an hour of the automated voice's directions, the dark forest swallows us up on either side. Suzy consults the map.

"After about three miles, you'll hit a side road without a name. Take a left there, and after another four miles, park. That'll put us in the vicinity. We'll head in on foot after."

I press my face to the car window, trying to make out something familiar, but all I see are black trees whipping past. I remember how I felt trudging through the forest last night. Like someone was watching. I hope they can see me now, whoever they are: the Three Angels, or the larger faceless mass of the corporation. I hope they see me coming and I hope they tremble.

Finally, we park and step into the frigid air. It takes time, but eventually Julian finds a clearing in the trees. Suzy leads us through it. She holds her phone in front of her and every few minutes raises a hand in the air, then changes direction. We walk in a tight huddle. I'm amazed by how silent everyone is, how gracefully they move through the solid dark. I try to mimic them, but I'm distracted by hope. *Let Peter be here, alive, okay. Let Peter be here, alive, okay.* I try to imagine him hiding in the trees: sore, bruised, exhausted, but alive. I try to imagine the smile he'll give me when he sees me. I hold on to the thought of it because the alternative makes my knees buckle.

Last night it took hours to find Frick's compound in the clearing. Tonight we trudge through the forest no longer than forty-five minutes before the trees in our path give way to open space. Suzy consults her phone, stops walking.

"Well," she says uncertainly. "It's within the coordinates."

I can't see over Colby's head, so I push to the front of the huddle. Diego hands me his flashlight, but I don't need it—the moon is high and bright; it illuminates the clearing like a spotlight. I feel Harp work her way to my side.

"No." She shakes her head. "This isn't right."

The huge structure we saw last night, Frick's compound, the gray-stone statues that stood before it—all gone. In their place is a huge pile of broken timber, insulation, brick, and stone. I see tire tracks crisscrossing the soil leading to it.

"How could they have done it that fast?" My voice sounds small in the dark. "What happened to everything inside?"

Diego steps forward, starts giving orders. "Julian, Birdie, Elliott, Kimberly—take the perimeter. Do not go farther than the edges. If you see something in the trees, shoot once and we'll come for you. The rest of you: Search the wreckage. Look for anything that would indicate the Church and the corporation have been here. Vivian, Harp—with me."

We're so close to where we found the truth last night that it's like being shot through with electricity—I feel the nerves at the nape of my neck tingle. We follow Diego to the edges of the rubble and answer the questions he asks—Where was the entrance? How many stories?—as best we can. His eyes are fixed on the debris, so he doesn't notice that I flinch every time I see a new, unfamiliar shape in the dark. Everything looks like a body—certain piles of crumbled brick, shards of wood and metal. Everything looks like Peter's body. Sweet Peter Ivey, who looked me in the eye and told me to run. What if he didn't get out before they tore the building down? Harp grabs my hand and squeezes. Her dark eyes are filled with worry. She's thinking it too.

"I don't know what I hoped we'd find," Diego mutters. "A piece of paper that says, 'We faked the Rapture; suck it, America'? They wouldn't leave anything important behind if they anticipated you coming back. And the fact that they tore it down means they did." He frowns. "I can't believe you made it in as easily as you did. It was across the country and in the middle of the woods, but you walked right in. Doesn't it almost feel like someone *wanted* you to find it?"

After a while, the soldiers begin to drag identifiable bits out of the larger pile: empty, misshapen drawers from file cabinets; insulation and bits of wire; shards of broken glass; a few dusty pillows; a bathroom sink. Diego has Harp and me inspect each item, but everything is exactly what it appears to be.

I can just about sense Diego getting ready to turn back when Harp yelps and dives into the refuse. She pulls something out—a large, gray, V-shaped stone.

"This was part of one of the statues!" she exclaims. "Adam Taggart's arm." She turns the shape to its side and I remember the way Peter's dad was memorialized in the statue garden: arms akimbo, proud expression. *She shall be burnt with fire.*

"Did you find anything else like this?" I ask the group.

Everyone shakes their heads except for Suzy, who notes a weird slab I think may be part of one of the Three Angels' wings. The sight of it is surreal, like a prop left over from a dream, the link between it and reality. But the militia still seems skeptical. Diego kicks carelessly at the stone wing, and I realize he's disappointed. These little bits of statue don't prove anything. The only thing they prove is that Harp and I have been here before.

"It isn't much," I say. "Nothing to topple an institution with, anyway."

Nobody answers. I hear approaching footsteps and turn to see Julian emerge from the dark, carrying something long and slim in his hands. I can't make it out. He hands the object to Diego. "Don't know if this is anything that means anything, but I found it propped up behind a tree outside the clearing."

Diego turns, holding the object up to the light of the moon, and the clouds shift, and I feel something soar inside me as I recognize it.

The sledgehammer from my parents' basement.

"That's mine," I say in a shaking voice, holding out my hand.

Diego gives it to me. We used the sledgehammer to break into the compound. I hadn't realized I did not have it until now. In my head I see Peter leaning against the car as I cross a Pittsburgh street with it propped on my shoulder, the slight sexy rise of his eyebrow.

That's a good look for you.

"We left it outside after we broke the window," Harp remembers out loud. She turns to Julian. "You found it leaning against a tree?"

Julian nods. "Yep. Sitting there, propped up casual, waiting to be found."

I run my hands along the heavy iron head, trace my fingers over the slim handle. Maybe there's a missive etched into the wood: *I'm okay. I'm on your side.* But the sledgehammer feels like it always has. The fact that it's here is the only message.

We trudge through the forest, leaving the clearing at our backs, while the predawn sky brightens to a deep, soft pink. When we see the break in the trees through which we came up ahead, Harp falls slightly behind, ducking to tie her shoe. I wait with her.

"Do you think Diego's right?" Her voice is soft—the militia is only a few yards away, and whatever she's saying she doesn't want them to hear.

"About what?"

"That it was too easy for us to get to the compound. That someone wanted us there."

She rests on one knee below me, looking up, her face drawn and troubled in the early morning light. I'm exhausted, drained of all my angry momentum; all I can do is shake my head. I begin to walk away. "No, Harp."

"Peter was the one who told us about the compound in the first place." She gets up and joins me down the trail. "He was behind the wheel as we drove into Point Reyes. He got us 'lost' near the start of the path. What if he knew where we were going all along?"

I wheel around to face her. "Why? Why would he have done that?"

"He's Taggart's son!" Harp insists. "Isn't it possible he could have had reasons?"

I don't understand why Harp is pushing at this impossibility, why she would want it to be true, but for her sake I try to look at it objectively. I think about Peter like he's not the first boy I ever kissed, like he never made me look at the stars when I was scared, like he never made me feel like I was invincible. It's true we made it to the compound with some amount of ease. It's true also—I feel a pang to admit it to myself—that he didn't tell us Adam Taggart was his father until he absolutely had to, that he might have otherwise never told us. But he is so much more than his father's son. And last night, he told me to run. Doesn't that count for anything?

"Please, Harp."

"Vivian—"

"Drop it, okay?" My voice rings sharply against the trees; a nearby bird squawks in response. "If you really believe this, believe it quietly. I don't want to hear it anymore."

Harp bites down on the inside of her cheek; after a moment, she nods. We follow the militia to the cars waiting for us. I'm sure Harp means well, but I can't look at her as we climb into the back seat and start the drive back to San Francisco. She's only looking out for me, I know, but she's distracting me from the most important mission I have right now: To find Peter. To save Peter. She's making me doubt myself.

I close my eyes so no one will talk to me, and soon the rumble of the engine has lulled me into a nightmare: pitch-black forest, the thin branches of trees whipping at my face. Something chasing me, I don't know what. A path that twists and turns but always leads to a body on the ground: my father, curled lifeless on his side. But I have to keep running. I go as long as I can without looking back, until I feel like I can't run anymore, and then at last I turn and the thing that's chasing me is there waiting, it has always been there, and I know at once what it is.

I recognize the blue of his eyes.

CHAPTER FIVE

I f I thought we'd be a natural fit with Amanda's militia because of how hard we fought to make it here, how hard we're
willing to fight to take the Church of America down, I was
wrong. As days go by, Harp and I are shut out of all knowledge of their ongoing plans. Diego treats us politely, but distantly,
like we're guests overstaying our welcome. He's disappointed that
the trip to the compound yielded nothing, and he's distracted
by whatever Amanda is planning. He gives us no sense of what
they're up to, though it's clearly something big. Yesterday we
watched Colby unload a small truck's worth of guns and ammu-
nition. And every time we try to enter Cliff House while Diego
runs a strategy meeting, he falls silent until Winnie escorts us
right back out again.

I hate being shut out. I almost regret telling Diego the truth
about the Rapture so quickly—it's as though the information is
his now, his to act upon as he and Amanda desire. I feel power-
less, restless. Peter is still out there; if I had any idea where he

might be, I'd go find him. But I can't talk to Harp about it—his name goes unmentioned between us, a source of a friction we both try hard to bury.

At least we feel safe. These are not the sleepy hippies that were the New Orphans: all day the soldiers train, run, research, and sharpen their individual skills. They're too busy to befriend us. Harp has flirted with them all—Julian, I notice, especially—but they won't let themselves be distracted from their mission. Suzy spends afternoons hacking into Church news feeds to look for evidence of the missing Raptured; she finds nothing she can use, but thoroughly dismantles the sites themselves, severing the corporation from its audience. Robbie and Kimberly are both accomplished sharpshooters—they take Harp and me out early one morning and let us watch as they snipe birds off the trees along the cliff side.

"Birds are quick," Kimberly notes in appreciation, raising the rifle she always carries strapped across one shoulder. "But they're no match for Dragoslav."

"Dragoslav?" Harp echoes, after the blast has exploded the stillness of the morning. We watch a flash of gray-white fall from a branch. "Did you . . . name your rifle?"

Kimberly smiles proudly, nods. "I have Serbian roots."

Elliott makes explosives. Frankie throws knives. Tiny Birdie gives daily lessons in hand-to-hand combat. Even kind, maternal Karen delights in showing us the ropy muscles of her calves—two days ago, she lifted a chair over her head with Harp sitting in it. When we're with them, I feel like I'm part of something big, something effective.

But more often, Harp and I are left to entertain ourselves while the militia discusses plans we're not at liberty to hear. Over a week into our stay in San Francisco, we waste time down by the wreckage of the old bathhouse, tightrope-walking along the stone edge of what used to be a swimming pool, while Diego and the others huddle inside Cliff House.

"This is *bullshit*," I seethe. "I could throw knives, if I wanted. I could be really good at it."

"You'd be amazing, Viv. You'd be an Olympic-level knife thrower."

Harp balances a laptop on one arm, unconcerned by the waves crashing precariously near. Ever since our faces appeared on the Church's feed, she refreshes it constantly. The battery on the stolen laptop has long since died, but Suzy gave us one of the militia's computers to track the progress of the Church's hunt for us. So far, we remain safely hidden.

"It's *sexist*, is what it is," I continue. "Because we're teenage girls, we can't be soldiers? We can't know what the big plan is?"

"It's not like there aren't women up there, Viv," Harp notes. "But I take your point. Diego's a little slimy. I haven't forgiven him for that 'trip to the mall' thing. Like, fuck *you*, dude. I don't even *like* malls. What does Winnie see in him, anyway?"

"Don't ask me." Yet another topic I'm not interested in discussing. Winnie's been so busy helping Diego that we've barely spoken since she rescued us.

Harp turns her attention back to the feed. I stare out at the ocean crashing white against the rocks ahead. It's beautiful here in California, and I am relatively safe, but I feel as if all my parts are held together by a single small knot at the center of me, and I'm slowly watching it unravel. My father is dead; my mother is not at all who I thought she was. Winnie and Peter are both their own mysteries. Even the thing that has given me purpose for so long now—fighting the Church of America—feels frustratingly beyond my grasp. Standing here staring out at the Pacific, I realize that everything I've been is literally behind me. I am standing at the edge of the United States and I am somebody new entirely.

Beside me Harp gasps at the screen. My heart lurches—*Peter!*—and I race to her side, nearly stumbling into the still waters of the pool. Silent in her shock, Harp holds the laptop out to me, and I gaze eagerly down at what she sees.

A picture of two men shaking hands in front of a large group, standing in a sun-drenched place I recognize as the Keystone base of the New Orphans. Goliath, their handsome leader, turns halfway to the camera with a megawatt smile. But it's the man whose hand he holds who makes me feel unsteady: ruddy-cheeked, broad-shouldered, pudgy, and bald, he's unmistakably one of the Three Angels. The caption reads:

> **Ted Blackmore, Church spokesman, and Spencer Ganz, representative of the New Orphans, sign the Treaty for the Spiritual Engagement of Our Nation's Young. Ganz and his associates will lead a three-month, $5 million campaign to engage underprivileged secular American youth in the word of Frick through community outreach, teen-oriented literature, and brand giveaways. All hail the righteous Frick for this glorious day!**

"Ted Blackmore," I whisper.

"I *told* you!" Harp does a small jig on the stone wall, the laptop bouncing with her. "I *told* you Goliath works for them! It makes sense they'd make it public—the Church looks like they've neutralized the Orphans and he looks like a big shot. Ha!"

"Look how upset they look." I point out the faces I recognize in the group behind Goliath and Blackmore—Gallifrey, Daisy, Kanye, so many others. At the end of the line, pregnant and uncharacteristically sullen, is Edie. "This must have blindsided them."

I hear a faint noise above us and look up to see a figure standing at the edge of the cliff, calling out my name. Winnie. I wave back. Harp scrolls through the rest of the press release and wades into the comments below, reading out choice Believer reactions: "'Thank God the New Orphans have come around to the side of light! The angels smile down on us this day!'" I watch Winnie jog around the perimeter of the ruins and down the steps. She makes her way along the rock wall to us. When she arrives, she's out of breath.

"I came to tell you—both of you—that guy, Goliath, the head of the New Orphans? They just put a story on the feed—"

I gesture at the laptop. "We saw it."

"Oh." Winnie takes a noisy gulp of air. "Really wish I'd walked, then."

She lingers on the wall with us, and though she says nothing, I can feel a strange tension in the air. Harp must feel it too, because she snaps the laptop shut.

"I guess the meeting's over, then?" she asks. Winnie nods. "Great. I'm starving. You know, it might be nice for you to pack us a little lunch, next time you kick us out to strategize. Nothing big—just a couple of sandwiches or something."

Harp bounds past us, heading back up to Cliff House. Winnie sits down along the rock wall and stares out at the horizon. I notice for the first time how pale she is, the heavy bags under her eyes. She looks a lot rougher than she did last week. "Are you okay?"

"I was about to ask you the same thing. How are you settling in?"

I shrug. "I guess pretty great, considering my mother hates me and I'm sitting around useless while the big strike against the Church gets planned."

Her expression stays carefully neutral. "Mara doesn't hate you."

I wait for her to elaborate, but she just gazes at the sea. I feel a twinge of annoyance.

"Well, I wouldn't care if she did. She's been an epically shitty mom, and I'm not going to beat myself up for calling her out on it. I should have done it *ages* ago."

Winnie picks absent-mindedly at a fingernail. Is she even listening? Or has she taken a side already, my mother's side? Winnie leaves Cliff House every evening to return to her apartment and my mom. She feels responsible for her. I imagine with a surge of anger the conversations they have—long ruminations on all the things I've done wrong, all the ways I've let Mom down.

"If you have some kind of problem with me," I say then, "just tell me."

Winnie starts at this. "I don't have a problem with you, Viv."

"Why aren't you talking to me, then? I've been here over a week, and we haven't had a single conversation."

"I'm sorry." Winnie stands up and faces me. "The truth is, I'm wondering if bringing you here was the right thing to do. This mission we're planning? This 'strike against the Church,' as you put it? It's bigger and more dangerous than anything we've done before. And you're here now. And you're—well—feisty. Diego told me how you insisted on going to Point Reyes. Don't get me wrong; if I were in your position, I'd be doing the same thing. But I don't want you on this mission. I don't want you anywhere near it."

"What are you planning?" I ask, not expecting a straight answer.

"An attack on Church headquarters," Winnie says. "Once we can figure out where exactly that is. Amanda wants us to set up a bomb and detonate it. She wants us to pick off the survivors as they run for safety. It's awful, Viv." Winnie shakes her head. "It's too much. Some of us are not going to come back from it. That's not the issue, for me. I signed up for this. I knew what I was getting myself into. What keeps me up at night is the idea of the employees inside. Not the people in charge. The low-level employees: receptionists, janitors, the cooks in the cafeteria. I can't stop imagining what their faces will look like the moment before we blow up the building with all of them inside."

I'm taken aback by her honesty, and by the plan itself. The rational part of me knows it's too much, but there's something else—some deep vindictive strain in me—that feels satisfied by it. I try to feel what she does for these people. I know not every Believer is evil; most of them must be like my mother, lost and afraid. I can understand a little why Winnie doesn't want to target them. But then a series of images flick through my brain: Goliath shaking Blackmore's hand, the smug smile on his face; the Three Angels in their robes, pretending to speak for God; my father taking the wine Frick hands him, my father drinking it. I shake my head.

"They knew what they were signing up for too. They know what the Church is."

Winnie cocks her head to the side. "So you think they deserve what they get?"

"I don't know." I echo something Grandpa Grant, my mother's father, once told me. "You make choices, and there are consequences."

"I wish I could see things as clearly as you do," Winnie says after a long moment. "It's really black-and-white for you, isn't it? Good versus evil, Believers versus Non-Believers, you versus the whole world."

"That's not how I *see* it. That's how it is." I stand up straight. "Anyway, you don't have to worry about me, okay? I can take care of myself."

Winnie's mouth twists into a grim smile. "Don't you think it's possible for me to believe that and worry about you at the same time?"

I don't know what to say. My thoughts stray back to Mom. If Winnie might die carrying out this attack, as she seems to believe is possible, what happens to my mother? She's confused and still Believer-inclined—if the Church gave her a second opportunity to be Raptured, I'm not sure she wouldn't take it. Who will protect her from them? I'm about to ask, but I hear a sound—Harp stands at the edge of the cliff where Winnie did, calling down to us. She waves her arms in wide circles. Winnie follows my gaze.

"Is something wrong?"

I strain to hear Harp's voice over the sound of wind in my ears. Her words travel down to me as an echo: "Another Angel! Another Angel!"

I race up toward Cliff House, Winnie at my heels. The two of us burst in, breathless. Diego and the others are gathered in clusters around laptops. They watch an identical moving image. As I approach, I see the face of the female Angel, a blond woman identified beneath as MICHELLE MULVEY, CHURCH OF AMERICA EXECUTIVE VP. A wide shot establishes her to be behind a podium in a crowded ballpark. HISTORIC DAY FOR THE CHURCH OF AMERICA! LIVE BROADCAST FROM CRUSADERS STADIUM IN LOS ANGELES, the ticker reads. I grip Harp's hand.

"God loves the United States best, out of all his nations," Michelle Mulvey announces, the amplification lending an echo to her cool, clear voice. "This we know from the Book of Frick, but also by looking into our own hearts. Frick tells us the Creator loves our boldness, our entrepreneurial spirit. So too does He love the way we've always led the world in industry, innovation, and moral righteousness. Today, the Church of America is so proud to embark on an audacious new initiative in that spirit. We proudly announce the opening of over seventy new Church branches worldwide—"

Julian hisses at the screen.

"—in countries such as Canada, Mexico, Italy, Iceland, Kazakhstan, and many others. Additionally"—Mulvey glances behind her, at a line of rigid, blue-uniformed men wearing helmets painted with stars and stripes and crucifixes—"we're honored to introduce you to the new Church of America police force—the Peacemakers—who will enforce Frick's justice in cities both here and abroad, seeking out dangerous enemies to salvation. Blessed are they! Today, we proudly embrace our fellow nations in this, our collective hour of need. God may not have made you American, but embrace His Church warmly and he might lessen the anguish of your spiritual torture when September twenty-fourth finally comes. Hail Frick!"

The stadium erupts into enthusiastic applause, and Mulvey waves like a beauty queen. Diego closes the laptop with an angry flourish. "The globalization of the Church of America," he mutters. "Probably should have seen that coming."

"Other countries didn't have the Church before now?"

I don't realize it's a dumb question until it's out of my mouth, and Harp gives me a weird look. Diego rolls his eyes.

"A few imitators have popped up here and there—I know a

Church of Great Britain made a stab at it last year—but nowhere is it like here," Julian explains gently. "And that's exactly what the corporation is taking advantage of. Things are dire all over— extreme weather, poverty, terrorism. But only here has someone provided such a convenient narrative for it. After the first Rapture, the rest of the world is starting to wonder."

"Our grandma back in Mexico has already hung a little portrait of Frick up over her mantel," Diego adds. "She calls him Santo Padre—Holy Father. Their market's going to expand like crazy once they spread the message overseas. Have you really," he asks me, with patronizing curiosity, "never wondered what was happening in the rest of the world?"

I feel my cheeks flush. The embarrassing truth is that I haven't. My scope of the world has been so small all my life: only in this last year—these last few months, really—has it widened to include the rest of the country. I knew the apocalyptic phenomena affecting the United States weren't limited to us alone, but I guess I never gave thought to how other countries were handling it. The Church permeated my own life so deeply, I assumed it had sunk its claws into all seven billion of us. But this is stupid, I realize now, and so self-absorbed. I remember something Winnie told me the morning I met her: the apocalypse isn't happening to me alone.

Diego paces in front of us, brow furrowed, hands clasped behind his back. "Amanda will send us to Los Angeles. If Mulvey's in Los Angeles, it's fair to assume that's where the Church of America's new headquarters are. When we find it, we'll plan the attack."

There's a sharp, uncomfortable tension among the nearby soldiers, and I get the feeling Winnie's not the only one with doubts. Harp's brow furrows.

"Attack?" she echoes.

Diego pauses. "We need to call another meeting. Winnie, could you please take Viv—"

"I already told her the plan," Winnie interrupts. "So they might as well stay. Harp, we're planning to target the current Church headquarters—which we can now safely assume to be in Los Angeles—with a coordinated, violent attack. Amanda wants no survivors."

The silence in Cliff House is electric. Beside me, Harp stiffens—I hear her draw a breath that she waits a long time to release. The soldiers hanging around all have bleak looks on their faces; Frankie watches Diego furiously.

"You know what will happen if you kill Mulvey or Blackmore, or any high-profile Church employee?" Harp asks. "You'll turn them into martyrs. You'll turn them into Frick and Taggart. You'll make them bigger and more powerful than they ever were."

"We'll also take them out of the picture," Diego replies. "And with their apocalypse three months away, and the second boat even sooner, that's enticing. You realize what another Rapture means, right? They're going to do it again and again, until they come up with something else, something big enough to keep people believing and buying. Listen." His tone gets strident. Harp has fixed him with an intensely skeptical look. "I appreciate your concerns, but you're not a part of this. We've weighed the alternatives, and this is the only viable plan."

"It's a stupid plan," Harp shoots back. "There's a better one sitting right in front of you, and it's so easy, and so effective, with so much less murder involved. Right, Apple?"

I turn to her. "What?"

Harp beams at my confusion, like she's just discovered she's the smartest person in the room. "Seriously? It's so obvious. We have the best possible weapon there is against the Church. It's the only thing in the world we have."

When I frown at her, Harp shakes her head. She still can't believe I don't get it.

"The truth, Viv."

CHAPTER SIX

J ust write it like it happened."

I sit at a desk by the windows—beyond the screen of Harp's laptop is the blue of the ocean. It's early the next morning, and the sky is the pale pink hue that darkens every afternoon into an alarming, fiery red no meteorologist seems able to explain. I'm exhausted—Harp kept me up late, working out the details of her plan, and when I slept I slipped from nightmare to nightmare.

"Viv," Harp says patiently beside me. "It's not that hard. We can fix it up after you've finished, make it sound snappy. Just tell it like you're telling it to me."

I sigh and stare at the screen. Harp has already typed in a headline: THE TRUTH ABOUT THE CHURCH OF AMERICA. I look up at her.

"You're sure this can't be traced back to us?"

She nods. "Suzy set it up and she's a genius. The Wi-Fi at this place is so well protected, the FBI couldn't track us down."

Suzy has her back to us at another desk, typing intimidating-looking code. She turns, frowning, at Harp's words. "The FBI could *definitely* track us down, if they wanted to. But the Church won't know how, and we'll be in Los Angeles by the time they realize what you're posting. That's when the real trouble will start."

"That's extremely encouraging, Suzy, thanks," I say, and she giggles.

"Look alive, Apple!" Harp grabs my head and turns it back toward the screen. "The fate of the world rests on your shoulders right now. No pressure."

Diego was reluctant to approve Harp's plan. Winnie finally convinced him that it couldn't hurt—though I think she pushed for it mainly as a way to keep me out of trouble. Now I stare at Harp's headline. Picking carefully at the laptop's keys with my left hand—my right still firmly encased in its splint—I begin to tell our story:

> We found the place late at night in Point Reyes. There
> were several statues out front that confirmed it as a
> Church of America compound.

"What the hell?" mutters Harp in my ear.

"I can't write if you're reading over my shoulder!"

"Yeah, clearly." She reaches over me, hitting delete until the screen is blank except for her headline. "You can't start at the end of the story. A lot of important shit went down before we got to the compound. You have to introduce yourself—that's what's going to draw people in, once they realize you're one of the girls on the feed."

"Okay." I nod. "That makes sense."

My name is Vivian Apple and I am 17 years old. I was
born in Pittsburgh, Pennsylvania.
    You may be wondering why I am writing this blog
post. Well,

I hear Harp groan and I look up at her. "What's wrong?"

"'You may be wondering why I am writing this blog post,'"
Harp reads in pinched tones, pushing an invisible pair of glasses
up the bridge of her nose. Then in her normal voice, she says,
"Come on, Viv. It isn't an assignment."

"You *literally* assigned it to me!" I exclaim. "Why can't you
do it?"

Harp makes a face. "I can barely spell, Viv."

"I've read your texts; you spell fine." I stand, stepping away
from the desk. "You're the interesting one. You're the one with
two working hands. Why don't *you* try?"

Harp stares at the laptop. After a moment she settles uncertainly into the chair. Her fingers hover over the keyboard for one
long beat. She looks up at me.

"I don't know how to do this! It's going to sound dumb!"

But I don't even need to encourage her. She turns back and
begins to type. I watch the words fly easily onto the screen.

What up, America!
Probably you're wondering what the deal is with
those two teen girls on the Church of America's news
feed. Probably you're like, "Better them than me, ha
ha ha!" as you and your family shiver like little baby
chicks in your homes trying to pretend you believe in
the word of Frick so that the Church doesn't come to

> your door to slap the stale bread crusts out of your
> kids' hands and burn your wives at the stake for their
> prostitutely ways. COOL LIFE, BRO! But guess what:
> I am one of the girls on the Church of America's news
> feed, and I'm about to tell you how they straight-up
> faked that motherfucking Rapture.

Harp pauses and reads what she's written. I see a little gleam of satisfaction in her eyes when she glances at me. "Too aggressive?"

I laugh and shake my head. "It's perfect, Harp. Seriously perfect."

Harp beams and keeps typing. I watch as she weaves our story: she begins with the Rapture's Eve party, then the tense days immediately following our parents' collective disappearance, Raj's death, my return to Pittsburgh, Peter, every stop we made on our journey across the continent. It's funny and quick, and I begin to feel a sudden sureness blazing through my veins, because who'd read this story and doubt the girl who wrote it? How could anyone who read it not *want* to believe her? Maybe the blog won't keep the militia's attack from happening—I'm still not sure I want it to—but at least, for now, it makes us feel less voiceless. I feel like more than a face on the feed for the first time since the Church published my picture—I feel like a human being again.

> Picture us, sweet reader: three bold and — dare I
> say — stunning (you saw the feed, you know we
> look like the stars of a romantic high school vam-
> pire soap opera; we are *babes*) American youths,
> standing there in front of Beaton Frick, who has just

admitted to poisoning a(n unclear) percentage of the so-called Raptured. We are not pleased. We're pretty much tearing through the seven stages of grief at warp speed, and my sweet buddy Viv (once a timid valedictorian type, now an increasingly fearless vixen and newly crowned make-out queen) is faster than anyone. She hits anger way before I do and how does she handle it? SHE STRUTS OVER TO FRICK AND BREAKS HER FUCKING HAND ON HIS CRAZY OLD MAN FACE.

"I didn't break it!" I protest. "It's only a sprain!"

"Poetic license, Viv. 'Sprains her fucking hand' doesn't sound nearly as good."

She types on, describing the Three Angels (Mulvey, Blackmore, and a TBD creep, all of them in some seriously weak-ass angel costumes, like literally they'd just wrapped themselves in sheets; it was embarrassing) and our escape. She doesn't share her doubts about Peter; maybe just for my sake she paints him as steady and noble, a romantic hero. She ends the post with an exhilarating plea:

> I swear by everything in this world I hold dear — my dead brother Raj and parties and gratuitous swearing and my best friend in this or any universe, Vivian Harriet Apple (note: I do not actually know Viv's middle name) — that this is true. Consider this: In your heart, do you honestly find it any crazier than the idea that your loved ones just beamed on up into heaven this past March, that if you kill enough sweet

innocent gay boys you'll get cleared to beam on up yourself? You've let me down a lot these last few years, America, but even I don't believe you're that goddamn stupid. So ponder this tale, sweet reader. If you find yourself believing it, I ask you to do three things only:

1. GET ANGRY. We should all be so pissed at the Church of America that we're willing to break our hands in the metaphorical punching of its metaphorical face. Take that fear you've been living with for three years — that distrust of your friends and neighbors, that nervous anticipation of September 24th, the supposed last day of this beautiful messed-up world — and turn it into unseemly stone-cold anger. Say to yourself, "The Church of America has fucked with the wrong citizenry!"

2. Tell someone else the story. Even if they don't want to hear it — especially if they don't want to hear it. The Church can kill me and Viv, but they can't kill the story.

3. Help us find the missing Believers. Before your Raptured loved one disappeared, did he or she say anything weird(er than usual)? Any references to random locations, upcoming trips? "I hear Minnesota is lovely this time of year"? Anything inexplicable left behind? Pamphlets titled *Things to Do in Denver Before You're Raptured* tucked inside their Book of Frick? Strange charges on credit card statements, confusing numbers on phone bills? We know firsthand from one Believer who escaped

Point Reyes that she'd been summoned to California weeks before the Rapture, told to move in secret. By any chance did the Believer in your life let the secret slip?

OK, that's it, you beautiful idiots. If you've got questions, leave them below. I've got nothing to hide except my current location.

xoxo Harpreet Janda, Fugitive

For more than three weeks, we wait.

Harp expected an instantaneous, explosive response, so we spend that whole first afternoon sitting by the laptop, refreshing the page, waiting for a comment. She shares it on her Twitter and her Facebook; she finds secular forums and subforums devoted to Rapture theories and posts the link in the comments. "The farther it reaches, the more people will buy it," Harp says. "And once they buy it, they'll pass it on." But there's no immediate response. Suzy shows us the stat counter she installed and we watch it faithfully, noting that there are in fact visitors—fifty-eight page views the first day, seventy-three the next. But on the third day, it drops to a dispiriting seventeen. Plus, there are no comments, no link-backs from other pages. Harp seems to be the only person spreading the story.

"It takes time," she says hopefully, more than once, "for things to go viral. You have to make them get seen by the right people."

Meanwhile, everyone at Cliff House relocates in shifts to the Los Angeles base Amanda has secured. We're to fully abandon Cliff House by the end of July. One night about a week after Harp posts our story, I wake to the sound of typing, to the now-familiar blue glow of the laptop screen. Harp sits in bed with her knees to her chest. The sky outside is black, freckled with stars, and the beds around us are empty—today Kimberly and Birdie left for LA with twenty others.

Harp sees me stir and quickly dims the screen. "Sorry, Viv! Didn't mean to wake you."

"Any comments?" I ask hopefully, pulling myself up on my elbow.

"Still nothing. I'm researching other Rapture theories. There are thousands, Viv. Blogs, hashtags, whole forums. Listen to this guy." She reads out loud. "'When will these sheeple accept what the rest of us have known since well before March twenty-fourth: that Beaton Frick and his ilk are extraterrestrial life forms who abducted the Raptured for their own nefarious purposes. They're long gone, folks—they're getting cut up like rare steak in a laboratory on Venus.' There are one hundred fifty replies to this guy, all praising his sound logic. I posted a link to the blog in the comments, but why would people like this ever listen to a story like ours?"

"I don't know. Some people will go for the most outrageous answer, I guess. It's a weird thing that happened—why not believe it's part of something weirder?"

Harp sighs and pulls up a different page. "This one's from a professor of psychology at NYU. She says, 'The Church of America resembles not a system of belief so much as a cult. Various factors—its charismatic leader, dogmatic principles, elaborate system of reward and punishment—raise red flags for those of us in the psychological community. While it would be intellectually irresponsible to hazard a guess as to the fate of the missing three thousand, one is sadly reminded of such tragedies as Jonestown and Heaven's Gate, mass murders and suicide pacts orchestrated by leaders who suspected their hold on their community to be slipping.'"

I sit up, electrified. "Harp, write to her! Send her our story! She can help us!"

But Harp shakes her head. "I can't. She's dead. Apparent suicide, although her family has questions." She looks up, and I see the distress in her eyes. "It's dangerous to say this stuff out loud. It's dangerous to tell the truth and believe it. If it's safer to say the Rapture was freaky alien shit—if believing that *people* did this could get you killed—why wouldn't you believe the freaky alien shit? And even if you didn't, wouldn't you want to? It's like the Believers: better to convince yourself you're a good person, that someone's going to save you, than to believe you might be as flawed as everyone else, and that in the end, you're alone."

"We can't control what anyone else believes. All we can do right now is speak up and hope somebody listens."

"But there's no time!" Harp exclaims in a tight voice. "Here's another article—a scientist from Iowa, who went missing last week. He says, 'We're dealing with alarming climate change across the globe, and it's not an act of God—it's manmade. We'll make it past September twenty-fourth without issue, but after that our path is unclear. We have maybe forty or fifty years until major food shortages slowly begin to eat away at the global population, and that's assuming something cataclysmic—an asteroid, a nuclear war, the explosion of the supervolcano underneath Yellowstone—doesn't occur first. We could conceivably slow this destruction down, but it would require huge overarching changes in the structure of our society—the kind of change we'll never achieve so long as we remain distracted by imaginary acts of God.'"

She stares at the screen a moment, then closes the laptop. I wait for her to lie down, but she doesn't.

"We knew that, Harp," I say softly. "We knew the Church doesn't control the weather. You said it yourself—it's definitely coming. Whether in three months or in three hundred years."

"I thought it would be much closer to three hundred years," she whispers.

I don't know what to tell her. I want our story to be the life preserver that keeps us afloat, but I'm starting to understand how little purchase the truth actually affords us in this world. I consider reminding Harp of the militia's plan—if nothing else, we can at least destroy the people who have so confused our dying world. But I know that won't bring her comfort. At the moment, it barely comforts me.

| | | | |

The next morning, I help Robbie pack supplies in the kitchen— he's leaving for LA with some others this afternoon. I don't know him well yet. Robbie's got a thirteen-year-old boy's surliness, plus the excuse of grief to keep him silent. Birdie told us his story: his mother went devoutly Believer and his father ran off, leaving him behind; Robbie left home shortly before the Rapture and doesn't know where either of them is today. I've never heard him speak more than monosyllables before, but today Robbie looks up from the pile of silverware to mutter, "I read your friend's blog."

"Yeah? Well, that makes one of you."

Fewer than ten page views yesterday. We had Suzy examine the stat counter, thinking maybe it was broken, but she claimed the number was accurate. ("I think you just have a really unpopular blog," she told us apologetically.)

71

"You think your dad is really dead?"

My body jolts, like I'm waking from a dream about falling. I haven't thought of my dad in a while. "I can't know for sure, I guess. I know he was at Point Reyes. I doubt he made it out."

"But there are a lot of people missing, right?" Robbie has dropped his monotone; he sounds curious, hungry. "Maybe he went somewhere else. Maybe he's still alive."

"We don't know that the missing people are alive," I remind him gently. "And even if they are . . . I guess I thought when I found my parents, that would fix things. I would find them alive—and I figured they'd be *sorry*. They'd become themselves again. But I don't think it works like that. Because even if they had been alive and sorry—that's three people who end up okay. And I don't think I could be content anymore, to be whole when so many others are broken. You know?"

"I get you." Robbie throws the silverware in a box with a metallic clang. "And even if they were *all* alive—they already made their choice. They chose Not Us."

He glances up from under his shaggy hair with a defiant expression, but there's a question in his eyes he still wants answered.

"Just choose your own family, Robbie," I tell him. "Choose the people who choose you."

We fall back into comfortable silence, broken finally by the sound of approaching footsteps. I look up and see Diego, looking weirdly unsettled.

"Vivian? Could I borrow you a second?"

I follow him through the main hall, into a cluttered back office I've never been in before. I've never seen him so uptight—he acts, more than anything, like a troublemaking student about to face the principal. Winnie stands just within the door, and Harp lounges in a chair, her legs kicked lazily over the side. Behind the desk in front of her is a woman in a wheelchair who can't be much older than Winnie. She has raven-black hair and severe bangs brushing the tops of her eyelids; she scrolls through her tablet, looking as if she is literally biting her tongue.

"Vivian," Diego says. "I'd like to introduce you to Amanda Yee."

"Hi," I say.

Amanda doesn't look up. I turn to Winnie, confused, and she gestures to the chair next to Harp with pleading eyes. I sit. We watch Amanda for what feels like five full minutes before she folds her hands on top of her tablet and turns a piercing stare upon us.

"I've just been reading your blog. *Very* fascinating stuff."

Harp and I glance at each other, and I see my best friend wondering the same thing I am: Is this a compliment? Before we can ask, Amanda continues.

"Here are my top three favorite things about it, in ascending order. One: I love the humor. So fresh, so clever. Two: I love that you spent so much time cozying up to Taggart's son. Does part of me feel like, why am I paying for these girls' room and board when they had Peter Taggart in their back pocket but weren't able to deliver him? I promise you I'm not bothered by the significant part of me that feels that way."

My cheeks burn and I've opened my mouth to protest—his name is Peter *Ivey*, I want to say—but though I know Amanda sees me, she keeps talking.

"Three, and this is the big one: I love that you went ahead and posted this extremely incendiary missive on Cliff House's servers. I love that I poured the better part of my fortune into the creation of the only instrument in the country that could theoretically take down the Church of America, and that said instrument is currently in jeopardy thanks to two fugitive minors who took it upon themselves to publish the sort of thing for which the Church *murders human beings* using the Wi-Fi for which *I pay.*"

"Suzy—" I start to explain.

"Suzy's good," Amanda interrupts. "She can keep you cloaked for the time being. But she's not a miracle worker. And that's what you'll need once the Church decides to take action."

"It's the truth," Harps insists. "It's what we saw."

"Do you think I doubt it? My point is only that you could have fashioned that truth into a far more effective weapon than the one you did. It's more powerful as a secret. We could've blackmailed the Angels. But you gave it away, and now it's a toss-up: Will the story gain traction? Will people believe you? If so, what will they do? Get angry enough to fight back? Because I think the best-case scenario is, you'll get a couple hundred who say, 'I'm never shopping in a Church of America megastore ever again!' And get a couple hundred more who say, 'I knew it!' but keep shopping there, because it's got everything, and for such low prices."

I don't like the reprimand, but I know Amanda is right. I look to Harp—the blog is her baby; she'll be crushed to realize we've ruined our chance with it. But to my surprise my best friend looks perfectly calm.

"You know what we need, right?" she asks.

"A time machine," Amanda supplies sarcastically.

"Money."

Amanda snorts, but she doesn't interrupt when Harp continues.

"Let's say you do, by some secular miracle, manage to kill everyone in the Church's LA headquarters. How many people is that? Maybe two hundred? The Believers who remain will spin it. You'll be terrorists; they'll have the Peacemakers hunt you down. Then your money's gone and so's your army. And so, most importantly, is the narrative about who is the good guy and who is the bad guy. It seems"—Harp sounds sympathetic—"like a really dumb investment."

Amanda taps her fingers on the table in a bored way, but I can tell she's listening. "So what would you suggest?"

"I suggest you pour your money into *me*," Harp says. "Into my fresh, clever voice. I've shared that post as far as I can, but I don't know how to get it read. I bet you could buy its way into the right channels. You could put it on news sites. You could put it in tabloids. You could probably afford to get it carved onto the moon, for all I know."

Amanda shakes her head. "It'll still be your word against theirs. You must know the Church will find a way to retaliate. They can be clever too."

"They can say whatever they want about me." Harp sounds a little rueful. "As long as I can keep writing. The only thing they've got that I don't is an audience."

There's a long pause. Amanda stares at Harp through narrowed eyes, and I feel Harp grow still beside me, like she'll lose her hold on Amanda if she so much as flinches. Just when I think the moment is about to end, that Amanda will demand we find another place to hide, she speaks.

"Okay. You keep writing your story, and I'll make sure it gets read. But understand this: the attack is happening." Amanda leans forward, gripping the table with her hands. She's a slight woman, but I find myself drawing away, afraid. "You don't get a say in that. Your new job is to get public opinion on our side. You're going to make it so that when the bomb goes off, the country understands that it was the only way."

Harp's mouth drops open. "No! That's not the point of the blog. That's not why I'm telling our story!"

"It is now," Amanda says evenly. "If you want to stay under my protection, that's exactly the story you'll be telling. Unless, of course, you've got somewhere else to go?"

| | | | |

The next day, Harp has eight hundred comments. Amanda has had the story reposted as an op-ed on all the major secular news sites. We wade through the responses together.

"'You're a dumb bitch and probably ugly and fat. Jesus hates you. Go back to Iraq I hope we drop a nuke on you God Bless USA,'" Harp reads out loud. "Well, that one covers all the bases."

I read another. "'This story is bullcrap lol tell your friend to watch her back no one does harm to the prophet Rick and lives to tell about it long story short I'll kill her.' The Prophet Rick? Oh, *oh!* He means me. He wants to kill *me!*"

"Well, he'll have to get in line. Pretty much everyone does. Wait, here's a nice one: 'Lord help these heathens by drowning them in their own filthy lies and suffocating them on the scum that is their foul transgression.' Signed UtahGrandma98."

"This is awful." I lean back in my chair after nearly all of the first hundred comments prove to be some variation on a racist death threat. "I didn't expect the most positive reaction to your post to be 'Saw your pic on the Church's feed you're hot message me.'"

"I knew the first wave would be angry." Harp scrolls through

76

the hundreds of comments that remain. "It's getting under their skin. There was nothing like this on the alien abduction forum. They're mad because it seems possible."

"Well, that's a good thing! Right?"

But Harp looks unconvinced. I know she's thinking of our meeting with Amanda—the justification Amanda wants Harp to provide. Now that Amanda has done exactly what Harp asked, and helped to spread our story at a level we couldn't reach on our own, it seems as though Harp has no choice but to fill her end of the reluctant bargain. But my best friend is still set against the attack on Church headquarters. Reading the hateful bile of these Believers has done nothing to sway her. I'm far less sure. If the Believers across the country won't listen to Harp, isn't it possible they need something bigger, some drastic, unimaginable action, to work as a shock to the system?

I decide to walk the trails on the opposite side of the cliff, to gaze one last time in the direction of Point Reyes. Ever since Harp voiced her crazy fears about Peter, I've had endless nightmares where he's chasing me. Last night, though—I blush, remembering it—I dreamed we made out at a party in front of a room full of people, and when we pulled away, the other partygoers were filming us, streaming the footage directly to the Church of America's news feed. I have to go and stare at the mass of land where I last saw him, to remember the person he truly is. Stepping outside, drawing my hoodie tight around me, I watch Winnie and Diego pull up. I haven't seen either of them since this morning, when they left before sunrise on a mission they didn't discuss. There are only seven of us left in Cliff House now: Frankie, Karen, Suzy, Julian, Diego, Harp, and me. The rest are in LA. There's something unsettlingly vast about the building now that it's nearly empty.

"Where have you two been?" I ask as they get out of the car.

But Diego just makes a face, as if to say, *You know I'm not going to tell you.* He pushes past me to enter Cliff House. Winnie watches him go, spinning the car keys around one finger; after a moment she gives me a sad smile.

"We were moving Mara," she tells me. I feel my blood go cold at my mother's name. "She can't come to LA, but she can't stay here—not in an apartment under my name, anyway. Amanda paid for a little house in the suburbs. We brought her there this morning."

I look away, up at the rocky cliff side, trying to collect my thoughts. It's not as if I imagined some tearful reunion—I'm too angry for that still, and anyway, I can't stray farther than the area immediately surrounding Cliff House. But some part of me must have thought my mom would seek me out, that she'd sense my presence here at the edge of everything and come to find me. Because the knowledge that she's no longer in the same city as me feels like an impenetrable wall falling down. I realize that I'll never see my mother again.

"I'm sorry." Winnie touches my arm. "I tried to arrange to bring you with us—to give you a chance to say goodbye—but Diego and Amanda thought it would be too dangerous."

I shrug off her hand. "That's fine. I didn't want to see her anyway."

"Come on, Viv. Of course you did."

There's something gently insistent in Winnie's tone. I bristle against it. What right does she have to tell me how to feel about my own mother? I remember the morning we met, how she scolded me to cut Mom some slack. "Don't forget you're the one she kept," she told me. Like it was a competition: Who did Mara Apple treat worse? But I'm the real daughter. I'm the one who thought for seventeen years that she was there for me. I'm the one who had to find out the hard way that she wasn't.

"No, actually," I say, increasingly annoyed. "I didn't. Do you seriously not get it? She left me alone to fend for myself. I didn't know she was alive; I didn't know where she was! I nearly got myself killed looking for her. And when I gave her the chance to save my life, to actually *be my mother*, she blew it. She cares more about getting on the second boat than whether I live or die."

Winnie's face blurs—I've started to cry. Embarrassed, I cover my face with my hands. I feel her put her hands on my shoulders to hold me steady, and I'm crying too hard to wrench away.

"I'm sorry I'm in the middle of this, Viv. I don't want to be. I want to be neutral, okay? I want to be Switzerland. You have every right in the world to be furious with Mara. She's been rash and immature and unreliable. But she loves you, I swear. Her love is flawed—it's really fucking flawed—but I don't think it's worthless."

I take a shuddering breath, slowly calming down. When I lower my hands, I see Winnie's face, close and troubled.

"But you know what?" she says softly, shaking her head. "You grew up with her. I didn't. You know best. So if you want to stay angry, stay angry. Just remember: you and I, we can be a family now. I want that, and at some point, I hope you'll want that too."

I'm too stunned to give her an answer, but Winnie doesn't wait for one. She squeezes my shoulders and walks into Cliff House. I make my way toward the trails. What Winnie suggests is exactly what I hoped for when I first learned she existed, exactly what I imagined as I climbed the stairs to her apartment the morning we met. Now the thought of it creates a weird, hopeful buzz inside me, but something else, too—a fear I can't bring myself to fully contemplate.

I'm running through Point Reyes again, the leaves underfoot soft and slippery, the thin branches of trees lashing at my face and arms, slicing deep bloody lines into my skin. It hurts, but I can't stop: I'm being chased. The night is black and impenetrable, and behind me I hear the thing's heavy breathing, the thud of footsteps, the snap of wind at its back. But when I turn to catch a glimpse, I can only make out a shadowy outline. I try to lift my head, to look directly at it, but something's wrong with my eyes—I can't focus on its face. It gets closer, fingers slimy at the back of my neck; I feel the heat of it. I know I should run faster, but I slow down, because I'm coming to a clearing I've been to before, where a figure lies limp with his eyes open. *No, no, no.* I try to slow down. *Not again—*

And then I'm in the passenger seat of my grandparents' car on a blank stretch of sunny highway. I hear the buzz of Harp's snores behind me, and when I look to see who's driving, I feel a rush of pleasure, because he's alive, he's here, he's whistling something sweet. He glances at me, and though I can't quite see his face, I can make out the parts of it that I like best—his lips and jawline and long eyelashes, and of course, that flash of bluest blue.

"Where are we?" I ask.

"California, of course."

"Where are we going?"

"Anywhere," he says. A cloud passes over the sun, and the sky above us turns red as fire. "I had to get you out of there. You weren't safe."

Yes, I was, I'm going to say. *I was with Winnie.* But I feel something clasp around my throat, the fingers of the thing that's chasing me, and, choking, I turn to Peter to beg for help. He stares at my neck for a moment, without interest; then again he begins to whistle.

"Viv!"

Help Harp, I'm trying to tell him; *she's screaming.* But then Peter is gone and I'm awake in Cliff House, aware of something heavy pressing down on my throat. An arm. I hear the sounds of nearby scuffling and then "Viv!" again, sharp and desperate. Harp is shouting my name, but then there's a thump and she's not shouting anymore. I hear a click and a light shines in my face.

"That's the other one," says the voice behind the flashlight. "Call it in, Randy."

CHAPTER SEVEN

I open my mouth to scream, but the arm around my throat makes it impossible to inhale. Where are Suzy and Frankie and Julian and Karen? Where are Winnie and Diego? I begin to pick out shadowy figures in the moonlight—four of them, plus the one holding me down. They wear the dark blue uniforms of the Church of America Peacemakers; I see crucifixes on their armbands. One is illuminated by the screen of his phone; he's young, not much older than me. I try to see Harp in my periphery, but nothing moves where she ought to be. I can't turn my head—afraid of what will happen if I do, afraid of what I'll see there.

"Yep, we got 'em," says the man—Randy—into the phone. "They match the picture on the feed . . . no, no accomplices present. Thank you, sir. Frick's blessings to you as well." He hangs up and addresses the group. "Blackmore says somebody's got to be helping them. We have to move."

Blackmore. The group springs to action. The one holding me hoists me up, sets me on my feet, but my legs tremble so hard I think they'll buckle. *No accomplices present.* Sometimes late at night, Julian goes on runs to the northernmost point of the cliff side and back. Sometimes Frankie patrols the caves around the pool to ensure they're all empty. But how can all the soldiers be gone now? How could we have made it this far only to get snatched up this easily? My arms are pulled roughly behind my back, and when I struggle, the person pulling them groans. I realize it's a woman.

Beside us, someone sighs. "Just knock her out. I'll do it, if you think you can't take her."

I move my head a fraction. The man who's just spoken leans over Harp's bed and scoops something into his arms. When he straightens up, I see Harp's body, limp and lifeless, her head lolling back on her neck.

"Harp!" I try to struggle out of the woman's grasp, and one arm gets loose, but then I feel a sharp blow between my shoulder blades, knocking the wind out of me. The man carrying Harp laughs; he moves toward the back exit. The woman pulls me against her with one arm. The other arm reaches toward the man with the flashlight.

"Can I use that a second?"

"Don't hit her too hard," he warns, handing it over. "Blackmore wants them alive."

My heart thumps painfully. I pull with all my energy against the woman's hold, but she's far stronger. I have less than seconds. If she knocks me out, there's nothing I can do to help Harp. I shout in frustration and feel the woman's arm rear back, the heavy flashlight in her fist. Then the room is flooded with light. At first I don't understand—I've never seen Cliff House lit. The Peacemakers react with panic. The woman freezes, but the other three retrieve guns from holsters I didn't notice before. The one carrying Harp drops her to pull out his, and in the second before she hits the floor, I see her arm jut out to break her fall.

"Easy does it," calls the man who seems to be in charge. He looks around, trying to identify the source of the lights. "Don't do anything stupid now. Let's talk this through—these girls can't be worth that much to you."

I look up, hoping to see Diego march in with guns blazing, the remaining soldiers flanking him, controlled and furious. But I don't see anyone but the Peacemakers, and Harp's body on the floor, eyes shut tight.

"Randy," the man mutters. "Call for backup."

Randy nods, taking his phone from his pocket. He hasn't quite brought it to his ear when I see a flash of movement from across the room and hear Randy's accompanying howl of pain as he drops the phone. He turns slightly and I see the knife protruding deeply into his hand. The man who held Harp is closest to the movement; he reacts quickly, shooting twice in that direction. There's a yelp from behind the bar. My stomach turns—Frankie.

"What the *fuck!*" Randy screams.

"Language, Randy!"

"Fuck you, Nelson—there's a *knife* in my hand." Tears stream down his face as he turns to where I'm held and points his gun at me.

"Randy, don't!" shouts the female Peacemaker. I feel her grip on me loosen just a little. "You're not thinking clearly!"

"They want her alive, Randy," says Nelson urgently. "We have to keep her alive. You swore on the Book of Frick."

"Yeah, well, that was before I got *stabbed in the fucking hand!*" Randy shouts.

He fires.

But before he does, in the half moment between his voice hitting my ears and his finger pulling the trigger, I drop to the floor as heavily as I can. The Peacemaker's hold on me breaks as the room explodes into sound and fire—I hear her scream, clutching her shoulder; Randy's bullet has hit her where my head just was. I hear the shatter of glass and Diego's unintelligible shouts from above; I hear the steady, deafening pop of guns from every direction. It isn't just the Peacemakers, but my people too—they've placed themselves at strategic angles on the balcony above, behind overturned tables and the wide oak bar. I roll under my cot, where my few possessions are piled. I grab my sledgehammer and crawl. There isn't time to think; there isn't time to breathe. Blood pumps in my ears, and I realize I'm whispering to myself: "Get to Harp. Get to Harp." Then someone reaches under the cot and grabs my arm; I swing around to kick out at him, screaming, unable to hear my own screams in all the chaos.

"Vivian!"

Julian drops to a crouch so I can see his face. He holds out his hand, and I push myself out from under the cot to take it; he leads me at a sprint, past the commotion, toward the exit. The air above us splits as a bullet flies past, too close; Julian pushes me to the floor and fires back. He drags me around a corner, and I hear a woman screaming—Winnie? Julian blocks me with his body, watching for movement, digging into his pocket with trembling hands. He throws a set of keys at me.

"Get out." He nods at the exit several yards to our left. "Get a car and bring it to the entrance. Wait five minutes. If no one comes after five minutes, drive. If one of *them* comes, go."

"No!" My ears are ringing from the gunshots and my voice is too loud. "I have to make sure Harp is okay!"

"We'll get Harp. Don't worry. Just go."

He looks at me with his deep brown eyes, at once assured and pleading, and I feel something in me — some wall I've built — give way. I take the keys and the sledgehammer and I run, ducking my head under my arms as though that will protect me. I burst through the back exit and race around the building, the cold air searing my lungs, the terrifying pops inside Cliff House muffled under the sound of wind in my ears. It's dark, but for the first time, a glow spills out onto the pools of still water beyond the cliff. When I reach Amanda's two remaining cars, my shivering hands struggle to fit a key into one of the locks. I accidentally scratch deep grooves into the paint. Then the key fits, the door opens, and I throw myself inside, turning on the engine but not the headlights. I race on screeching tires to the entrance, reaching to throw open the passenger side doors. I check the clock: 12:14. Five minutes, Julian said. But how does he expect me to leave when those minutes are up, if Harp is not here beside me?

"Come on, come on," I whisper. I try to keep my eyes away from the clock for as long as I can, but they dart back there of their own accord after what feels like forever — 12:15. I listen for gunfire. But either it's stopped or I can't hear it over the tinny, wheezing sound I recognize as my own breathing. I check the clock again.

12:16.

I kill the engine, throw the door open. I step into the night again, holding my sledgehammer close to my body. I move toward Cliff House, but the front doors burst open then, and Winnie rushes out, half dragging an ashen Harp beside her. Winnie has a gun, and Harp carries her laptop — both appear to be uninjured.

When she sees me, Harp wrests her elbow out of Winnie's grip and runs to embrace me. Neither of us seems able to speak. Winnie breaks us apart and pushes past me, climbing into the driver's seat. "We have to move," she says.

"What about the others?" I ask as Harp and I crawl into the back seat.

"We'll meet them in LA." She floors the gas, and we race away from Cliff House. I have only a second to look back at the building, hoping I'll see someone leave it. But no one does.

| | | | |

We drive south, merging onto the interstate slightly before two a.m. I listen to Harp breathe heavily beside me. I wait for my teeth to stop chattering, my ears to stop ringing with the echoes of gunshots. But they never do. When I feel like we've put enough distance between us and San Francisco, I whisper the question I'm so afraid to ask:

"Is everybody okay?"

There's a long pause, but I know Winnie heard me—she shifts uncomfortably in her seat.

"Suzy took that first shot, after Frankie threw the knife," she tells me in a dull voice. "She was still breathing when we left, but she didn't look good."

Suzy's face floods my mind—her dimples and big green eyes. Her brow furrowed as she hunched over her laptop, fingers playing across the keyboard like a piano. I can hardly pretend I knew her well, but she was good and brave, and she helped us. I shudder, feeling a painful knot form at the back of my throat. Harp coughs lightly.

"I think . . . Karen got hit too," she says tearfully. "I saw her across the room right before you pulled me out, Winnie. There was . . . there was a lot of blood."

Winnie doesn't react for a long moment. Then she slams her hand down on the steering wheel. "Fuck! Everyone was running around, prepping for the move. The one moment none of us were watching you, and this happens. How could we have been so *stupid?*"

Neither Harp nor I reply. Winnie goes quiet; she continues to drive at exactly the speed limit, no more, no less, so as to draw no attention to us. Her silence turns into a physical presence that I have no wish to push up against. It seems obvious to me how the Church of America found us—they have to have tracked us down through the blog. They were quicker than Suzy thought they'd be. I'm sickened by guilt. I keep thinking of the small, surprised shout I now think must have been Suzy taking a bullet. I close my eyes and try to let the sound of Harp's typing fingers lull me into calm, but it doesn't work. I can still see their faces so clearly.

Three hours into our drive, Winnie pulls into a rest stop to get a cup of coffee. Beside me, Harp frowns at her screen and lifts the laptop, moving it slowly from one side of the car to the other. When she catches my look, she says, "I'm trying to pick up the rest stop's Wi-Fi. I want to check the feed."

The feed. I can only imagine what the Church of America will say when they discover what happened. If none of the Peacemakers survived, they'll paint us as unhinged; if any of them did, if they found any identifying information about Amanda's militia, we'll all be in danger.

"Bam!" Harp points to the full signal strength and pulls up the Church's website. I lean over to see. Our faces are still in a sidebar—WANTED FOR SPIRITUAL THREATS, the caption reads—but we're not the top story. There's a headline in a peppy bright blue font. PRAISE FRICK! PRAISE THIS MIRACLE! Animated angels flank the words, cute and chubby-cheeked, doing a celebratory dance. Below is a video. Harp looks at me, worried.

"Play it." I feel a wave of anxiety creep up my spine. Anything that makes the Church of America this happy is sure to be bad.

Harp presses play. The camera focuses on a podium in some swanky outdoor setting, fresh flowers and fountains. Beside it stands Michelle Mulvey in an evening gown, smiling at someone off camera. There's a smattering of applause as Ted Blackmore approaches the microphone. I inhale through my teeth in anticipation.

"For the last three and a half months," Blackmore begins as the unseen crowd hushes themselves, "I've spoken on behalf of the Church of America. I consider myself a good man, a devout man—" He's interrupted as the audience cheers; he gives them a shy, grateful smile so convincing even I'm slightly won over. "However, there are good men, and there are angels. And as we know, my predecessor, Adam Taggart, falls into that last category.

"A week ago, I had a dream. I dreamed the blessed Mr. Taggart and I were in his office, consulting the Book, drinking hot cocoa, as we so often did before he went to his reward. In the dream, I voiced some of the struggles I currently face. 'Brother,' said I, 'how can I encourage your people on their path to salvation? How can I speak for them, in a world tormented by evil, by grown men lying with other men'"—his voice gains resonance and the crowd begins to murmur, calling out, "Amen!"—"'by women who turn their backs on their hearths and descend into promiscuity, by atheists who deny you, by Believers who fail to honor you with their hard-earned dollars'"—Blackmore shouts now, and this last he booms in a furious snarl—"'by *little girls who spread lies to save their own wretched skins!*'" The audience sounds like thunder; the list has worked up a fury in them. Blackmore feigns exhaustion, takes a long sip of water. Mulvey hands him a towel, with which he gratefully mops his brow. When the crowd finally quiets, he continues.

"In my dream, I asked the Enforcer: 'Isn't there anyone in this blessed country who'll join me? Isn't there anyone who can help spread Frick's word across this troubled land?' And I'll tell you what happened next: Taggart said nothing at all. He looked me in the eye, pushed the Book to me, and pointed to a passage. It was the parable of the Starbucks. *'Dost thou recognize me as thy own Father?'*" Blackmore quotes reverently. "*'You are my child.'*"

"Harp."

She looks at me. I hardly realize her name has come out of my mouth — a drowning sound. I want to warn her of something, but my brain is all white noise. I can't find the words even to think them. I want Blackmore to stop talking. I need him to stop talking.

"When I woke up, I meditated on that a long while," he continues, "not knowing what it could mean. But soon enough, I found out. What the Enforcer meant was that his work on this doomed planet was not quite finished. What Taggart meant was that he would send us someone he himself could speak through, a man with Taggart's own convictions, his own unparalleled brain, his own blood.

"His only son."

The audience gasps, but I barely hear them over the high-pitched buzz in my ears. We watch Blackmore step back from the podium and another person enter the frame to shake his hand. "No no no no no," I hear Harp murmur in horror beside me; she lifts her hands to cover her mouth. I feel a sour pit form in my stomach and I know I'm going to be sick, but I have to watch it first; I have to see it happen. The new person turns from Blackmore to the cheering crowd, and you can hardly make out his face at first because the flash of cameras turns him into a streak of white light, a ghost. For a second there's a look of surprise on his face, but then it melts into a warm smile. When the flashes stop, there's only him and the audience's delight with him: his handsome face and his long fingers waving. The letters pop up in the lower left-hand corner of the screen: PETER TAGGART, NEW CHURCH OF AMERICA SPOKESMAN.

Peter steps up to the microphone and coughs once, shyly, while the crowd grows still. Blackmore and Mulvey stand off to the side, beaming proudly at him.

"Thank you," Peter says. "Thank you. Frick bless you."

CHAPTER EIGHT

The first time I heard Frick address a crowd was right after I attended Church services with my parents after their official conversion. The mass was mostly benign, and I found it weirdly engaging. People came from miles just to kneel at Frick's portrait. The pastor told wild tales—recounting miracles Frick had supposedly performed, describing tortures Non-Believers would face in the months between the Rapture and the planet's ultimate obliteration. Everybody stood to sing "Jesus (Thank You for Making Me American)," a song I'd noticed creeping ever more insistently onto the radio station that played on the bus to school. I remember looking down the pew at my parents and discovering with surprise that they knew all the words.

I decided then that the Church of America was strange, but probably harmless—Mom and Dad seemed happier than they'd been in months, and everyone was so cheerful, so sure of their fate. I didn't think to fear it until we were home, until I opened my laptop and searched for videos of Frick, curious to know more about the weaver of this elaborate fiction. I spent three hours watching YouTube videos of him preaching to crowds in Seattle, Houston, Indianapolis, Washington, DC—as he moved across the country, his speeches grew more and more convincing. It was not because the content made any more sense, because it only became harsher, more scattered. It was because Frick had honed in on the personality that made people fall in love with him. He began with winsome, folksy charm, peppering his speech with a lot of "y'all" and "folks" and "God bless America," before growing fevered in his predictions and condemnations. He ended always on a pleading note, eyes slightly misty, like he was truly worried about the crowd before him. In retrospect, knowing how tenuous Frick's grasp on sanity was, I imagine he struggled to pull off that initial friendly charisma—the desperation that succeeded it was the real Frick bursting through. But at the time, that first Sunday, as my bedroom grew dim around me and my eyes went glassy from the glow of the screen, all I understood was that Frick was charming and dangerous and he was winning.

In his first appearance as Church spokesman, Peter went a different route. Barreling down the highway toward LA in the pre-dawn hours, I compare Peter's speech to the many of Frick's that I've seen. He didn't scream like Frick used to; he wasn't sweating at the end like he'd run a marathon. If I had to describe Peter Taggart's persona, I'd have to say he acts not entirely unlike one of the two people in this world I thought I could trust: Peter Ivey. He's gentle, handsome, kind, quietly insistent. If you believe him—and who could blame you for believing him?—it's because you can tell, without knowing anything about him, that he's a genuinely good person.

We only watched his speech once before Winnie returned to the car, but it was short and straightforward. I already have it memorized.

"Friends and Believers." He read from notes but glanced up periodically to hold eye contact with the crowd. "Thank you for this gracious reception. As a longtime Believer, and the proud son of one of its prophets, I am humbled to stand before you today as the new voice of the Church of America. I may be young, but like my father before me, I'm devoted to Frick and his message. In my first act as Church of America spokesman, I'm excited to announce that Pierce Masterson, the Church's most brilliant scholar, has discovered in his research the projected date of the second Rapture. It will occur September twenty-third this year—one day before the apocalypse." The crowd broke into an excited babble, and Peter paused. Then he looked directly into the camera and said, "These are dark times, but together we wield the most powerful weapon against a world intent on sin and deceit—belief. Trust your heart above all things. Thank you."

And then the adoring throng erupted, and Blackmore and Mulvey flanked Peter to wave together, and that was the end of the video.

"Are you all right?"

I can barely hear Harp's whisper over the hum of the engine. It's the first she's spoken in hours. I see how exhausted she looks, her eyes a little bloodshot. She grips her laptop tight to her chest, her knuckles white.

"Later," I reply. Winnie will have to know—Diego, Amanda, and everyone else will have to know—that this person we trusted, this integral part of the story we're trying to tell, lied. That he was working with the Church the whole time. For now, though,

I can't handle the idea of anyone other than us three—Harp, me, and Peter—knowing the extent to which I was duped.

Harp reaches across the seat and puts her hand on mine. The weight of it reassures me. I look out the window at the Los Angeles skyscrapers materializing in the predawn light, and without really thinking about it, I lift my other hand to my chest, clutch the sledgehammer pendant that hangs there, and yank it hard, so the string holding it around my neck snaps in two.

| | | | |

In LA, I watch billboards flick past advertising Believer-friendly films, all rushed to production in the last year: *Prophet: The Beaton Frick Story; The Second Boat: Judgment Day; My Wife's the Devil 2.* They star actors whose sordid secular scandals I still recall from pre-Rapture days, who now pose with upturned eyes, hands folded in prayer, and simpering smiles.

Winnie turns onto a long commercial street lined with tall palms and kitschy shops with brick façades painted a rainbow of colors—lime greens, tomato reds, bubblegum pinks. The sun has risen and the sky's a cheerful artificial blue—the first blue sky I've seen in a month. This is how I imagined California, before these last weeks in blustery San Francisco: all seems bright, optimistic, and utterly synthetic. Winnie parks in front of a small bookstore—The Good Book—and we climb onto the sidewalk and into a dry, furious heat. Harp and I slip off our sweatshirts. All of us glance cautiously up and down the sidewalks. But it's still early—only a little before seven—and we're alone on the street. Winnie takes a deep breath.

"This is the bookstore I told you about." Her voice is oddly loud. "Let's check it out!"

"It's not even seven." Harp frowns into the shop's darkened windows. "I don't think they're open. And anyway, is this really the time for shopping?"

Winnie ignores her and pushes through the surprisingly unlocked door. Inside is a musty smell, shelves stuffed to capacity with used paperbacks, a magazine rack in one corner, a wire stand of GREETINGS FROM LA! postcards. There's an unnerving Church of America display on one table: leather-bound Books of Frick, spiritual memoirs by Believer basketball players (*Dunking with Jesus*), and a pristine hardcover entitled *Mysteries of the Second Boat Revealed*. Behind the cash register, I realize, is Robbie. He sits up, making a halfhearted attempt to look professional, but he's in the middle of a mammoth sci-fi novel, and the surprise on my face makes him beam.

"Can I help you, ma'am?"

Winnie sticks to a script I don't know. "Do you have a self-help section?"

Robbie nods, letting his expression go serious to match Winnie's tone. "Through the red door in the back and straight up the stairs. Knock twice. You can't miss it."

She leads us past the stacks to a red door onto which someone—maybe one of the soldiers, feeling cheeky—has tacked a promotional poster of Beaton Frick holding a copy of the Book. The text at the bottom says: READ! IT'S WHAT JESUS WOULD DO. Winnie opens the door onto a dark staircase.

"The storefront was Amanda's idea," she explains as we climb. "She thought we'd be more inconspicuous right in the middle of everything this time. Of course, that was before we were attacked . . ."

She trails off. At the top of the stairs, Winnie knocks twice on a door, and after only a second, it's thrown open. Diego stands in the frame, eyes wide and worried.

"I told you not to stop for anything!" He croaks in his panic, and as Winnie steps inside, he catches her by the arm and pulls her into an embrace. "We got here half an hour ago—I thought you got caught. I thought—"

Winnie slips her arms around him, murmuring into his ear. I take in the rest of the room—it's a large loft apartment renovated into a command center, with rows of desks and laptops against one wall, a big-screen TV playing the Church of America's official twenty-four-hour news network on mute. Elliott hovers by the kitchen, muttering tersely on his phone; when he catches sight of Harp and me, he turns his back without acknowledging us. Birdie and some others huddle on a couch against one wall, their eyes red from crying—Diego will have told them about Karen and Suzy. Kimberly stands in front of the TV with the remote in her hand, and when she catches my eye, I open my mouth to greet her. But her face goes hard.

"Great life choices, Vivian. You must be so proud."

Behind her on the screen is Peter's earnest face in the video we watched early this morning—the ticker reads TAGGART'S WORK ON EARTH: NOT DONE and, in smaller letters, THE PROPHET'S SON REVEALED DURING CHURCH FUNDRAISER AT CHATEAU MARMONT. Everyone here has read Harp's blog; they know about Peter and his father. They know Peter stayed behind while we ran; they know he and I were together. The only things they don't know are the things they can't, the things even Harp doesn't understand: the way he looked at me, like I was the person most capable of surprising him; how softly and sweetly he kissed me; how easy it was to believe him. Diego watches me carefully, his arm around

Winnie, who stares at the screen in horror. I don't know what to say to them, but luckily, Harp takes over.

"We were just as surprised as you," she says, moving in front of me as if to shield me. "We never had any reason not to trust him."

I could weep with gratitude. Harp has every right to rub her good instincts in, to revel in how wrong I was—but instead she's protecting me.

"Except, of course, for the matter of *who his dad was*," Kimberly notes sarcastically. "Which he was totally up front about, if I remember correctly?"

But of course she knows he wasn't. I remember with a plunging feeling asking him, "Can we trust you?" He said, "Always." He looked me in the eye.

"I'm sorry," I say. "We were stupid—*I* was stupid. Harp never wanted him along in the first place; it was all me. You have no idea how much I regret it."

"You realize what this means, right?" Kimberly is unappeased. "He's all over your story, and now it turns out you were spectacularly wrong about him. People are going to wonder—what else are you two wrong about?"

There's a long pause as each and every person in the room turns to us.

"We're not lying about the Rapture, if that's what you're trying to say. And if that's what you're trying to say, why not come out and say it?" Harp's teeth are clenched; her body coils with energy. I put my hand on her shoulder, afraid she's going to rush at Kimberly.

"We don't think you're lying about what you saw, Harp," Birdie sniffles. Kimberly shoots her a glare. "*Most* of us don't, anyway. It's just . . . you have to understand. It was going to be hard for them to believe you as it was. But now? When this person you claimed was on your side is the new face of the Church? It's going to be a lot harder. Won't people assume you're lying, or crazy? Won't people think you're just trying to get attention?"

I glance again at the TV, at Peter's face—bigger now than it was on Harp's laptop, nearly life-size. They're showing the part of the speech where he looks directly into the camera. *Trust your heart above all things.* I feel a surge of anger. I want to break down the front door; I don't want to rest until I've found him. I want him to feel what I feel, this hurricane of sorrow and humiliation and anger; I want him to know what he's done. By giving his face to the Church of America, he's made it impossible to beat them. He's taken everything I've done, everything I've sacrificed—these last desperate months, my relationship with my mother—and made them meaningless. I want him to know what he's done to me. I want to make him feel it.

| | | | |

That night, Amanda's army holds an impromptu memorial service for Suzy and Karen. They light candles Amanda has provided in case of power outages and crowd into the command center to sing secular songs and tell funny stories of conversations on the seawall with Suzy, of the way Karen always treated them like family. No one states the obvious—that the Peacemakers came for Harp and me, that it's because of Harp and me that their friends are dead. Winnie is warmer toward me than ever, and Julian praises my quick thinking during the attack. But I see the looks that Kimberly and Colby give us when we walk into the room, and I know they would rather it had been us who died in San Francisco.

Luckily, there are plenty of other things to worry about in Los

Angeles. Everyone is hard at work preparing for the attack—they train endlessly, practice shooting targets deep in the recesses of Griffith Park, and trail Peter, Mulvey, and Blackmore in small groups. Eventually they determine the Church's headquarters to be a hotel called the Chateau Marmont, the same place where Peter was first introduced as spokesman. The pinpointed target means it's only a matter of time until Amanda chooses a date for the attack. Meanwhile, heat blasts through the windows, and there's an ongoing drought that leaves the faucets dry. The fridges are stocked with plastic water bottles, but we can't shower, and as the hot days drag on, everyone's hair goes greasy; the loft acquires a sour stench of sweat. Still, we know we're lucky: according to the Church of America News Network, which Diego keeps on at all hours, the drought has already killed thirty people and counting in Southern California. It means disease and dangerous food shortages across the nation, and that's just some of the bad news within a small radius. The Church of America News Network also reports the assassination of the British prime minister on the steps of 10 Downing Street; an aggressive new strain of malaria killing nearly ten kids a day in China; mass shootings in Texas, Ohio, and New York; and one day, causing Robbie to cry out loud, me. They show my school picture, plucked from my freshman yearbook. Diego turns up the volume.

"The Church can now publicly confirm that the first of these dangerous enemies to salvation is named Vivian Apple, age seventeen, originally a resident of Pittsburgh, Pennsylvania. Her last known whereabouts were San Francisco, where she participated in the gruesome murders of five of the Church of America's blessed Peacemakers."

I feel my face go numb. My mouth moves noiselessly, trying

to utter the defense I'm too shocked to articulate. On the screen, my face cuts to Harp's.

"Her accomplice is one Harpreet Janda, and she is the author of a—truly disgusting—post currently making the rounds in the blogosphere."

The shot of Harp's face fades to Peter behind a podium at the end of a long drive, an ornate white building behind him. "It's pure fiction, of course," Peter says, sounding confident. "We've consulted with the experts—Pierce Masterson and other prominent ministers worldwide—and they agree that even *reading* it is a sin grievous enough to preclude passage on the second boat. Chapter eleven, verse eight: *'If the secular heathens spit lies in thy ear, it is thine own sin should thou start to listen.'*"

A reporter calls out, "Can you comment specifically on the allegations that you were in a relationship with one of the enemies to salvation? A Vivian Harriet Apple?"

His expression changes then to one I've never seen on his face before, a painful smirk. "Come on, guys, you know I can't kiss and tell." The reporters laugh. "But we all know that the Book of Frick encourages us as men to convert as many sinful temptresses as we can. Let's just say I was trying to do my duty as a Believer—does that work?"

The newscaster returns, chuckling to himself at this. "We spoke to Brendan J. Winters, a former classmate of these heathens, who can shed some light on their background and motives."

Harp emits a pained sound, something between a scream and a growl—they've cut to B.J. Winters, a late-adopting Believer, part of the gang that killed Harp's brother, Raj, back in Pittsburgh. He looks thinner than I remember, and terrified, though it's impossible to miss the gleam of excitement in his eyes as he answers.

"Well, it was no secret that they were both staunch Non-Believers. I didn't know Vivian well, but there were rumors that she was deep into the occult—like, witches and stuff. As for Harp"—B.J. cracks a small, hateful smile—"you don't have to be as devout as I am to know she was trouble. Her brother was openly homosexual, and both she *and* Viv were known around here for being . . . you know, slutty. It was actually kind of a game for them, I think—they'd throw themselves at upstanding young Believers in the community and try to tempt them into sin using their deceitful feminine wiles. I bet you anything Vivian tried to do the same with our blessed spokesman, Peter Taggart, but clearly he's made of stronger stuff." He pauses, maybe to gauge whether he's been brutal enough. "Plus, I can't be the first to wonder if Harp maybe had ties to Muslim extremists?"

Stunned into silence, we watch as the ticker below B.J.'s face reads APPLE AND JANDA: CONFIRMED WHORES/POSSIBLE WITCHES/ DEFINITELY VIOLENT ANTI-AMERICAN TERRORISTS?

| | | | |

We all make mistakes when it comes to dudes, often because they manage to delude us into thinking they're good people, rather than swamp monsters wearing cute boy masks. (The most recent of these mistakes for me personally, BTW, was Goliath, aka Spencer Ganz, aka Shithead.) It sucks, but such is life. Viv and I are not ones to hold a grudge — unless, of course, said swamp monsters go on national television to call us lying sluts!

We trusted Peter because he knew things about the Church we didn't, and he was nice to us. For a while, it really seemed like he was treating my girl Viv exactly how you want to see your best friend treated: with care, and respect. They never did anything but kiss — but even if they had, would that give him any right to do what he did? To lie to us, lead us into danger, turn on us, sell us out? Even if you buy their story instead of ours, what the fuck is wrong with you that you consider Viv's supposed sin (being a babe, enjoying a good make-out) a bigger transgression than all of Peter's?

And furthermore, WITCHES ARE AWESOME.

"I can't believe he tried to Magdalene me," I say for the millionth time, watching Harp aggressively bang out her latest screed. We lie together on the bed I've claimed on the third floor, where I've spent the two weeks since Peter's press conference hiding under blankets, sobbing, trying to talk myself down from panic attacks. "How could I have been so dumb? I always thought if someone made the effort to Magdalene me, I'd see it coming a mile away."

Harp reads over her post with a frown. Yesterday Amanda appeared for a strategy meeting and instructed Harp to keep blogging, as the Church's condemnation of us is bringing in more readers than ever before. She had a few of the more tech-savvy soldiers work to cloak the Good Book's servers, and though none of them have Suzy's talent, it's assumed she's bought us at least a little time. Amanda told Harp to avoid the subject of Peter Taggart at all costs, but I could have told her this was a lost cause.

"Girls who get Magdalened aren't *dumb*," Harp finally replies, continuing to type. "The only mistake they make is in trusting the dudes they have sex with. It isn't their fault that the dudes are so goddamn untrustworthy."

I catch the flint in her voice. Harp has had a lot more sex than I have at this point (which is to say any), and I know B.J.'s accusations have gotten under her skin.

"You're right," I say. "I'm sorry. I'm just embarrassed."

"I know." Harp's voice softens and she stops typing, turning to look at me. "Try to turn it into anger instead. Anger's a lot more useful."

That isn't hard. The idea that Peter's aim in complimenting and kissing me, in making me symbolic sledgehammer necklaces, was only to have sex with me, convince me I was a sinner, and prod me into conversion is infuriating. How unfair that the Church took this private, magical thing—the shivery pleasure I took in touching Peter, in being touched by him—and turned it into a weapon to wield against me. I hear the chipper voice of the Church magazines chirping in my brain: *You're in a relationship with a boy who treats you as his emotional and spiritual equal. You feel a desire to express your affection through physical acts that will bring mutual pleasure. Do you (a) go for it! Sex is a natural gift from God, and a lot of fun so long as you do it safely!; (b) get him to propose! Sex is only fun if you do it in a Church of America–approved union! Plus, babies are so cute!; or (c) seek guidance from your local pastor for your sinful thoughts and ask for tips on expressing your love in a holy, nonphysical way? TRICK QUESTION! The answer is (d) the fact that you even momentarily considered having sex out of wedlock proves that you have no place in God's eternal kingdom, you reprehensible slut.*

Is that what Peter was thinking every time he put his mouth on me? Was he imagining the thumbs-up he'd get from Jesus once he managed to make me repent?

The door to the third-floor loft opens, and Winnie enters. She smiles when she sees us. "Hey, guys. What sort of occult shenanigans are you getting yourselves into this time?"

"Just your standard hocus-pocus," Harp answers, closing her laptop and getting to her feet. She stretches. "Who's on shift in the bookstore right now?"

"Julian."

Harp grins and tosses her hair. "That's what I was hoping you'd say." She goes bounding out the door, leaving Winnie and me alone together. My sister looks disheveled, her long hair loose in a bun, stray wisps falling around her face. She sits on the edge of the bed.

"You okay, buddy?"

"Oh, I'm fine, you know. Dealing with my reputation as a murdering enchantress. Coping with the fact that the dude I fell for was a lying scumbag. Coming to terms with the guilt of having caused the deaths of two innocent people. The usual."

Winnie frowns at this last bit. "You think you caused Suzy's and Karen's deaths?"

"It doesn't seem like a coincidence that the day our post about the Church gains traction is the day the Peacemakers arrive at Cliff House. We got the story read and they got killed. Is there any other explanation?"

"There are *dozens* of other explanations," Winnie insists. "Suzy had been hacking into Church-affiliated websites for months— maybe she inadvertently left traces. Someone could have followed us—any of us, Julian, me, Diego—back from an outside trip and seen you. One of our soldiers might be selling the rest of us out. Why would you tell yourself it was all because of you?"

I look away. I know she's not wrong, but I don't feel ready to be talked out of this guilt.

"Viv," she says. "I don't want this to come across as condescending, okay? But this is part of what being a soldier is all about. People are killed around you—suddenly, meaninglessly. And to get through it, you have to understand that sometimes there's nothing you could have done to stop it. Suzy and Karen? They were one of those times."

"How do you know?"

"Because the other times feel different. Like . . . this planned attack, for instance." Winnie shakes her head. "I've been trying so hard to get Diego to fight Amanda on it. It won't work. It's messy and it's pointless and innocent people are going to die."

"Not that innocent."

Winnie looks shrewdly at me. "No. Not that innocent. But, Viv—do you honestly want Peter to die? Like that?"

I'm angrier than I've ever been before—I'm more furious with Peter than I was with the Angels when I assumed they'd caught or killed him. My anger's not as useful as Harp says it is. It's unfocused and overwhelming. And the truth is I don't know what it means yet—right now I don't know what my fury is capable of making me want, making me do. Before I can tell Winnie this, though, I hear a clattering sound. Harp has burst into the room. She's clutching an armful of items and she has an expression on her face I can't quite decipher—some combination of joy and deep sorrow. She rushes to me and drops a hardcover book in my lap. It's the title I noticed when we entered the bookstore our first morning: *Mysteries of the Second Boat Revealed*. The author's name is Pierce Masterson.

"Pierce Masterson." I look up at her. "They keep saying that name. 'The Church's most brilliant scholar,' Peter said."

Harp nods and finds her voice. "Look at the inside cover."

I open the book. The author photo shows a man with a thin face, a high hairline, eyes so pale they're nearly translucent. He smirks at the camera, and I grin back. Because this is not the first time I've seen him. He sat to the left of Michelle Mulvey on the screen in Frick's compound.

"The third Angel." I hand the book to Winnie. "Pierce Masterson is the third Angel."

"Oh my God." Winnie stands, staring at Masterson's photo. "We should have known—this dude's everywhere. I'll catch up with you later—I need to go tell Diego."

She races from the room, book in hand, and Harp waits for the door to slam behind her before giving me an issue of our favorite Church magazine, *Godly Girl!* There's a grinning all-American boy on the cover, and my eyes skip over the headlines (SECOND BOAT FASHION: 167 UNFORGETTABLE LOOKS FOR YOUR DAY OF ASCENSION; CAN GOD READ YOUR TEXT MESSAGES?), but I'm not sure what I'm supposed to be seeing here.

"Thanks, Harp, but I've read enough of this shit to last me my possibly very short lifetime."

Harp shakes her head, pokes her finger so hard at the cover that she knocks the magazine out of my hands. "The cover model, dummy! Look at the goddamn cover model!"

I pick *Godly Girl!* up again and force myself to look at him. He's older than we are, with gold ringlets and tan skin. He wears a T-shirt and blue jeans and smiles disarmingly, broad forearms crossed carelessly across his chest. He's very handsome, and just looking at him, at the confidence in his warm eyes, I can tell he knows it. It's this quality, this self-assuredness, that makes me finally recognize him. When I do, I let out a faint cry and search for his name in the text. It only takes me a moment to find it.

Dylan Marx: Our Godly Gorgeous New Fave Spills the Deets on His Apocalypse Plans—and Describes His Dream Wife!

Somehow, Raj Janda's old boyfriend has ended up a Church of America cover boy.

CHAPTER NINE

H arp and I sit side by side, the issue of *Godly Girl!* splayed across our knees. We consume the feature on our old friend Dylan Marx with the same level of rapt absorption as the hormonal tween Believers for whom the magazine is written.

Dylan appears on five pages of *Godly Girl!* Four are just photos, primly sexy shots of him in a variety of dumb poses: rowing a canoe in a checkered button-up; in a tux, holding a bouquet toward the camera, glancing shyly through his curls; kneeling before a portrait of Frick, palms together, solemn eyes focused on the prophet's face. *"What the fuck is this?!"* Harp says each time I turn the page. "What the fuck is this?" At the corner of each page is a list of prices on all the clothes he wears, available at the Church of America website. What this is is an ad. What remains unclear is how Dylan ended up in it.

On the fifth page there's an interview we snatch up hungrily, eager for any clues as to why Dylan is shilling menswear for the

Church. Instead we find questions such as *Can you describe your dream girl?* and *What do you look for in a potential wife?*

"She has a penis," Harp remarks, deadpan, "and is, in fact, a man."

I shush her to concentrate on Dylan's reply:

> I love girls of all shapes and sizes, but when I settle down, it will be with a woman who loves the same three *F*s I do: food, football, and Our Heavenly Father!

"ARE WE IN HELL RIGHT NOW?" Harp shouts in my ear. "Vivian, I think we might be in my personal hell!"

The questions never stray far from the territory of *Do you like girls/Jesus?* and *How much do you like girls/Jesus?* All Dylan's answers read to me as desperately insistent that he likes both very, very much. (*"The perfect date? That's easy! Taking a girl to church is the surest way to find out if she's the one for me! Girls look prettiest when they're lit from within by God's holy light!!"*) The interview is surrounded by pastel hearts proclaiming Dylan's virtues: *Handsome! Devout! Your Boyfriend Would Look Great in These Clothes!* It's only in Dylan's last answer that we receive any insight into how and why he ended up in *Godly Girl!*'s pages:

> **Not to be all frowny-town, but how did you feel about being left behind? And what are you doing to prepare for the arrival of the second boat!?**
>
> I was initially bummed! My parents embraced eternal splendor in March, but Frick had different plans for me and my little sis, Molly. I've spent this

time between Raptures digging deep into my faith to figure out where I went wrong. Luckily, Frick sent me a sign! I was on a bus to New York with Molly in April when I met the Church scout who got me my first modeling job. And then I realized Frick wanted me to stay behind and encourage Believer girls to stay holy and virtuous, no matter the temptation! Now I'm truly giving back to my community—and getting to wear all these cool, affordable clothes isn't so bad either! [Laughs.] As far as the second boat goes—I plan to look my best, in my new boot-cut Church-brand jeans. I can't wait to greet the Prophet Frick in style!

"Are *we* doing this, somehow?" Harp asks incredulously. "Is there something about us that makes all the boys of our acquaintance turn belatedly evangelical? Maybe we're, like, too *raw* in our intelligence and sensuality."

"I don't think the rawness of our sensuality was ever an issue for Dylan." I reread his final answer, trying to make sense of it. "This is too ridiculous. He has to be faking it. Don't you think? The scout spotted him on the bus and Dylan saw easy money, plus stability for him and Molly. So he let the Church believe he believed. I can see him doing that—can't you? It's not like he ever had any sympathy for the Church of America."

"Neither did Peter," Harp points out.

"But we knew Dylan longer, and a lot better. And Raj knew him better than either of us. I can't imagine Raj being wrong about him."

Harp has a faraway look on her face. I wonder if she's thinking about the last time she saw Dylan: when she lashed out at him, blaming him for Raj's death. I watch as she grabs her laptop and searches Dylan's name. Together we marvel at the results. I'd searched for him before—two months ago now, in Keystone— but nothing came up. I hadn't searched since because I was afraid of what I'd find. I thought he was dead—as far as we knew, he'd been on the East Coast during the devastating Hurricane Ruth. But we soon figure out that this push to make him famous is recent and aggressive. The image search is a treasure trove along the same theme as the pics in *Godly Girl!*: Here, Dylan smiles sultrily in front of an American flag. Here, Dylan stands knee-deep in the ocean in a red, white, and blue swimsuit, beckoning to the viewer. Harp finds his Twitter (*PGH boy in the City of Angels! Prayin' for the second boat!*); he has two hundred thousand followers. He tweets in the same cheerful tone as his *Godly Girl!* interview:

Great shoot today over @StyleVirgin! Classy &
modest just as @FatherFrick would want. Think you
guys are gonna luv these pics! #GodblessUSA.

Wow! I love my new @ChurchofAmerica brand water carbonator. Gotta get my fizz on! Seriously tho
they make a great product.

#LazySaturday working on my car! I am a car buff!
Total dude thing. Keep holy the Sabbath tomorrow!

Asked to be the new face of @ChurchofAmerica
cologne for men: Eden! Soooooo #blessed! Smells
great.

I'll b @theGrove this afternoon doing a
promo event with @GodlyGirl! Come say hi!
#Frickblessyou!

It isn't the most egregious of the Church's crimes, but my skin crawls at the way they've turned my friend Dylan—whom I loved in Pittsburgh for being smart, sly, and sharply sarcastic—into this brainless walking advertisement. I'll never understand why Believers cling to this kind of language, this relentless empty optimism, plus all! those! exclamation! points! Maybe the corporation uses it to offset the doom preached on a daily basis—if the corporation's language matched Frick's, people would be too depressed to leave their homes to buy the Church-brand cologne and kitchen appliances. On her screen, Harp pulls up a map of the Grove, apparently a shopping center, which Dylan mentioned in a tweet from just a few hours ago. She traces its proximity to our current location.

"Five and a half miles," she notes, standing and heading for the door. "Doable. It looks like there's a bus we can take . . . we'll have to get the fare somehow. I have no cash. You think Amanda leaves a stash around?"

"Wait—what are we talking about?"

Harp makes a disbelieving face at me. "You don't seriously expect me to sit here while Dylan Marx is alive in the same city we are—do you?"

"Harp, come on." I trail her downstairs into the command center, empty now as everyone is scattered across the city on their various missions. "You think you can waltz into a Church-sponsored event and out again with no repercussions? They're looking for us. They have the whole country looking for us."

"Exactly!" She throws open drawers, searching for secret petty cash. "It would be *so* stupid for us to try this that no one in their right minds will expect it. It's the perfect cover!"

I watch her move to the kitchen. Harp opens a cabinet above the stove, takes out a black tin, and removes the lid. "Ha!" She holds up a wad of small bills. Her grin fades when she sees the anxiety in my expression.

"You don't have to do it, Viv. Just because I'm doing it doesn't mean you have to. You don't magically turn back into the old Vivian Apple every time you make the choice to abide by the rules. But I have to go. Because Raj loved him, and you're right—that's not the real Dylan. They're making him do it or he's doing it to survive, but that isn't him. And maybe I can help him get away from them."

It's true that I don't want to take chances. I feel like we're already pushing the line with Amanda's militia—Kimberly thinks we're liars and the others think we're reckless; Diego's impression of us as useless teens would probably not be turned around for the better if we were seized at a *Godly Girl!* event in the middle of a bright Los Angeles day. I don't want to betray Winnie's trust. But I look at Harp's face, at the determination set into every line, at that little glimmer of mischief, too—she wants to see Dylan. She's going to see Dylan. And if she's going to get caught, I won't let her get caught alone.

"Lead the way, old sport," I tell her.

| | | | |

We'd be most incognito in our old Church of America–approved apparel: modest long-sleeved shirts and ankle-length skirts to hide our skin, the source of all temptation. But when Winnie brought us new things to wear, she somehow didn't anticipate our need to blend into a crowd of tween Believers. We try to make ourselves look as different as possible from the pictures of us on the feed. Harp raids the others' bags for bits of disguise; she finds a baseball cap for me and a pair of wire-framed glasses that blur my vision but make me look a few years younger. My sprained hand has mostly healed—Frankie took the splint off last week— but my fingers are still stiff, and I struggle to pull Harp's hair into two tight pigtails. "Hustle up, Apple!" she commands; we don't know how much time we have until the soldiers begin to trickle back home. When we assess ourselves in the bathroom mirror, I note that we don't really look different—we're recognizably ourselves, just more ridiculous. Harp's expression is sober, but she's not deterred.

"Let's move," she says.

By the time we walk down to the bookstore, Julian's shift is over, which is a relief—he and Harp have this new flirtation, but still I think he'd have stopped us if we tried to get past him. Robbie sits behind the counter. When we walk in, he looks up from his book.

"Where are you going?"

Harp replies simply, "Out"—but one look into Robbie's eyes and I panic.

"Amanda asked us to go on a mission . . . for the blog!" I blurt. "It's secret, so you can't tell anyone."

Untroubled or uninterested by this burden, Robbie shrugs and returns his eyes to the page. When we step outside into the brutal glare of the sun, the searing dry winds blowing down on us, shivering the leaves of the palms overhead, Harp gives me a look.

"What?"

"You are terrible at lying, Viv. Embarrassingly bad. Have I taught you nothing?"

At the stop down the block, I'm expecting a normal public city bus to pull up, so when the gleaming white shuttle that arrives turns out to be a Church-sponsored one—Sacrificial Rides—I feel a cold sweat break out over my skin. I stand back, ready to let it pass, but Harp pinches my arm and gestures me forward. "It's the only bus there is," she whispers.

Onboard, I feed my fare into the machine, avoiding eye contact with the driver, hyperaware of the security camera above. There's a large cluster in the center of the bus: elderly women, boys with skateboards, wealthy tourists with sunburned faces. Harp slips into the crowd with ease. I move awkwardly, too aware of my body. One of the skaters glances up as I push my way behind him, and when our eyes meet I instinctively smile—then freeze. My face is visible, but it'd be weirder to duck my head, to hide. So I stand there, smiling politely at him, hoping my eyes don't reveal the terror I feel, until the boy, apparently taking me for a crazy person, makes a face and turns away. When I glance at Harp, I see she's watched the whole exchange with an incredulous look upon her face.

Sacrificial Rides is more expensive than public transport used to be, and it shows in the sleek, clean interior of the bus, the small televisions hanging over every other seat, each of them playing the Church of America News Network. I stifle a gasp as I recognize Pierce Masterson's thin face on a split screen beside one of the newscasters.

"Mr. Masterson, could I get you to just lay it out for me? It's August fourth; we have less than two months left until the Rapture happens—what can we expect from these last weeks of our time on earth?"

"Happily, Scott." Masterson has a reedy voice, and as he continues to speak, his face takes on a sleepy self-satisfaction. He looks like a cat, I realize. I half expect him to purr. "As we move through August and into September, I expect we'll see the very fabric of human civilization begin to unravel. Democracies will fall and class warfare will erupt—meanwhile, deadly storms will continue to ravage the nation from coast to coast. The Book of Frick talks of a death toll of tens of thousands. Now"—he draws himself up—"some scholars of Frickian theology believe this to be an exaggeration for dramatic effect. But I say that's heresy."

"Well, you can bet I'll put money on your interpretation. Now take us through the last two days of the world. What will that look like for the people left behind?"

"Well, I imagine the morning of September twenty-third will be quite familiar to all of them—waking to find loved ones gone, ruing their presence on a dying earth. But luckily, they won't have too long to dwell on this self-reflection. Within forty-eight hours, the earth will be destroyed. The exact amount of time it will take for the Lord to destroy the world is unknown, but a careful reading of the Book of Frick reveals we can expect it late in the evening on September twenty-fourth. What we *do* know is that a wretched hellfire will cover the surface of the planet and devour everything that's left. The pain, as I understand it"—he wears a false, pitying smile—"will be absolutely excruciating."

It takes us forty minutes to reach the Grove, and by the time we do, I'm sick to my stomach from the sound of Masterson's sneering voice in my ears. Harp and I exit the bus into a sunny plaza swarming with people. At its edges, under the dubious shade of the palms on the parched grass, there's a small tent city—signs reading NEED FOOD AND WATER, PLEASE HELP. Beyond is the dazzling shopping complex, shimmering in the heat—dozens of expensive stores and well-maintained cobblestone paths. The only evidence of the drought is the elegant stone fountains that sit every couple hundred feet, bone dry.

We make our way through the crowd, keeping space between us at all times. We're not sure where exactly Dylan's event will be, but then Harp points out a pair of Believer mothers in their long skirts and bonnets, shepherding three giggling tweens in matching modest dress. "Bethie," one of the mothers snaps, "what does Frick say about such unseemly behavior?" One of the girls stops laughing, looking chastened. *"'The voices of young girls give Satan pleasure and Jesus untold grief,'"* she quotes back. We decide to shadow them.

In the center of the Grove is a white tent with a crowd of young Believers gathered at its mouth, and a banner reading FRICK BLESS YOU, DYLAN MARX! to let us know we're in the right place. But we're dressed all wrong—surrounded by this sea of demure femininity, we might as well be wearing mesh tank tops and thigh-high leather boots. Luckily, the crowd seems too focused on the prospect of Dylan to pay much attention to the heathens in their midst—they stand on tiptoe, strain forward, attempting to catch a glimpse. They're very quiet, trying hard not to please Satan. I remember being twelve, killing an afternoon in the mall with my old best friend, Lara Cochran. Outside the food court, we stumbled on a performance by a boy band on the rise. The girls thronging the stage that day were slightly older, totally wild: jumping, shoving, holding up suggestive signs with neon lettering. Above all, they screamed so loud you couldn't hear the band. They were completely undone by desire. I tried to edge closer, fascinated, but Lara hung back, looking revolted. "They're like *animals*," she said disdainfully—prime Believer material before there even was such a thing.

These silent Believer girls could not be mistaken for animals—

they cower under the eyes of their mothers and God. Still, I feel their quiet yearning, all the more powerful for being contained. I'm unsettled by it. I know as well as anyone the strain of being good, and I wish I could convince them it isn't worth it. If I weren't trying so hard to stay anonymous, I'd start screaming and pushing; I'd start a riot.

The meet-and-greet line forms with a hushed excitement. I get in it while Harp makes a loop around the tent. She's gone a few minutes, and every second she's not in my sight is agonizing: I imagine a Peacemaker seizing Harp's skinny arms, dragging her off into parts unknown. I sigh in relief when she reappears, tugging thoughtfully at one of her pigtails.

"Okay," she says in an undertone. "He's nearly alone up there—there's a woman at the table who seems like an assistant; she sells posters of the *Godly Girl!* cover to the girls, and he signs them. There's also a Peacemaker right behind him—just one, and he doesn't look particularly speedy, so if worse comes to worst, we could probably make a break for it?"

"'We could probably make a break for it' is a sentence that should never end in a question mark, Harp. But okay. Anything else I should know?"

She shakes her head and then grins. "It's really him, Viv. I got a good look, and it's just—Dylan! He looks so good. He's alive!"

Her excitement is infectious; I grin back at the thought of him at the end of the line, shaking the hair out of his eyes in his casual way, probably desperate for a cigarette. It's like holding a piece of home in my hands, to think of him so near.

Harp appraises the line behind me. She nods. "Okay, I'll go back there. We're too recognizable together. Once Dylan sees you, he'll make a point of talking to you alone."

"Wait, what?" I shake my head, panicked. "Harp, no! It's too dangerous to split up, and anyway—what if he pretends not to recognize me? How am I supposed to get him away from his handlers?"

"Don't worry!" Harp says as she walks away. "I'll come back when I think of something!"

But she doesn't come back. I think I know why Harp has formed this horrible plan—she's wary of facing Dylan after the way she last spoke to him, when she blamed him for Raj's death and insisted she never wanted to see him again. But I can't help wishing she'd just suck it up. I stand in the slowly dwindling line, fidgeting in my stolen glasses, feeling the sweat pool at the small of my back. I watch as Believer girls collapse onto the pavement, either from heat or from the pressure of repressing their imminent sexual awakenings. As I get closer to Dylan—close enough to see huge posters of his face on either side of the tent, his dimpled grin beckoning me nearer—his fans around me work themselves into as much of a frenzy as their decorum allows. The girls in front of me, their hair tied back into somber braids long enough to sit on, grasp each other's hands, tense and jittery. Behind me, I hear the squeak of a little girl's voice as she recites an endless list of Dylan facts: "His favorite football team is the New Orleans Saints! He likes hiking, sailing, and bowling! *I* like bowling! And he has a sister, and she's the same age as me! And he's *so* handsome!" Her mother whispers, "He's very godly, Trudy, but keep your voice down—you know it's a sin to speak wantonly of the opposite sex."

Soon there are three groups in front of me, then two. I watch girls run off ahead, clutching signed posters to their chests. Now I can hear the friendly murmur of Dylan's voice as he greets his fans: "Good afternoon! And what's your name?" I try to find Harp behind me. But all too quickly, the girls with the braids in front of me get their posters signed and step away, one trying to suppress a squeal, the other looking pale, leaning against her friend. Right as I step forward, Dylan turns to ask the Peacemaker for a bottle of water, and the man sets off in search of one. Dressed in a crisp button-down and shiny boots, Dylan leans back to flick lazily through an expensive-looking phone. It's so hard not to simply call out his name.

"Forty-five dollars for a small poster, seventy-five for a large," says Dylan's handler. She's in a modest black skirt suit and her upper lip gleams with sweat.

I slip my hand into my pocket but I already know I have nowhere near that much.

"Uh . . ." I try to pitch my voice higher. "I just wanted to say hi?"

She sighs and glances up with disdain, but seems to look right through me. "Dylan has a very full schedule—if you want to say hi, buy a poster."

Dylan stays focused on his phone. "Relax, Marnie. It's not gonna kill me to say hello." He glances up in a jokey, perfunctory way and says it: "Hello."

I watch his smile hang there a moment as the panic reaches his eyes. Then his face falls. He drops his phone on the table and stands. I feel the muscles in my legs tense—he's about to say my name; I need to run before he gets the chance—but then I see how pointedly he stares away from me. When he speaks, he sounds calm.

"Marnie, I need a bathroom break."

His handler leans to the side to gauge the line. "Can it wait twenty minutes? We're nearly done."

"No," Dylan insists. "I really have to go. Look, it's in my contract that I get at least one fifteen-minute break at every event. I never make a fuss, but *legally*—"

Marnie throws her hands in the air, aggravated. "Fine!"

I step away slowly so as not to attract her attention and head for the public restroom to our left. Behind me, I hear Marnie call out, "Make it quick, though! I'm the one who has to answer to Peter Taggart, you know!"

I don't hear Dylan's response. A moment later, someone shoves me hard from behind, and when I look up, I see him making a beeline for the men's room. I speed up to slip in behind him, hardly thinking about what will happen if anyone else is inside. But the blue-tiled bathroom is empty—Dylan crouches, moving from stall to stall to check, and when he finds no one, he whirls around to face me, eyes blazing.

"What is wrong with you?" he hisses.

"I think etiquette dictates a greeting more to the effect of 'So happy to see you alive and well in these troubling end times, old friend.'"

"I'm not happy to see you! Seeing you is confirmation that you're actually deranged! The Church of America is looking for you and you respond by accusing them of mass murder; you wait until they call you a terrorist to show up at a *crowded Church event*—"

"I thought it was a sin to read the post." I stand by the door, hoping Harp has seen me leave the line, that she's followed. If she hasn't, the next time the door opens, I'll have to run like hell. "You're never going to get on the second boat with that kind of browser history, no matter how dashing you look in your boot-cut jeans."

His face goes pale under the fluorescents, and when he speaks again, his voice is soft and controlled. "I'm glad I could bring you such amusement during these dark days."

"Dylan—"

"Really, it's a comfort. Frick knows how doomed you are. There's a bull's-eye on your back, Vivian, and if I can bring you some laughs before the Church takes aim, I'll consider it an act of charity. I'm trying hard to give back while I can."

"We were worried," I say, feeling uncertain. Were we right to think that Dylan's Believer posturing was entirely an act? "We thought we could help."

"You have a weirdly optimistic concept of the position you're in. Thank you, but no thank you. I don't need the help of a known heathen."

"Dylan." I stare at him hard, but his expression is blank. "Come on. It's me."

He turns, focusing on his own reflection in a mirror above the sink. He adjusts an artfully tousled curl. "Get out of here, Viv. Okay? Go back to hiding in caves, murdering Peacemakers, whatever it is you do these days. I'll pretend I didn't see you—it's a sin against Frick, but I'll do it, for old times' sake."

I take a step back, frightened. But at that moment the door bangs open, and to my relief Harp bursts in. Dylan jumps at the sound. When he turns and sees her, his mouth falls open. She moves toward him, determined, and I want to warn her—*it's not safe; he's not our Dylan anymore.* But Harp doesn't even acknowledge my presence in the room. She and Dylan face each other; they wear identical expressions of surprise and sadness and lingering anger. He and Harp are bound together for life: they're the ones who loved Raj; they're the ones who buried him. I lean against the door with all my weight, and wait for someone to break the spell.

"You look," Harp says after a long moment of excruciating silence, her eyes welling with tears, "so fucking *stupid* on the cover of that magazine."

Dylan covers his face with his hands. When he takes them away, I see he's laughing and crying. "At least I'm not a slutty Muslim extremist! At least I have that going for me!"

They each take a couple of steps forward, meeting in the space between to throw their arms around each other. After a moment Dylan lifts Harp's small frame up into the air; she squeals.

"This is so weird, you guys," I tell them.

Dylan pulls away first, wiping his eyes with his forearm. "You have to get out of here. Don't worry about me. I'm okay."

"How do you know you can trust them?" Harp grips his arm and doesn't let go. "How do you know they won't get rid of you once they don't need you anymore, once you stop making money for them?"

He shakes his head. "I don't! But it's better than the alternative—if I hadn't met Marnie on the bus, Molly and I would've headed straight into Hurricane Ruth. But I did. And they spent a few months polishing me up, making sure I was 'on message,' and now I'm here, in Hollywood, and Molly's safe at a Church boarding school in Colorado. She has three meals a day, and water, and friends, and the corporation doesn't know I'm—" He stops himself, swallows. There's no one in the room except us, but still he's afraid to say it. "They don't know of any reason to take me out of my room in the middle of the night and shoot me. I've locked that part of me away."

"And what if you slip up?"

"Not going to happen. I play the part extremely well, Harp. Vivian can attest." Dylan nods at me, a hint of a smile tugging at the corner of his mouth. "I admit it's not an ideal situation, but I'm safe . . . which is more than you two can say."

"It doesn't bother you at all," I say, "that you're on the wrong side?"

He laughs a familiar laugh—wide-eyed, gently teasing. "Viv, come on—don't you get it? It's a luxury to be able to choose a side. I'm trying to eat, access clean water, keep Molly safe . . . I don't have time to have ideals. Look, I won't pretend every person who works for the Church of America is perfect, but they're more than you make them out to be. A lot of them are just trying to do what they think is right."

Harp watches the faucet drip. I know that for her the idea of helping Dylan, of rescuing him from the Church's clutches, was a way of turning back time. She wasn't there when Raj was killed, and she must feel the way I do about my father—that if we'd just been able to change the situation in one microscopic way, everything that happened after would have been different.

"Dylan," I say. "You need to know something. There's a militia planning an attack against the Church—an explosion at the Chateau Marmont."

Dylan's expression goes rigid. "Is this a joke?"

"No. We're not sure when it's going to happen yet—but they have the means, and they're going to do it. If that's where you're living, you need to get out of there."

He turns to Harp, like she'll assure him that I'm only playing around, but Harp has raised a trembling hand to her eyes. She's just realized, as I only did moments ago, that right now, Dylan doesn't need to be rescued from the Church as much as he needs to be rescued from Amanda Yee.

"How am I supposed to get out of there?" he asks, pacing the damp, dirty floor. "It's in my contract that I have to stay at the Chateau for the duration of my employment—and if I lose my contract, Molly loses her tuition. Oh, God. Guys! What am I supposed to do?"

"Maybe you can talk to Marnie about going on vacation for a while. Tell her you want to visit Molly before the second boat?"

"Even if she agrees," Dylan notes, "which she won't—Marnie lives at the Chateau too. I'm supposed to waltz away and leave her there, knowing full well she's about to get blown up? I'd have to warn her, too. I'd have to warn everyone! But—what am I supposed to say? Where am I supposed to have gotten this information? If they find out I know you, *how* I know you . . ."

He stops and bends over the sink, heaving. I think he might be about to throw up. He can't warn the Church of America about the attack. If they traced him back to us, they would find out about Raj. That would put both Dylan and Molly in danger. I put my hand on Dylan's back to comfort him.

I have an idea then. Possibly a profoundly stupid one.

"What if," I suggest, "you got us into the Chateau? What if you helped us meet with Peter Taggart? I'll warn him myself. He's powerful enough that he could get the Church to relocate. And I'm pretty sure he'd believe me."

Harp snaps her gaze toward me, eyes bright with alarm. Dylan laughs weakly. "Ha ha, Viv. I really don't see how a showdown with your ex-boyfriend is going to help. Although can I just say, I'm impressed? No doubt the betrayal was a blow, but that boy is cute. I frankly didn't think you had it in you."

"I'm not joking," I say.

He pauses, then looks back at Harp, who continues to say nothing. She retreats to the opposite corner, as if to put as much distance as possible between herself and this idea.

"You'll get caught," he points out. "They have Peacemakers at every entrance."

"You can tell us when the building will be closest to empty; you can help create a diversion. All we need is an open door, Dylan."

He seems speechless. The last time we saw each other, I was only Harp's compliant sidekick, a pleasant, dull presence in his apartment. Now Dylan turns helplessly to her, as if she'll rein me in, get me to stop asking the impossible.

But Harp shrugs. "A simple yes or no, Dylan."

"It could still backfire for me, easily. So why should I?" he asks, sounding both confused and defiant. "I've spent months making these people trust me. Why should I put myself at risk? Why should I put *Molly* at risk, just because you've gone full adrenaline junkie?"

"Because otherwise I can't promise you won't be in the building when the bomb goes off," I say, and Dylan recoils. "Also—because it's what Raj would do."

This plan is brand-new; it arrived fully formed in my mind only seconds ago—tell Peter about the bomb; have him convince the Church to move out of the Chateau; give Amanda no option but to cancel the attack—and part of me hopes he'll be so angry with me for invoking Raj that he'll refuse. But after a long moment, Dylan sighs. He takes a pack of cigarettes from his back pocket, shoves one into his mouth, and glares at me.

"The guilt, Apple, my God. You should start your own religion."

CHAPTER TEN

Dylan has to finish appeasing his adoring crowd, but first he tells us that a week from tonight, next Friday, most of the Chateau's occupants will be at a fundraiser in Laurel Canyon. Dylan believes that will be the ideal time for us to enter. We'll have to scope out the building, just as Diego and the others have been doing every other night; we'll have to familiarize ourselves with the entrances and the Peacemaker presence there. Dylan tells us to meet him at midnight tonight, on a back road behind the Chateau; he'll help us case it to the best of his ability. He gives us hugs—mine a little stiffer than Harp's—and returns to his place under the tent. Harp and I wait a few minutes, then make our way back through the Grove.

"Have you ever noticed," Harp mutters as we start the long trudge back to the Good Book, not wanting to test our luck again with Sacrificial Rides, "that you have a weird habit of escalating situations to their most dangerous possible outcomes? It's sort of pathological, Viv. I say, 'Let's see if we can dig up dirt on the Church of America'; *you* say, 'Let's drive across the country and break into their secret compound.' I say, 'Let's go see our old pal Dylan'; *you* say, 'Let's sneak into Church headquarters in the middle of the night so I can yell at my ex.' Peter isn't just some guy from school you hooked up with who never called—believe me, if he was, I'd be all about the dramatic cafeteria confrontation. I'd help you slash his tires in the parking lot. But he isn't. He's the sort of person who could have us killed, if he wanted to. I mean, has it ever occurred to you, Viv, that you might have a problem of some kind?"

"They're going to kill him," I say quietly. "Amanda's militia—they're going to kill Dylan, and Peter, too. They're the faces of the Church, and that's where they'll start."

Harp doesn't say anything for a long time. When she finally speaks, I can barely hear her over the traffic whizzing by.

"If you do manage to warn him, they're going to see it as a betrayal."

She doesn't have to tell me who "they" are—I know. Amanda, Diego, Julian, Kimberly, Robbie. Winnie. The people who have protected us, who have worked hard to hide us from the Church. Not to mention Suzy. Not to mention Karen. I feel sick.

"But Winnie was right," I tell her. "None of it's black-and-white; the whole thing is in-between space. It's like Wambaugh told us: don't see groups instead of people. Granted, a lot of Believers are terrible people—but they're still people! Maybe it's absurd that it took Peter turning Believer for me to get that, but I *do*, and we just—" I take a breath, overwhelmed with the weight of what we're discussing for the first time. I picture him in a room somewhere, the moment before detonation, just as Winnie imagined. Brushing his teeth, drinking a glass of water, staring out of a window, not knowing. This is the part that kills me: that for him it will simply be a blink into oblivion. One second he's here, the next he isn't—his giddy, surprised laugh and his blue eyes and the beating heart of him gone, because of something done by my friends, my sister. Gone. "We can't let it happen, Harp."

She watches me catch my breath. "You want to break in to the Chateau. You want to make contact with Peter. You want to do all that without getting caught. I mean, Jesus, Viv, to pull that off, you'd need—for lack of a better word—a fucking miracle."

"I know," I say. "But at the very least, I'll have you?"

Harp laughs. Though we're exposed—all these cars speeding past, with who knows how many pairs of eyes—she takes my hand. "Duh, Viv. We'll warn him. And if through some miraculous turn of events we don't die in the process, just know I'll always be here, coming up with cockamamie schemes for you to turn into full-blown suicide missions. For the rest of our lives. That's just the kind of friend I am."

The walk is hot and endless. Harp's pigtails loosen and frizz; I feel a sunburn flare on the back of my neck. Both of us are tired and hungry, painfully thirsty. Harp navigates with uncertainty a circuitous route off the busy highway, cutting between houses and behind shops and restaurants. It takes nearly two hours, and by the end of it I'm exhausted and dizzy. She reaches the bookstore before I do, and I feel an ache of longing watching her slip through the front door, imagining the air conditioning now on her skin. By the time I enter, she rests against the counter, guzzling from Robbie's water bottle. He nods as I approach, bemusement in his eyes. As always, the shop is empty. Harp passes the bottle to me.

"So they're still not back? Huh," Harp says. "Long day for them."

"Yeah," Robbie replies. "We got word from Amanda last night

that we're doing the thing at the hotel place in exactly four weeks, I guess. Diego's ramping up training."

I try to catch Harp's eye, but she pushes herself back from the counter and heads for the red door, before turning abruptly on her heel, like she's just remembered something.

"Robbie," she says, "you have a set of keys to the cars, right?"

He nods. "Yeah. We all do."

"Amanda said you need to lend me yours—Viv and I need a car, see, for the mission she's sending us on, and she figured you didn't need yours, since you can't legally drive."

He scowls and digs into his pocket, pulling out the jingling keys. But he doesn't hand them over yet. When he speaks, he sounds defensive. "I'm a good driver—Diego taught me how. And anyway, it's not like traffic cops are even a thing anymore."

"I know." Harp rolls her eyes in commiseration. "But—Amanda's orders."

I watch Robbie's arm cross the distance between himself and Harp. In the moment before he drops the keys into her open hand, he turns to look into my eyes. I'm too self-conscious about how badly I lie to attempt it, so I just smile. This seems to appease him, and he lets them go. I watch Harp catch the keys and put them in her pocket.

| | | | |

That evening is like every other evening—we gather on the second floor, eat a simple meal, and watch the Church of America News Network in silence. There's a brief consultation with Masterson about Harp's and my possible motives ("It's clear these girls are doing Satan's bidding—the question is simply, what has he promised them in return?"); a long segment on Peter's immense popularity among Believers, with footage of him visiting a tent city, offering paltry loaves of bread; and a weather report on the arid, howling winds that are currently battering the windows in their frames. They're called the Santa Ana winds, the meteorologist explains, and they're noteworthy for their power, heat, and dryness; they increase the risk of wildfires, and legend has it they cause aggressive changes in people's moods. "In a city already poised on the brink of apocalypse," he muses, "one bad temper could have a catastrophic chain reaction."

Kimberly hits mute. "Well, that's a cheery thought."

About a half hour before midnight, once everyone has headed up to bed, Harp and I sneak down the stairs and through the bookshop, out to the street where the cars are parked. Harp hands me Robbie's keys and I drive. She pulls out her laptop, where she'll take notes. I'm nervous about every aspect of what we're currently doing—I scope the streets we cruise down for any sign of cops or Peacemakers or random mobs of citizens driven mad by the Santa Ana winds. A few nights ago, the president issued an emergency nationwide curfew of eleven p.m., an attempt to cut down on the spikes in violent crime from coast to coast, but if the news is any indication, it's had no effect—perhaps, as the Church newscasters hint, because he did not authorize the Peacemakers to enforce it.

"What are you thinking about?" I ask Harp, to distract myself from my nerves.

"Oh, just reading some blog comments. I'm getting a thousand a day now."

"Oh yeah? How many have compared you to Hitler at this point?"

"A little under two fifty, but I'm not really keeping a tally." Harp frowns at the screen. "People are starting to talk about where they think their Raptured relatives went. I took screen shots of the important ones. 'Hi Harp, thank you for revealing the TRUTH! I want to tell you about my mom, Mona Patterson, eighty-five, MISSING SINCE MARCH'—blah blah, this woman's whole life story, and then—'I checked credit card statements, like you said to, and guess what? She bought a one-way ticket to Cleveland the week before the Rapture. I SAY IT'S SOMETHING SINISTER.' And here's another: 'If what you say is true that explains a lot. My husband believed and our marriage was really in trouble, but about three weeks before the Rapture he planned us a romantic weekend in Nashville. We had one beautiful night together, and when I woke up he was gone. Haven't heard from him since.' I don't get it," Harp says. "How many different cities were the missing Raptured summoned to?"

Shortly before midnight, we turn off Sunset onto a steep, twisting road. We pass the entrance to the Chateau, close to the highway—a long iron-gated driveway leading up to the stark white building, ivy crawling up its walls. Under two glowing torches a couple of sleepy Peacemakers are stationed. Harp shrinks into the shadows, but they glance at our car without flinching. I can't let my gaze linger, but I'm struck by how weird the Chateau looks, so ornate and old-fashioned in the middle of this weird city. It isn't particularly tall, but it's imposing, overlooking the twinkling lights of Hollywood. I turn the corner and continue up the curved lane past extravagant, abandoned houses. At the top of the hill, I turn onto the twisty street Dylan told us about and park in an empty house's driveway. We wait. After about fifteen minutes, I see blond curls bouncing beneath a sweatband as Dylan comes jogging up the sidewalk. He wears a white tank top and short red shorts. Harp unlocks the back door for him.

"Dude." I turn in my seat to study him. "Have you ever seen, like, a single movie before? This is your stakeout attire?"

"You didn't say anything about what to wear!" Dylan exclaims. "And anyway, I told Derrick—the Peacemaker at the kitchen entrance—that I was going for a run. I wouldn't go for a run in a black ski mask, would I?"

He advises me to do a loop. The Chateau is built into the hillside, and the roads behind it are curving and narrow. As we drive, we study the hotel's white stone façade and the black iron gate—taller than any of us—that protects the Chateau's perimeter. Dylan tells us we're approaching the kitchen entrance, then ducks—Derrick, the Peacemaker who guards that door, is peering intently into the car as we pass. I turn my face away as best as I can, feeling exposed by the lamps hanging from the walls of the Chateau, and it isn't until we're far away from the Peacemakers, back on Sunset Boulevard, that the three of us are able to breathe. Dylan points out a thicket of trees beside the hotel, a few shiny palms peeking through—this is where the Chateau has a small number of bungalows, where a few of the Church's distinguished employees, Dylan included, reside.

"I don't think Taggart's in a bungalow," he says thoughtfully. "I never see him by the pool. If I had to guess, I'd say he's on the sixth floor, the top—I know that's where Blackmore stays."

It's too dangerous to do another loop and risk Derrick's suspicion—the Peacemaker is built like a professional wrestler. We pull into what used to be a gas station across the street, and Dylan describes the hotel's interior in great detail. I hope Harp is paying attention. Because all I can focus on is the lit windows of the sixth floor. I try to imagine which one of them Peter is behind. I try to imagine he knows I'm coming.

In the week that follows, we stick to this routine: On the four nights Diego himself isn't doing surveillance at the Chateau, we wait until everyone's gone to bed, sneak out, and drive to the hotel, which we observe from all angles until shortly before dawn. We watch the guards at the front gate end their shifts at two thirty a.m.; we watch their impossibly prompt substitutes appear. We note that Derrick, the Peacemaker at the kitchen exit, ends his shift approximately ninety minutes before—no one comes to replace him, but a security camera hangs over the door. Late on Monday, we watch a black car pull up the drive, and a man who looks like Ted Blackmore steps into the moonlight before entering the hotel. Twice Dylan joins us, showing us pictures on his phone of Molly in her school uniform (navy jacket, starchy white bonnet), and laughing with Harp about bad habits of Raj's they're trying not to forget. The other nights it's just Harp and me, increasingly tired and spooked about our plan. On Thursday, twenty-four hours before we plan to break in, a breathless Dylan scampers up to the car and dives in, his expression anxious. He lies flat across the back seat.

"Don't drive," he hisses before I can start the engine. "I may have been followed."

"Fuck!" Harp slips below the line of the windshield.

"I was down in the lobby with Marnie, and I saw Peter Taggart walk past, with Blackmore. They got on an elevator, so I decided to trail them. I ran up the steps as fast as I could and I caught up with them on the sixth floor. Peter went into a room—619. So there's that. But then a Peacemaker came up behind me, all 'What are you doing?' and I said I was just stretching my legs but

I could tell he didn't believe me and now I'm going to die here because of you two; I'm going to die cowering in the back seat of a midsize sedan!"

We wait a long time, but the ominous knock of a Peacemaker at the window never comes. After about twenty minutes, I take a tentative peek outside. Nothing.

"We're okay," I say, and Harp and Dylan reluctantly lift their heads. "But, Dylan, you shouldn't stay, just in case. We've got it from here."

He frowns. "You do? What, exactly, is your plan?"

Harp looks at me—we haven't discussed it in detail yet; we have only the barest sketch. I've been counting on something foolproof hitting us over the course of the week, as we've sat here watching and worrying. But nothing has.

"We're coming back tomorrow, at one thirty in the morning. We're going in through the kitchens, after Derrick goes off duty."

"What about the security camera?" Dylan sounds dubious.

"We'll—" I glance around, as if the answer is here in the car with us. "We'll throw, like, a hoodie over it, or something."

Dylan groans. "Have *you* ever seen a single movie before? I can unplug the camera from the inside just before you arrive. You'll have a window of about five minutes before the Peacemakers watching the feed realize something's up. How are you going to get through the door?" He waits a beat, but we have no answer. He shakes his head, but I can tell he's secretly a little pleased. "I can make sure it's unlocked during that window."

"If I didn't know you better," Harp muses, "I'd think we weren't the first people you've covertly snuck into a heavily guarded hotel."

"Maybe you shouldn't assume you're the only people who've ever covertly snuck in." He raises an eyebrow at our blank looks.

"This is the Church of America we're talking about, ladies. They talk a virtuous game, but surely you realize not all Believers are angels? I've picked up on a few tricks along the way. How do you plan to get up to the sixth floor?"

Another snag I hadn't anticipated. "Quietly?"

"Pathetic." Dylan's laughing now. He reaches into a pocket and pulls out a thin plastic card on a lanyard, reading BELLA—STAFF. He hands it to me. "An employee pass. It'll get you into the service elevator at the back of the kitchens."

"Dylan!"

"I've been cozying up to a housekeeper." Dylan grins. "She thinks I'm cute. I told her I lost my pass, and could I just borrow hers; it'll only take me two days to get a new one."

Harp reaches back to swat him playfully on the arm. "Look at this! This is the rascally Dylan Marx I know and love! You incorrigible scamp! Where have you been hiding?"

But Dylan doesn't answer. Even in the dim light of the car, I can see a weird tension in his eyes. His grin stays in place, but it seems forced now. "Listen, if you get caught—"

"We would never tell them how we got in, Dylan," I assure him. "I swear."

He shakes his head. "If you get caught, or even if you make it but I don't see you before September . . ."

"We'll see you before September, dummy," says Harp, "and after September too. The world's not really ending, remember? You're gonna be stuck with us a *long* time."

"Right." Dylan doesn't sound convinced. "Well, look—be safe. Okay?" He leans forward and kisses us on our cheeks and then, without another word, slips out of the car and into the dark, hot night. We watch him jog away into the shadows.

CHAPTER ELEVEN

We crawl into bed above the Good Book shortly before dawn, moments before the others begin to stir. I lie awake, eyes shut to the rising sun streaming in through the windows, listening to Winnie and her friends prepare for another day of training. The weight of what we have to do presses down upon me. I try to remind myself that if we succeed in warning Peter, Winnie will not have to help attack the Chateau Marmont—a mission she doesn't believe in, a mission that could kill her. If we succeed, there's a chance Winnie won't see this last week of furtive planning and sneaking out as a betrayal. She might even be grateful for it. But right at this moment it's hard to believe we'll succeed. Once the soldiers have left and after we've given up on the prospect of sleep, Harp reads from her comments a new flux of theoretical destinations of the Raptured: Billings, Boise, Boulder. I can't concentrate. I am thinking only of Winnie. If we're caught tonight—and how could we not be?—I will never see her again. I explain to Harp why I'm distracted, and I can tell by her frown that she understands.

"I just wish we could say goodbye," I tell her.

Later, after the soldiers have returned to the command center, all of us cluster around the television together, watching the Church of America News Network in our usual, irritable, terrified way.

"You guys," Harp suddenly addresses the group, "are so boring."

No one responds. I see Kimberly roll her eyes at Colby. I watch Harp, unsure of what she's doing—all I know is that she has a glint in her eye I recognize from what feels like a long time ago, the arch easiness that always comes with her burgeoning plans.

"I mean it," she tries again, after a minute. "Don't you ever have fun? Don't you party? When we were with the New Orphans, there were parties *every night*. Epic ones—music, so much booze, everybody grinding up on each other, going nuts . . ."

"I thought you said the New Orphans were useless." Diego raises an eyebrow. "I thought you said they were pawns of the Church."

"Uh, yeah?" says Harp. "That doesn't mean they don't have great parties."

Julian gazes at her, tapping his bottom lip with his finger. Winnie watches the screen, but she seems to be trying not to smile.

Diego says, "Well, I'm sorry being a soldier is not the nonstop rave you were expecting."

"I'm sorry for *you* guys," Harp replies. "You never take any time to unwind. If that works for you, no judgment! If it were me, though . . . well, never mind."

"If it were you, what?" Julian asks.

She gives him a sad half smile. "Life is short. Shorter for a soldier. If it were me, I'd want to have some fun before I gave up my life for my—extremely honorable!—principles."

Julian frowns. Robbie stares at Harp; he looks slightly pale. But everyone else appears to ignore her. Just when I think they must be unusually immune to Harp's particular charms, Elliott gets up, leaves the apartment without saying a word, and returns twenty minutes later with a paper sack from which he pulls five bottles of tequila, four bottles of vodka, and a bottle of whiskey. He stays silent, but he unscrews the cap on the whiskey, holds the bottle up to Harp in a solemn salute, and takes a long, eager sip.

No one has to say it's a party for it to become one. After some prodding from his cousin, Diego busies himself in the kitchen, and a mix of delicious smells—roasting garlic, sautéing onions, fresh cilantro, sizzling meat—begins to waft into the room, making everybody hungry and a little giddy. Harp pours tequila into a couple dozen glasses and, when she runs out of glasses, directly into some soldiers' mouths. But the soldiers are shy with one another—they remind me of myself the first time I went to a house party with Harp, one night last July. I was unnerved by the presence of fellow students, most of whom I'd never spoken to outside the context of history projects and French study groups. "Who did you expect to be here?" Harp asked incredulously, and then she dragged me around to every person there, forcing me to say hi. "You guys know Viv, right?" she'd say. "I'm taking her on as my protégée."

I watch her perform the same magic tonight, easing everyone out of their formality with a drinking game she invents on the spot. She turns up the volume on the news and shouts, "Every time they say the word 'sin,' we drink!" Within ten minutes, everybody is red-cheeked and giggling, though Harp (who, like me, hasn't had a sip) is horrified. "Jesus, I didn't realize how much they used the word 'sin'! They're getting so wasted!"

But nobody seems to mind. It's funny to watch the uptight

façades fade away, the real personalities shine through. Diego serves us a huge, warm, fantastic meal, which we eat on the floor, balancing paper plates in our laps: rice and beans; creamy guacamole with lots of salt and lime; bread dripping with melted butter and roasted garlic; golden-brown, smoky pork chops we have to cut into thirds for everyone to have a piece; orange slices for dessert. Robbie—who has somehow managed to sneak a couple of shots of tequila despite Frankie's scolding eye—turns on music as the plates are cleared, and everyone drifts into groups of twos and threes, chatting in corners about the things they don't have time to care about anymore: books and bands and old secular TV shows. Kimberly and Julian invent new cocktails, mixing Elliott's alcohol with every liquid in the fridge—they taste, spit in disgust, fall over each other laughing, and try again. Birdie and Colby sway together in the center of the room, slower than the beat of the song, while beside them Robbie performs a frenzied dance, banging his head, kicking indiscriminately, creating a wide berth around him. On a couch in the corner, Diego has his arm around Winnie; he murmurs into her ear, and she sips happily from her glass, nuzzling close to him. He planned to go to the Chateau himself tonight, for another long stretch of surveillance, but clearly that plan has been forgotten.

Harp makes rounds with the bottles, and when she empties one, she opens another. Around eleven, people begin to drift up to bed, but not before tossing their arms around Harp and me, insisting we do this every night. By eleven thirty, only a few remain—Diego and Winnie; Kimberly sprawled across a couple of desk chairs, snoring deeply; Julian, lying on the floor; and us. I catch Harp's eye—we'll have to leave soon. She stands, kicking gently at Julian's feet. He moans.

"You should go to bed," she says. "Do you need help?"

"I need *you*, Harp." Julian grabs her ankle. "Can't you see I'm in love with you?"

She struggles to hide a smile, and to my surprise I can make out just the faintest flush of color. "You're drunk," she says, laughing, trying to pull away.

Julian grins and lets go. He reaches up, and Harp takes his arm with both hands, pulling him to his feet. "Don't minimize my feelings, girl. That's cold. That's damn cold."

We watch him stumble out the door and up the stairs. After a moment, Diego and Winnie follow. Winnie stops to pull me into a loose-armed hug, and when she moves away, she wears a sleepy smile filled with so much love, I feel a pang of guilt, like a knife between my ribs. Diego pauses at the door. "You guys coming?"

"We'll clean up first." Harp nods to the empty bottles, dirty glasses, paper plates.

"Listen—thanks for that. I didn't realize how much we needed it . . . but I guess you did."

Harp smiles, but I notice the tightness around her eyes.

"How did that measure up to your New Orphan parties?" Diego asks.

"It was like a hundred million billion times better," Harp says truthfully, "in every way."

| | | | |

When Diego is gone, Harp opens her hand to show me a watch on her palm—I recognize it as Julian's, and though we'll need it to make sure we're on schedule, I'm not sure I want to know how Harp came about such Dickensian pickpocketing skills. We clean quietly, aware of Kimberly's slumbering body—if we wake her, we'll never leave. Slightly after one, when all footsteps upstairs have finally ceased, we make our way out, mindful of every creaking floorboard, the deafening pounding of our two hearts in the dark. It isn't until well after we've gotten into the car and left, until there's a mile between us and our protectors, that we manage to speak.

"So . . ." I begin, eager to think of anything but what we're about to do. "Julian, huh?"

I don't have to look at Harp to know she's blushing; she shifts in her seat, and I can practically feel the sheepish pleasure radiating from her skin. "He's just drunk. If I had a nickel for every declaration of love I've received from a drunken stranger . . ."

"He's not really a stranger, though. We've known him over a month. *And* he's cute." Harp stays silent, and I'm so jittery I keep prodding. "Don't you think? Come on, you can't pretend he's not cute."

"It doesn't really matter," Harp replies quietly. "He'll probably be dead in three weeks, so why bother thinking about whether he's cute or not?"

I have the drive to the Chateau memorized by now, and when I park in our spot in the driveway of the abandoned house, I can almost convince myself we're still on stakeout. But this time, we step outside. We're wearing the clothes Winnie brought us when we first arrived at Cliff House—dark, practical, and easy to run in. Harp was disappointed at the time ("Couldn't she find anything with sequins?") but now these nondescript outfits fit the bill; we blend in easily with the night. We pad down the twists of the hill. The wind blows unpleasantly warm, knocking my hood back, exposing my face; I have to tie the strings tightly at my chin. There's an exotic California smell on the air: sage and lavender. It's completely foreign to me, so uncomfortably new that I feel an ache in my stomach, a helpless longing for my house in Pittsburgh. I push the feeling away. I could never be content in that house anymore. I'm not even sure such a house could contain me.

The gate behind the Chateau opens to the kitchen entrance— there's a cluster of garbage cans reeking of rotting food, a single light above the back door. The security camera hangs over it. I check the time: 1:29 a.m. We can only hope Dylan was able to unplug it. I try the door he promised would be unlocked and it opens. I step into the kitchen and freeze. I'm waiting for an alarm to ring, a voice to shout, "Intruder!" But nothing happens. Harp slips in behind me. We stand still, letting our eyes adjust to the dark. Harp brought a flashlight, but we won't use it unless absolutely necessary. We want to be shadows. The kitchen is huge; stainless-steel hoods and stoves gleam in the light peeking in through the door. I see a line of copper pots on the wall, a block of knives. Dylan told us security makes a loop every twenty minutes: we have to move.

The service elevator is at the opposite end of the kitchen, around a dark corner, across from what appears to be a meat locker. I press the button and cringe at the thunderous sounds: the whoosh of the elevator's approach, the deafening ding as its doors open. There's no way it didn't wake the whole hotel. We clamber in and I wave Bella's ID in front of the sensor, press the button for floor six. When the doors seal us in, Harp turns to me with a wide, slightly manic grin.

"You know, Viv, when we started hanging out, I don't think I understood *quite* how much sleuthing I'd end up doing. I'm not complaining! I'm into all this hardcore Nancy Drew shit. Maybe we should consider costumes next time, though? Or props? Comically overlarge magnifying glasses?"

I don't answer. I can hardly hear myself think over the hum of anxiety that thrums through my body, making my teeth chatter.

The floors tick by, too quickly; three, four, five, and we're there. The doors open on red carpeting and white walls, gold lanterns hanging from the ceiling. About twenty feet away, the hall makes an L shape, and it's down that longer section, Dylan says, that we'll find Peter's room. I check the time again: 1:40. I hear feet treading carpet in the unseen part of the hall; I put my arm out to stop Harp from strutting forward. There's a closet to our right and I dart into it, dragging her with me, hoping as we close the door that the guard hasn't reached the hinge of the hallway in time to see the flash of our movement.

It's cramped—extra towels and sheets folded along built-in shelves, a vacuum tilting in one corner. Instinctively we crouch to make ourselves smaller. The footsteps grow louder, closer. Harp claps her hands over her mouth. I can see the outline of the guard behind the slats of the closet door, his blue legs in a wide stance; he pauses.

There's a crackle of static and then a voice. "Hey, Jerry," the Peacemaker says, "what do you call a sleepwalking nun?"

Another crackle, then a muffled voice at the other end of the walkie-talkies. "What?"

"A roamin' Catholic!" The Peacemaker chuckles. Across from me, fingers still pressed to her lips, I see Harp's shoulders shake. I glare at her in reproach, but I start to feel the blood return to my fingers—we see the guard turn and walk back the way he came. "I love that one. I should tell Mulvey when she gets back from the fundraiser—it'll crack her up."

"Yeah. Okay. Hey, Bob—you still on the sixth floor?"

"Leaving now."

"Grab me a towel? I just spilled Coke *everywhere*."

"Sure thing"—and there's not even a moment to panic, because Bob's shadow looms in front of us once again, and alarm-

145

ingly, the doorknob turns in his hand; he's opened it half an inch, and my thoughts are a whir: *I'll throw myself at him; I'll scratch out his eyes; I'll buy Harp the time she needs to get out of here.* But then the hallway is filled with movement and distant murmurs and Bob closes the closet door.

"Evening, Mr. Blackmore," we hear him say, as footsteps approach. "You're earlier than we expected!"

"Ah—hi there . . . Bud, is it?" The oily voice of Ted Blackmore seeps under the door. Harp grips my arm, digging her nails into my skin.

"Bob." Bob sounds a little annoyed.

"Bob." Blackmore sounds even more annoyed at having been made to repeat it. "So sorry. Quiet night, I hope?"

"Very, sir. When you folks are out at these fundraisers, the place is just about deserted—it's a little spooky, to be honest with you. Almost haunted!"

"Well, Bob," Blackmore replies snippily, and I hear a door across the hall open, "you'll want to watch who you make observations like that to. Remember the Book of Frick: *'In this world there be no spirits but the Holy Spirit.'* Chapter eighteen, verse sixty-two. I'm sure you don't want to give off the impression that we believe in ghosts."

"Oh—no, sir! I was just—well, of course I don't believe in—"

"Let's hope not," Blackmore interrupts him. "Now, I really must sleep. Thank you for all the work you do, Bob. Frick's blessings to you."

"And to you too, sir." Bob sounds confused, but the door has already closed on him. There's a pause, and Harp's nails dig in deeper, but then he wanders off, muttering (*"There be no spirits . . .'* I only said it *felt* haunted!"), having forgotten all about the towel for Jerry below.

I count to ten and then pull my arm out of Harp's grasp. We have to do it now or we'll never do it.

We stand and open the door. I step into the hall. There's no way to cover ourselves—we shouldn't be here; if someone were to see us, there'd be no explaining ourselves away. We move swiftly down the hall, trying to be noiseless, trying to feel like air; we take the right-hand turn, watching the door numbers flick by: 627, 625, 623, 621. And then there it is. Harp has a credit card out to jimmy the lock—whose it is and how she got it I have no idea; she leans forward, but some self-destructive instinct kicks in, and I raise my hand to knock: three times, loudly.

Harp jumps back at the sound. She looks around, panicked eyes searching for a reaction, but there's only silence up and down the hall. Behind the door, too. I raise my hand to knock again and Harp grabs me to keep me from doing it, and that's how we're standing—my arm in the air, Harp clutching my wrist desperately—when the door finally opens.

He wears a white button-down shirt with the top button open, an untied black bow tie limp around his collar. He has a new hollowness under his cheekbones, deep circles under his eyes. His eyes are the worst part—that cool, alien blue. We stare at each other a long moment before he seems to understand what he's looking at, but then I see his eyebrows rise, his jaw go slack. I wait for him to shout, to give us away, but he's silent. Harp's grip on my wrist tightens. It's like staring at the ghost of someone long dead, someone you loved who now wants to hurt you. I catch his scent—wood smoke and cinnamon—and my head goes fuzzy; I'm flooded with longing, and I'm furious with him for making me feel it. I tug my hand out of Harp's grasp and tighten my fingers into a fist—I am going to punch Peter Taggart in the face. I am going to punch him until all the bones in my hand are ground into dust. I don't get the chance, because what happens next takes me so completely by surprise: his shoulders slump; his open mouth stretches into a feverish, incandescent grin; and Peter steps into the hallway, where at any moment all three of us could be seen, to pull me into his arms.

CHAPTER TWELVE

When my surprise fades, I act swiftly. My raised fist is pressed between our bodies and I yank it free, then slam it hard against Peter's shoulder, pushing him away. He stumbles back into the room. Harp follows and I enter after them, closing and locking the door behind me.

"I'm sorry." A shiver goes up my spine at the sound of his voice. "When I saw you there, I thought—you're angry, of course. You have every right to be angry."

"You can't just go around *hugging* people," Harp snaps. "Use some common fucking sense. You really think Viv's in the mood to *hug* you right now?"

"I'm sorry," Peter says again, sounding nauseatingly convincing. "Seriously—I don't know what I was thinking. I was just so happy to see you."

He looks at me intently, and I look away. I note how dull the room is—cramped white walls, large white bed, none of the Old Hollywood elegance of the Chateau's façade. Harp just stands there, seething. When neither of us speak, Peter continues.

"Listen, you have to know not a second has gone by where I haven't thought of you—both of you. I didn't know if you were alive for so long; I didn't know if you were okay"—he takes a breath—"I didn't know if you knew about me. I can't imagine what you think of me, but I promise you that you can't possibly hate me as much as I hate myself."

"You'd be surprised," Harp snorts.

Peter's face flushes; he stares miserably at the floor. I try to breathe calmly, in through my nose and out through my mouth, so that when I finally speak I'll appear composed—cool and in control of myself, not a girl easily Magdalened. But this performance of his—all woe-is-me and Frick-forgive-me-for-lying-to-you—is a hundred times more infuriating than it would be if he were just honest, if he would just admit he conned us before alerting security to our extremely immoral presence in his room.

"You know what I wish I'd known before I got involved with you, Peter? Besides *anything*?" My voice is low; it seems to usher from some primal part of myself, the part that wants to rip his throat out with my teeth. I see a flash of fear behind his eyes. "I wish I'd known what a superbly talented *actor* you are. You just inhabit these roles you play. You're believable as Peter Ivey, Non-Believing dreamboat; you're believable as Peter Taggart, bombastic Church spokesman. I would even believe *this*—our pal Peter, the rational Believer—if we hadn't already been played by you so many times before."

I see a muscle twitch in his jaw, but I don't stop; I don't want to give him the chance to respond, the chance to win us over once again.

"I'm glad the Church brought you to Hollywood, Peter. I think this could be a great place for you. No hard feelings. In fact, Harp and I are here as friends. We thought you should know there's a small militia planning to detonate a bomb at the Chateau Marmont in three weeks. Don't ask for details," I say, because Peter's head has snapped up. "That's all we can tell you. Liar though you are, we didn't like the thought of you dying here."

I reach into my pocket and take out the remains of the sledgehammer necklace; I toss it at Peter's feet. He gazes at it, but his expression doesn't change.

"Now," I continue, "if you want to call the Angels and let them know we're here, I think the least you can do—as someone who pretended to care about us once—is give us a head start."

Peter just stares at the sledgehammer pendant. He finally looks up, bewildered.

"Wait, why would I call the Angels?" he asks. "If they find you here, they'll kill you."

Harp laughs. "What a great coup for you—Taggart's son ensnares girl heathens! Not to mention the brownie points you'll get with God. High-fives all around at the pearly gates!"

The frown hasn't left Peter's face. The second he looks at the telephone next to the bed, the second he takes a half step toward us, I'll get out of here; I won't be caught in Peter's room.

"Hang on," he says. "You guys don't think—do you think I'm a Believer?"

I look at Harp and Harp looks at me. She wears an expression that seems to say, *Was he always this stupid?*

". . . Yes?"

But Peter's started to pace the room; he runs his hands through his hair and stares at us in disbelief. "All that stuff about acting . . . You thought—I get it now, but when you said it I just thought—I assumed you guys knew what I was doing; I thought you were just disgusted by it."

"What you're doing . . ." Harp echoes, confused. I feel a light,

151

fluttery feeling at the center of me—a flare of hope not yet tangible enough to trust.

"I mean, you should be disgusted! Don't get me wrong! But how could you think—I didn't realize—how could you possibly believe that I *believe?* I was standing *right there with you* when Masterson and the others showed up in their angel costumes."

Harp rubs hard at her temple, like she's got a headache. I barely register what Peter's saying. The relief is like a drug in my bloodstream, making me confused and drowsy.

"You're not actually a Believer."

Peter looks at me and laughs the way he did the first time I ever made him laugh, at Harp's Rapture's Eve party—like he's caught off-guard by the joke, so giddily surprised to be laughing. "No, Viv. Jesus Christ! Of course not."

It's happening too quickly: I'm letting my guard down too fast. *Pull it together, Apple!* I hear a voice in my head admonish. It sounds like Harp.

"How are you their spokesman, then?" I demand. "Last I checked, the Church of America wasn't totally big on recruiting teenage atheists to their PR team."

Peter sighs as he collects his thoughts; he sinks to the edge of the bed. When he looks up at me again, the laughter has drained from his eyes. "Vivian, this wasn't some brilliant scheme of mine. I don't have anything close to a scheme! Every morning I wake up and think, *What do I have to do today in order to not get murdered?* And then I do it. It happened by accident, and it's kept me alive—but that doesn't mean I'm proud of it. It also doesn't mean it's been easy."

"Oh, boo-hoo!" Harp waves her hand around, to indicate the clean, air-conditioned hotel room in which we stand. "It must be a real trial, reciting Book of Frick proverbs on TV, going on fancy black-tie adventures with Ted fucking Blackmore, sleeping in a nice warm bed every night. What suffering!"

For the first time, the pleading, penitent expression on Peter's face slips a little. He cocks his head and looks at her. "You two don't exactly look like you've been starving on the street. You look like someone's taken you in and given you unlimited Internet access—yeah, I know about the blog." He smirks at the inquiring expression on Harp's face. When he looks at me and sees how unyielding I've forced myself to be, the smile fades. "Look, you guys ran. Back at Frick's compound, when the corporation came after us, you ran. I'm not scolding you," he adds, because Harp has opened her mouth to protest. "I wanted you to run! I *told* you to run! But I didn't run. So my options were different. I'm not saying they were less. I'm just saying they were different.

"At first I thought I'd be able to catch up with you. I'd calm down Frick and my dad, and we'd be able to catch up. Then it would be simple, right? We'd get them in front of a camera and everyone would know the truth. But they were freaking out. My dad was upset that I was there, and Frick—he didn't understand what he had done, exactly, but he knew the Angels were angry. The two of them wouldn't move. And I knew I was stuck then—I could see the corporation's cars from the front door. I had to improvise. My only thought was, *Stay alive, stay alive, get to Viv and Harp.*" He pauses a beat, his stare fixed beyond me, so he doesn't see the heat rush to my face. "When the Peacemakers arrived— just guards then, I guess; they hadn't been rebranded yet—I told them who I was. I told them my real name. I said I'd come to pay homage to what I thought was my father's point of Rapture. I pretended to be confused about what he was doing here, alive. Confused but overjoyed—'Praise Frick! What a miracle!' You get the idea."

"They believed that?" Harp sounds skeptical.

"Sort of." Peter shrugs. "They were suspicious, but what were they going to do? Shoot a kid claiming to be Taggart's son on sight? Blackmore arrived at dawn to interrogate me. I stuck to the story—devoted son, Believer, Frick be praised! That's where my apparently superb acting skills came into play. But I'm not sure I was actually that convincing—he just wanted to believe me. From what I gather, Blackmore doesn't test well with hardcore Believers. As spokesman, he never really matched that all-powerful kind of thing my dad did so well. When we spoke, he figured he could use me—he figured he could use my name. He brought me here to LA, vouched for me to Mulvey and Masterson, and they'd just decided to make me the new face of the Church when Harp's first blog post went up."

"About that." My voice is still hard. "How much have you told the Church about us?"

"Practically nothing," Peter assures me. "They'd seen you on the security feed, so I couldn't pretend I hadn't gone there with you—I said I'd met you along the way and you'd given me a ride. I told them I'd tried to convert you, but you freaked when you saw Frick; you ran. Even if I'd wanted to tell them where you went, I couldn't—I had no idea! These days, I try not to ask about you— I try not to act too interested. I worked hard to make Blackmore trust me. I meet with him every day"—his voice sounds a bit thin, and he pauses to swallow—"and every day I think he's going to tell me that they have you, that they've hurt you."

"Didn't Blackmore find the blog suspicious?" Harp asks. "Wouldn't it poke holes in your whole act, for him? I went into, like, serious detail about your make-out history."

Peter's mouth twists. "By the time you posted, I was in too

154

deep. Blackmore likes me a lot, and plus, he wouldn't have wanted to admit to Mulvey and Masterson that he was wrong about me. I told him you'd made it up, and that's exactly what he wanted to believe. I was his best weapon against you. The second they made me public, everything you said looked like a lie." He cringes, a little apologetically. "Also he thought . . . he thought maybe if the Church made me public, you'd turn up wherever I might be."

He politely avoids my eyes, and I'm grateful—my face is so hot I feel feverish. I hate that Harp was good enough at conveying how I feel about Peter that the Church was right about me.

"They were more confident in that than I was," he adds, "being a swamp monster and all. I figured you were angry I was playing this part. Which, again, you should be. I sold you guys out. I made you look like liars. I said . . . terrible things about you on TV. I have no right to hope you'll forgive me."

But when he glances up at me, I see that he does hope. Peter looks uneasy, quietly embarrassed, but still hopeful. Harp stares at me too. I realize they're waiting for me to make the call: Harp will follow my lead when it comes to Peter, and as much as he likes Harp, it's me Peter wants to hear. It's too much to process right now, an equation I'm not yet capable of solving. All I know is, I believe him. Maybe it's because his story seems plausible, but maybe it's just because I want to—because even now, every nerve in my body feels raw and electric by the nearness of him.

"If you hadn't convinced them you were on their side, they would have killed you," I say. "You did what you had to do."

Peter looks rueful. "Maybe. But somehow I can't see you doing it."

There's an uncomfortable silence. Harp twists a strand of hair around her finger—I can't tell whether or not she really buys the story. Peter leans forward, elbows on his knees. I remember again my first conversation with him: we sat side by side on the steps of the abandoned mansion the night before the Rapture, flirtatious but unable to actually communicate, both of us weighed down by the unwritten future, both of us preoccupied by the people we were and the people we wanted to be. I feel that same awkwardness now. If there were any time, I'd sit with Peter tonight until I understood every thought in his head and he understood every thought in mine—but it's late. We'll have to leave soon if we don't want Diego and Winnie to know we've been gone.

I clear my throat. "We should probably talk about that attack."

"The bomb." Peter sits up. "Right."

"Winnie—my sister—she's part of this group. They're funded by a woman named Amanda Yee. Amanda wants to bring the Church to its knees, violently. She plans to have them detonate a bomb, here, in three weeks. Do you think you can convince the corporation to move out of the Chateau before then? Ideally, they should get out of Los Angeles altogether—they should move far enough away that Amanda doesn't have time to regroup."

Peter considers this. "I can definitely try. I can tell them I heard a tip from a donor at the fundraiser. But I don't see them leaving Hollywood before the apocalypse—not if they're planning what I suspect they're planning."

I hear the careful note of uncertainty in his voice. Harp looks sharply at him. "What? What do you suspect they're planning?"

He takes a breath. "First of all, you have to understand that as high-profile as they've made me, they still haven't admitted to me that they faked the Rapture. When Blackmore and I first spoke that morning after we broke into the compound, he told me I might have *thought* I'd seen Frick and my father in the flesh, but that what I actually saw were manifestations of the Holy Spirit, welcoming me into the fold." He pauses to shake his head at the memory. "He's stuck to that line the whole time, and it's been easy for him to do it, because I haven't seen my dad or Frick since—I don't know where the corporation's hidden them now. I don't know what they did to the missing Raptured, and I don't know what they have planned for the apocalypse. As far as I can tell, the majority of Church employees are in the dark about all of this. The Three Angels know, and maybe some people directly beneath them, but everyone else seems to think, or at least hope, that it's all really happening.

"But here's what I do know: Without Frick, the Church is more fragmented than it used to be. The Angels are the perfect encapsulation: Michelle Mulvey's only concern is the corporation—developing new products, marketing aggressively, keeping the money rolling in. Ted Blackmore is all about the public face—recruiting new Believers, making sure the old ones continue toeing the line. Masterson . . . he's the one who really worries me. He's the one telling the stories. He interprets the Book as he sees fit, and lets that interpretation color everything Mulvey and Blackmore do. He has the same values as Frick, without the excuse of paranoid schizophrenia. The good news is, they're not on the same page; I think you'd only need to play them off one another to make the whole corporation implode. The bad news is, they know it. And I think they're trying to get that unifying force again.

"They hold these fundraisers every week. Big mansions in Beverly Hills, Brentwood, Malibu. Hollywood people, lawyers, producers—people with money. I get up and give a speech Blackmore's prepared: welcome, Frick smiles upon us, and so on. Then every one—*every single speech*—makes reference to a messiah. 'If we continue to abide by Frick's word, to show him our devotion through our actions and our generosity toward his Church, he'll have mercy on us. He will send us a savior.' It gets a big response: cheers every time. They've raised millions so far. But the thing is: there's no messiah in the Book of Frick. He's straightforward about that. 'Don't believe in a savior; there's no such thing.' The way Frick saw it, the chosen would be saved and the rest of us destroyed, and nothing—no one—would be able to stop it."

A knot begins to form in my stomach. Harp shakes her head slowly in dawning horror.

"And the other thing is—okay, maybe this is me just being paranoid, but every morning this week, at the end of my daily meeting with Blackmore, his assistant arrives with his eleven o'clock appointment. They all look the same: friendly-looking white guys with long hair and beards . . ." He looks almost sheepish. "They bring headshots."

I don't know what to say. Peter's theory is absurd, but I know enough now about the Church of America to know they've never let a plan's abject absurdity stop them. I glance at Harp and see she's fixed Peter with a disbelieving smile.

"Are you seriously suggesting," she asks, "that the Church is trying to cast a messiah?"

"It makes sense, if you think about it. They can't keep killing off their devoted faithful—that's a terrible business model. My guess is, they're trying to find the right person: someone young and willing to be bought. Then, on the day of the apocalypse, they drag him in front of the cameras—maybe alongside a miraculously resurrected Frick and Taggart—and boom: they never have to worry about pulling off a Rapture again. They create millions of new Believers on the spot, and best of all, they've got the celebrity spokesperson to end all celebrity spokespeople. They've got Jesus fucking Christ."

"But . . ." Harp shakes her head like she's trying to dislodge the awful story from her brain. "Seriously, how stupid do they think we are?"

"I think they think we're pretty stupid," I say, putting my head in my hands. "Or at least they think we're desperate. Believers will buy the story because they *want* to—better that than to believe we're doomed. And if Peter's theory is right, it's not like they'll convince everybody—but they'll convince enough to make a profit by."

"The good news," Peter points out, "is they'll probably stop killing people."

"But they'll get away with killing people in the first place!" Harp exclaims.

"Not if we make people believe our story before the Messiah appears," I say, thinking fast. "If we can find proof—real evidence that the Church of America faked the Rapture—then they can drag out all the fake messiahs they want and it won't do any good." My friends look at me with hopeful expressions, like I've just noticed said evidence here in the room. I shake my head. "We need to find the missing Raptured."

"How are we going to do that?" Harp asks. "I've been asking for information on my blog for weeks, and no one's given me anything concrete, just various cities that may or may not have anything to do with it."

"I don't know. But if we could find even one, if they were willing to tell the world what happened—"

"They'd have to be alive for that to work," Peter notes gently, "and I don't see how they could be at this point without us knowing about it."

I know he's right. Peter's closer than any of us to the Three Angels, and even he has no clue where the missing Raptured could be. We spend another twenty minutes telling him everything Harp's blog followers have told us, everything that vaguely resembles a clue. But then the three of us lapse into uneasy silence. I feel exhausted and discouraged. It's strange how similar this feels to other hours I've spent with Peter—huddled in his apartment outside Pittsburgh, examining his mysterious mail; tracing our route to Point Reyes on a map in Sacramento—and how different at the same time. We're polite and uncomfortable, suddenly strangers. I feel a tired ache behind my eyes, like I've been crying, like I'm about to. It's time to leave.

Harp is nervous about escaping the Chateau by the same route we took in, the one that will bring us past Ted Blackmore's door. Peter suggests the fire escape outside his window. He pulls it open, letting in thick, heavy heat and the quiet chirping of crickets. Harp climbs out first, moving quietly down the side of the building before dropping smoothly onto the pavement. I make out her dusky shadow giving me a thumbs-up from the sidewalk. I move to follow, but then Peter touches my arm.

"You know I'm sorry, right?" His voice is tender as a bruise. "Because I'm so sorry. It's been killing me, imagining you seeing the things I'm saying. What you must think of me."

I remember him on the Church of America News Network, that smirk on his face when he said, "Come on, guys." For the first time, the thought of it doesn't send a shiver down my spine. Maybe it's just because he's standing here in front of me, his expression open and sad, his skin on my skin. This is the real Peter. If only because I want him to be.

"I know. I'm not going to pretend like it didn't suck, but I get why you did it."

Peter smiles weakly. "I can't believe you heard all those things I said about you—all the things I said about everything!—and *still* you didn't want me to get blown up. That's . . . kind of a superhuman level of goodness, Viv."

"I'm not human, though, is the thing," I point out. "I'm a witch."

It takes him a second, but then he laughs that pleased, surprised laugh again, my very favorite of his laughs. My body reacts before my brain can—I cross the foot of space that separates us to kiss his laughing mouth. It is warm and wet and tastes sweetly of champagne; I run my hands across his broad shoulders. He's so surprised that at first he doesn't move, but then he grasps the back of my neck with his hand, sending sparks down my spine. I feel like I'm no longer muscle and bone, but pure liquid. It's the happiest, the most relaxed I've been in months. After a few long moments, I pull my head back, slightly dazed. Peter holds me tight against him, looking stunned and delighted. We both start laughing.

"What were you saying?" I ask, when he finally lets me go. I glance outside and see Harp on the ground, waiting anxiously. "That you're sorry or whatever?"

"Something like that, I think." Peter shakes his head. "Hard to remember now—it seemed really important at the time."

"Well, you're forgiven. Just keep looking at me like you're currently looking at me, and you will always be forgiven."

Peter laughs and moves forward to steady me as I throw one leg over the window ledge. "Okay, but in general? I'm not sure that's a sound policy. You could get yourself in a lot of trouble with a policy like that."

"Trouble!" I echo, incredulously. The night air is warm on my skin; I lower myself out of the window to let it swallow me up. I feel clever and messy and vibrating with life. "You think I can't handle a little trouble? Watch the news sometime, Peter Ivey. I'm a motherfucking enemy to salvation."

CHAPTER THIRTEEN

I don't have to explain to Harp the slight spring in my step as we return to the car; she takes one look at me when I drop to the pavement beside her and makes a face. "Oh, Viv. Don't you know how to play hard to get?" But Harp can never stay too unhappy when I'm happy. Despite Peter's messiah theory and the impossible mystery of the missing Raptured, we're both a little giddy on the ride back to the Good Book. Harp scans the radio for something upbeat and secular, and we make do dancing away our frayed nerves to a poppy jingle for Church-brand toothpaste: "For a smile as white as the robes of Jesus!" I still feel the scratch of Peter's bit of stubble around my mouth; I remember our kisses with a shudder of pleasure. For the first time in a long time, I realize as we park in front of the Good Book and try to compose ourselves, I feel *young*—sneaking out with my best friend, kissing cute boys. I feel like an actual teenager.

We slip in through the bookshop and climb up the stairs, thinking longingly of the beds waiting for us. I'm so buzzed on the night's various surprises—We didn't get caught! Peter's on our side! We might have figured out the Church's plan, and we're going to try as hard as we can to stop them!—that I don't notice until a split second too late that the knob of the second-floor door is turning.

Then it is open, and Diego stands there.

Harp gasps. My mind runs through a string of weak excuses— We heard a noise? We needed some air?—but my head goes blank when Diego steps aside and I see the rest of them behind him, waiting: Winnie by the kitchen, staring stonily at the floor; Amanda beckoning us in with a manic, false smile; and, worst of all, poor Robbie, slumped on the couch, red-eyed.

"Here you are!" Amanda's voice is ice-cold. "See? Not to worry, Winnie. They were probably just taking a midnight joyride, like two average red-blooded American teens."

"Where were you?" asks Winnie in a muffled voice, and I realize she's been crying. "When Kimberly came to bed and you weren't up there, we thought at first—"

"How long have you been doing this?" Diego sounds disgusted. "Robbie told us he gave you the keys a week ago, for a 'secret' mission I sure as hell know nothing about. What is the matter with you two? You made me swear to protect you." He turns his dark-eyed glare on me; I have to look away. "We're putting ourselves at risk, protecting you—this is how you repay us?"

I feel sick. I glance at Harp; she has a distant, slightly bored expression on her face. This is how she hides herself from hurt: she transforms herself into stone, makes herself impenetrable. But I feel like an open wound. I force myself to look at Robbie. Winnie's distress would be bad enough, but Robbie—he's trying to sit still, but I can tell by the jerky motion in his shoulders that he's crying.

"Robbie—" I say. He looks up at me, wary and embarrassed. We've made a fool out of him.

"Go to bed, Robbie," Amanda says firmly, and without a word, he gets up and pushes past us to the steps.

"Don't punish him," Harp says in a would-be careless voice, but there's a pleading hitch in it that tells me she feels terrible, too. "We talked him into it."

"He's a soldier in this militia, and he should know better." Amanda's voice snaps like a rubber band; any second now she'll be screaming.

"This isn't a militia, lady." Harp still sounds casual. "This is a group of people you've convinced to kill themselves for your personal vendetta. Don't call them a militia just because it makes you feel better about the fact that they're going to die."

Winnie and Diego stand very still and show no reaction to Harp's words. But Amanda takes a deep breath through her nose. When she speaks again, it's with the silky smoothness of a businesswoman.

"Vivian, would you be so kind as to tell me where you were tonight?"

"Um . . ." I feel Winnie watching me, willing me to give an answer that will satisfy. "Just driving around? Like you said. We've been—you know, we've been cooped up a lot, in the apartment, and we were just feeling kind of . . . stir-crazy?"

There's a brief moment where I think I've convinced her. She nods, as if taking this in, then laughs gently. But when she speaks, Amanda says, "You are frankly the worst fucking liar I have ever met in my life." She glances down at her nails, like she's too bored with me to even look at me. "You're no longer welcome here. You are no longer under our protection. I'll give you an hour to get out."

Winnie stiffens almost imperceptibly. Diego gives Amanda a sharp look.

"Amanda," he says, "the Church of America is looking for these girls. If they find them, they'll be killed. We can't just turn them out on the street."

"Well, maybe they *should* be killed, Diego! Because really, what good are they doing us? We had an arrangement—they could stay so long as they built up support for violent measures against the Church. But all I see on that blog are long screeds about this idiot's romantic woes"—Amanda sneers at me—"and dull posts about where Believers were vacationing before the Rapture. I mean, what is that shit?"

"That's me trying to find proof that the Rapture was faked," Harp snaps. "Something we'll need in order to actually get rid of the Church of America. I know you're not so deluded that you think this attack will actually work, so why aren't you putting any of your resources toward finding the missing three thousand?"

"How *dare* you question my methods," Amanda snarls, wheeling closer to us. "You have no actual idea of what it takes to create change in the world—you're fucking *teenagers*."

"Amanda—"

"I don't want to hear it, Winnie! So long as the Church is looking for them, these girls are poison. This isn't an orphanage. This isn't a home for wayward kids. We don't have time to raise a couple of needlessly reckless fugitives. Especially now. Because, frankly, you know—she's not entirely wrong." Amanda nods to Harp. "Not everyone's going to make it out alive with this mission, and the ones that do will be on the run. I don't intend to adopt these two once the Baby-Sitters Club"—she gestures dismissively to Winnie—"breaks up for good. I'm busy trying to recruit to make up for the numbers we'll lose in the attack."

I clench my jaw. Amanda is right. We're not helping her cause. If anything, her army's protection of us has only hurt them. She's well within her rights to kick us out, to stop providing beds and food we've in no way earned. Even though I am weak with fear that Diego, still standing solemnly near the door, is about to comply, I understand that Amanda is right. But still I feel a surge of anger toward her, the heartless way she's spoken of her soldiers' lives. *The numbers we'll lose.* As if they don't have names or faces or personalities. As if one of them isn't my sister.

Winnie moves toward us now from across the room; she steps in front of me. Diego falls back, and I realize she's the one who's going to do it. I've pushed too hard at the bond between us; I've let her down. Winnie doesn't want to be my family anymore. It makes sense that, as the one who brought us into Amanda's militia, Winnie will be the one who ushers us out of it. But still it's hard to look into her eyes as she fixes Harp, then me, with a hard stare. Her eyes look so much like my own.

Winnie turns then, standing in front of us, shielding us from Amanda.

"These are *children*," she says. "These are *girls*. As bright and brave as they are, they'd be in danger out there. They'd be in danger even if the Church wasn't looking for them, and you know it. You know what Believers think about girls. You know what they're capable of. You told us when you recruited us that this would be an effort to put things right. How is this the right thing to do? Maybe it's because you're alone, Amanda"—her tone becomes softer, sympathetic, and I notice a muscle twitch in Amanda's cheek; she looks furious—"but you don't understand. We're more than just bodies. Vivian and Harp are going nowhere."

I glance at Diego to see if he objects, but he just frowns, like he's not sure whether or not he's in charge anymore. Amanda glares up at Winnie, but I see the raw, confused hurt on her face. It's hard to keep everybody's separate threads of tragedy in my mind at a single time; it's hard to remember that all of us, Believers and Non-Believers alike, have had something taken from us. Some invisible knot that holds us all together. The knowledge that there are things worth living for. I don't think Amanda knows that. Somewhere along the way, she's forgotten.

"When you're gone," she tells Winnie after a pause, "they're not my problem."

CHAPTER FOURTEEN

Friends, lovers, enemies:

Viv and I are touched by your responses to our story — the comments, questions, heartfelt support, racist vitriol, all of it. We're so happy you're listening. Muchos gracias to the Church for covering our story every single day on the news! HUGE spike in page views. Apparently you weren't convinced by that whole "God hates blogs" thing they attempted to make stick. Kinda sloppy, right? The Angels are losing their touch.

Sorry we haven't been around lately. We've been busy collecting information about the Church with which to successfully overthrow them. I've got all my Muslim extremist buds on board — I called them and they were like, "Oh, totally, Harp, we are behind you one hundred and fifty percent!" and Viv was finally able to get in touch with her coven. But we've hit a wall, and we need your help.

Let's talk about our missing fellow citizens, folks. I've gotten a lot of comments with possible leads; we seem to keep coming back to the same twelve cities: Billings, Boise, Boulder, Nashville, Cleveland, Fort Worth, Tulsa, Santa Fe, San Antonio, Minneapolis, Wichita, and Grand Rapids. But after that, the well runs dry. Folks in these cities, I beg you: LOOK AROUND. NOTICE ANY WEIRD NEW NEIGHBORS? FRESHLY DUG GRAVES? These people went somewhere, and we owe it to them to figure out where. I know what you're thinking: Harp, this post gravely lacks in your usual fast-paced wit and wordplay. And you're right. But Viv and I are beginning to understand what the Church has planned for Apocalypse Day. And it's big and it's stupid, and if it works, we'll never be rid of them. So if you love this country the way we do, the things it's really and truly about — The separation of church and state! Hot dogs on the 4th of July! Gratuitous sex and violence on primetime TV! — you'll help us right this ship. Please, PLEASE, help us find the missing Raptured.

EAT A DICK, BEATON FRICK.

xoxo, Harp Janda, Citizen

Things start to feel different in the weeks after Winnie stands up to Amanda. It's a relief to no longer be keeping secrets from Winnie—after she stood up for us, I told her where we'd been and what we'd been doing. I wanted her to know Peter was on our side. And the soldiers seem to understand that Amanda's not truly in charge anymore, that she can be questioned. It must give them hope, because they're looser now, less afraid. Though the attack still looms horribly on the horizon, and Diego seems tenser than ever, spending every night casing the Chateau, Winnie's friends are more relaxed and easy with us than they've ever been. Even Kimberly's starting to crack—one morning before she leaves for training, she pauses in the doorway and turns to Harp and me, asking, with a slight hint of accusation, "Is it true that you two broke into the Chateau Marmont last week and snuck into Peter Taggart's bedroom?"

"Who told you that?" I ask.

"Winnie told everyone yesterday at training. She said you went in through the kitchens and out through the fire escape, and didn't get seen even once."

"Yeah," Harp replies in a cool, bored voice, focusing on her laptop screen. "It's actually pretty easy to do, if you're not completely stupid."

Kimberly nods at us. "Respect, ladies. That shit is hardcore."

Only Robbie treats us coldly now—I sort of think he'll never forgive us. He's always been quiet, but since Amanda caught us and he got the blame, he's downright stony. If Harp or I so much as edge near him, his face turns a painful purple, and he pays such hard attention to everything that isn't us, I wonder if he's trying to will us out of existence. This makes it hard to apologize to him. One night after dinner, while we watch the Church of America News Network, I slip beside him and speak before he can notice I'm there.

"What we did was wrong," I whisper. "It was disrespectful and we shouldn't have done it. I'm so sorry we got you in trouble; I regret it—"

But he leaps to his feet before I can finish. "Do I have permission to go to bed?" he asks loudly of the room at large, and Winnie stares at him, confused.

"You're a human being, Robbie. You never have to ask permission to go to bed."

He glares at her, then turns on his heel and stomps upstairs. Harp gives me a sympathetic look from across the room. She's permanently attached to her computer now—in the last few days, she's started what she calls "an intriguing correspondence" regarding the missing Raptured. But she won't give me details, so I know the theory she's been offered doesn't satisfy her. Next to me, Julian chuckles.

"Don't take it personally, Viv. He's thirteen."

"Yeah. I guess." But that only makes me feel worse. I'm not that much older than Robbie. I remember how small and useless I felt at thirteen. I think of Robbie's orphan status. It makes me sick to think how alone I've helped make him feel.

"And anyway, maybe he's just affected by the *Santa Ana winds!*" Julian wiggles his fingers, adopts a spooky old-movie vampire voice. I laugh weakly and turn back to the television screen, where the weather report drones unsettlingly on.

But it's hard to find much humor in the idea that the weather is turning us all into angry violent shells of our former selves, because to some degree, it seems to really be happening. Each day the Church of America News Network has some new horrible detail to report. Most of the major cities across the globe are beset by riots—ongoing collisions between protestors and police officers, fires, mass killings. Murder and suicide rates are at an all-time high. Following reports that police officers nationwide have fled their positions in droves and that the National Guard has been stretched to its breaking point, the president diverts federal funds toward the Church of America's Peacemakers, giving them temporary but official status as guardians of the law. It's a chilling development, but also it's unclear how effective it is, because things continue to fall steadily apart. Here in Los Angeles, there's a breakout from Twin Towers Correctional Facility, which Masterson on TV casually attributes to the influence of Satan.

Everyone still trains in anticipation of the attack, but no one seems to know whether or not it's actually happening. We haven't seen Amanda since we got caught, and Diego shuts himself away, refusing to answer anyone's questions about the campaign. Peter still conducts press conferences at the gates of the Chateau Marmont, so it's clear he hasn't successfully convinced the Church to move, and Harp's blog commenters still offer largely unsatisfying conjectures as to where the missing Raptured can be found. My friends and I are running out of time.

When Harp and I were honest with Winnie about where we had been the night we were caught, Winnie made us promise we wouldn't attempt a secret jaunt to see Peter again. I'm grateful to Winnie—I feel closer to her than ever before—but I still don't know that I ever intended to keep the promise. One night, with only a week remaining until the proposed attack on the Chateau, I wait for the others to fall asleep around me, for the rustling of sheets and the sound of Harp's typing to give way to deep breathing. When all is still, I climb out of bed and dress quietly in the dark, then pass through the door and down the stairs. I'm dizzy with the rush of having pulled it off, and I have a brief moment of delicious self-satisfaction—*Hardcore!* I congratulate myself, as Kimberly put it—thinking of Peter's face when he sees me, how pleased and surprised he'll be. I smile at the thought of it, and push open the door into the Good Book.

I freeze. A figure stands behind the counter, flipping through a magazine by the glow of her flashlight. She shines its light on me.

"*J'accuse!*" Winnie whispers.

She closes the magazine and bounds around the counter to

where I stand, frozen, feeling like a fool in my black hoodie, my hand still on the knob. I brace for her anger—massive and totally righteous. Winnie stood up to Amanda for me—she put her livelihood on the line—and this is how I thank her? But when she gets closer, I see my sister is smiling.

"I had a feeling you'd try it again sometime," Winnie explains. "I've been waiting down here the last few nights, wondering when you'll make the attempt. Nothing feeds delusions of invincibility quite as effectively as sneaking in and out of Church of America headquarters without detection, am I right?"

"I just needed some fresh air," I say in a tentative voice, and Winnie rolls her eyes.

"Seriously, kid, who taught you how to lie? Because you should really write them a sternly worded letter; they did not do a good job." She gives me a gentle smile. "Come on, Viv. Let's go upstairs, all right? There's still some of Elliott's vodka up there; let's just hang out and have a nice chat about boys."

It doesn't sound entirely unappealing. But I stand my ground. "I have to go, Winnie. I have to see him."

She looks disappointed. "Why?"

"Because . . ." I wish I had an answer other than the silly-sounding truth. "Because I want to. I miss him, and I'm worried about him. Maybe I wouldn't be quite as worried if I knew for sure that your boyfriend wasn't going to go ahead with this attack."

This hits a nerve. Winnie pulls back slightly, but then she sighs. "I wish I could tell you. But Diego won't even talk to me about it right now. I have no idea what he has planned. Most of us are against the idea, for sure—but they're loyal to him, and he's loyal to Amanda. If he decides it's what we have to do . . ." She trails off, sounding worried.

"Why are you with him, Winnie? I'm sorry," I say, because she's given me an annoyed look, "but I really don't understand. He's so—I don't know—condescending. Like, why wouldn't he just talk to you about whether or not he's going to go through with the attack? You're just as smart as he is, if not smarter. You're just as brave as he is, if not braver."

Winnie gives me a wry smile. "I think you have an inflated sense of my worth, Viv. But I'll take it." She pauses, thinking. "I don't know. I know what he is. I've been with him for a while now. He definitely gets confused sometimes—he manages to convince himself that he alone is responsible for taking down the apocalypse. Which you, by the way," she notes, "can be just as guilty of. But I believe he has a good heart. And I don't know! I just love him. Are you in love with Peter?"

She asks it like it's the simplest thing in the world to know.

"I don't know," I say, truthfully. "He's kind and good, and I think he'd be those things even if we didn't live in this particularly messed-up world. But if I knew for sure I was going to live to a hundred and die peacefully in my sleep, would I want to spend that whole long life with him? I guess I'm not sure yet. I hope to make it to a point where I have the time to wonder about that."

Winnie is quiet. After a long moment, she says, "I owe you an apology. I'd been assuming that when you snuck out to see him, you'd be doing it in a brainless hormonal fog. But I should know you better than that by now." She takes her keys out of her pocket and tosses them to me.

"I'm not your mother. If you think this is something you have to do, go ahead and do it. But for God's sake—take care of yourself, okay?" She heads back to the red door, stopping before she passes through. "As soon as Diego tells me what's going on with the attack, you'll be the first to know. Okay? Be safe and hurry back—I'll wait up for you."

| | | | |

When I drive past the Chateau a half hour later, the hotel seems weirdly busy, blazing with light despite the late hour. I see a well-dressed crowd mingling in the lane leading to the entrance. I drive through the winding maze of streets on the hill behind the Chateau and park on the back road. As I make my way down the narrow street to the hotel, I wonder, *Is this crazy?* for the first time. The fact that Winnie let me go makes me think it isn't, but then again, Winnie doesn't always seem so very sane herself. I duck my head low; I'm considering how to get around the security camera outside the kitchen door. I don't notice until too late a man in a white apron smoking a cigarette outside the gate, watching me approach.

I freeze. The man exhales a thin plume of smoke.

"Are you from the agency?"

Logically, I know this is the point where I should turn on my heel and run. But instead I say, "Yep?"

"Thank God." He takes my hand, dragging me into the bright, bustling kitchen. He must feel me tug back in my fright, because his grip gets harder. "Oh no you don't. You were supposed to get here *two hours ago*. Did you not bring a shirt?"

Panicked, I shake my head. The man groans, disappearing into a closet. It's like I've been cut loose inside a nightmare; I'm taking a test in a language I don't understand. Chefs are piling hors d'oeuvres onto wide shiny platters; bow-tied servers are standing by, looking impatient. It's confirmation, a little too late, of my suspicion: this was crazy. Why did I think I'd be able to pull it off? I have a brief flash of awareness of the nervous breakdown my old self—quiet, orderly Vivian 1.0—would have at this moment. But I don't move. The man returns with a button-down white shirt and a clip-on bow tie I dutifully change into. He retrieves a white bonnet—the preferred modest headwear of female Believers—and jams it hard onto my head. "We're *never* using your company's services again," he hisses before placing a tray covered in brimming glasses of champagne onto my arm and pushing me into the packed lobby.

It's a small room, but so full it's difficult to pass through. I feel slightly safe under the cover of the bonnet, but there are too many people here; it's impossible to keep my eyes on all of them at once. I inch through the crowd, glancing around wildly for Peter. As guests lift glasses from the tray, it gets lighter but more awkward to balance. Everyone seems absurdly rich and very drunk. I notice with annoyance that there's no adherence to modesty here: I see short skirts and plenty of cleavage, bare necks adorned by jewels. I guess if you have enough money, the Church will overlook a selection of your sins. I see Blackmore hunched low and murmuring into the ear of a miserable-looking Dylan; a woman trills loudly a few feet away, and I realize it's Michelle Mulvey. My arm begins to tremble. If I drop the tray, all eyes will be on me. I decide to abort; it's time to bolt before anyone gets a good look at my face, but then the last glass of champagne is lifted from my tray and someone grabs my elbow.

"Seems like you need a refill. I'll help."

Peter. Relief floods through me; I struggle not to throw my grateful arms around him. He steers me by the elbow through the lobby and down an empty hallway. He hesitates before a large coat closet, then pulls the door open and throws me in, following quickly. He closes the door behind him. The closet is stuffy; it smells like ancient wool. Peter flicks on the bare light bulb above us.

"Have you lost your fucking mind?"

My knees go shaky and my breath is coming out in a ragged wheeze, but I laugh in spite of myself at the look on his face. "Possibly, Peter. I'm not going to lie to you: it is very, very possible."

"This isn't funny, Viv. It's not safe. You could have been stopped by a Peacemaker; you could have been stopped by just a random crazy person. Last night there was a drive-by in front of the hotel—three people shot dead for no reason at all, as far as the Peacemakers could tell. For no reason! And that's just outside. This is the worst possible place for you to be. Mulvey was three feet from you! Do you have any idea what would have happened if you'd been seen?"

His voice is so angry. I feel annoyed, defensive. "I have many ideas," I say, ticking them off on my fingers. "The Angels capture me and kill me. They capture me, torture me, and then kill me. They make me tell them where Harp is, and they kill her, too. They string my body up on the Hollywood sign as a warning to slutty lying witches everywhere. At this particular point in my life, ideas about what will happen to me if I'm seen are pretty much the only ideas I have."

Peter's expression softens. He pulls me to him. "I'm sorry. I was just scared. When I saw you out there—it was like seeing a ghost. My heart stopped."

"I know, I know. I was planning to be a lot stealthier than this, but the head waiter saw me and everything went to shit. Probably I shouldn't have come in the first place, but I needed to see you. As far as we know, the attack is next week, Peter. Next week! Why are you still here?"

We break apart and I see the grave look on his face. "I tried to convince them something big was coming. But when I wouldn't tell Blackmore the name of the donor who gave me the tip . . . I don't know if he just doesn't trust me anymore, or if he thinks I'm as crazy as my dad, but I've tried all I could and he's not listening. You think they're honestly going to go through with it?"

"I don't know yet. We don't have anything solid about the missing Raptured, and Amanda wants this place gone. It's possible my sister's group will refuse to go through with it, but even if they do . . . Amanda will find others. What about the Messiah? Any developments?"

Peter shakes his head. "I haven't seen Blackmore meet with any actors in a while, but that could mean anything—maybe he was already cast; maybe I'm wrong about the whole thing."

We stare at each other. Peter has a sad, helpless look on his face, and I feel like my head's about to split open from stress. How easy everything would be, I realize, if I didn't feel responsible for everything that's coming, like Winnie says I do. If Harp and I had never driven to California, if we'd never seen Frick in the compound, I could just be like the thousands of other Non-Believers right now—frightened, clueless, waiting for the end, but without the excruciating feeling that change is right at the tips of my fingers, yet impossible to grasp. I feel like crying. But then I notice that Peter's mouth has flicked up into the barest hint of a smile.

"You look," he says, "completely insane in that bonnet."

I laugh loudly, and he covers my mouth with his own. I let the tray fall to our feet and grab him by the lapels of his jacket. We're being reckless and I know it, but something about him—the shape of his lips, the heat of his skin beneath his shirt, his grip at my waist—makes it worth the risk. He lifts me up and I slip my legs around his hips; he presses me against the wall of the closet and holds me there, kissing me. When he finally pulls away, his hair is adorably messy and he wears a satisfied grin. He lowers me to the ground.

"They're going to notice I'm gone, if they haven't already. I should get back."

"Stay here. Tell them you were trying to Magdalene a wayward caterer." I tug at the front of his shirt, unwilling to let go. "You saw the lust in her eyes as she offered you champagne, and the Holy Spirit compelled you to show her the error of her sinful ways."

Peter smirks, mischievous. "That might work. Unfortunately I'd have to admit defeat—you've still got, like, a ton of lust in your eyes."

I lean in to kiss him again. "Maybe you're not trying hard enough?"

"Vivian," says Peter, fake serious. "I swear on the Book of Frick that I'm never going to try very hard to get the lust out of your eyes. I really, really like it there."

Again, a shadow of the old Viv passes over me. She'd be blushing right now, hiding her face from Peter's sight, trying to convince herself he didn't mean a word of it. How many simple pleasures I denied myself, because I thought that was what goodness was. How stupid that it took me until the end of the world to realize it was something else entirely. Peter takes my hands into his and squeezes.

"When will I see you again?"

I shiver. "I don't know. Before next Friday, for sure. If the militia decides to go through with the attack, I'll come for you— Harp and I will come for you. We'll get you out of here."

"That's going to be harder than you're making it sound," Peter tells me. "And even if we pull it off—what about the rest of them?" He waves his hand in the direction of the party outside the door. "What happens to them?"

"I don't know," I say helplessly. "We'll think of something, okay? I promise you we'll think of something. In the meantime, keep trying to convince Blackmore that it's a credible threat. The second I know what's coming, I'll be back to tell you directly."

Peter says nothing, and I smile at him despite my nerves.

"Aren't you going to tell me it's too dangerous?" I ask. "It's an unnecessary risk? You wish you could protect me; if anything ever happened to me, you'd never forgive yourself . . . ?"

"If anything happened to you," Peter says firmly, "I'd never forgive the person who did it. But I'm not going to lecture you, Viv. Why would I? I've never met a person more adept at handling herself than you. The last thing my girlfriend—my smart, stubborn badass of a girlfriend—needs is my protection."

I feel my cheeks go pink. Peter has always considered me ten times more capable than I consider myself. There's something so intoxicating about being seen that way—the more convinced he seems of it, the more he convinces me. But that's not the reason I feel a happy glow like a sip of whiskey warming my insides.

"You just called me your girlfriend."

Peter kisses me lightly on my forehead, nose, lips. "Get a hold of yourself, Apple," he says, before he heads back into the party. "I'll give you my varsity jacket after we stop the apocalypse."

| | | | |

I wait a few minutes, and then I slip out and pass through the kitchen with ease, concealed by the bustle of activity among the waiters, by the look of determination on my face, like I have a destination in mind and it's the next plate of shrimp cocktail. I glide through the back door without anyone stopping me, and once I'm past the fence I break into a run, shedding my bonnet and bow tie on the way. My heart pounds the whole drive home—thinking of Peter's scent, his warm proximity—but also it's like Winnie said: right or wrong, I can't help but feel invincible, slipping through the Church's fingers again and again, like water.

CHAPTER FIFTEEN

The next few days that follow are at once endless and far too short. I can't sleep more than a couple of hours a night; I don't have nightmares anymore because I don't sleep deeply enough to get them. I'm worried and exhausted, waiting each day for Diego to confirm whether or not they'll carry out Amanda's plan, but he's more inaccessible than ever, and Winnie has no insight. I can feel the cracks in the soldiers' resolve deepen, a tension humming under the surface of everything, ready to explode. When they aren't training, they run in and out of the command center throughout the day, checking with Harp for updates on the missing Raptured. But she's evasive with them; she won't give them a straight answer, and on Wednesday, when Colby storms out, dejected by her nonresponse, I ask, "Did anything ever come out of that correspondence you mentioned?"

Harp continues typing, staring at the screen like she hasn't heard me.

"Harp?" I say, louder. "Hello?"

"What?" She looks up, seemingly dazed. "Did you say some-thing?"

But there's something false in her tone, like she's feigning confusion. "What's going on?" I ask. "Why won't you tell anyone what you're working on? Why won't you tell me?"

Harp pauses. "I don't know if it's for real yet, Viv. It seems kind of impossible that it's for real. I don't want to get anyone's hopes up until I'm sure."

"There's no time to be totally sure," I point out. I want to sound reasonable, but my voice comes out high and slightly pan-icked—I'm worried for Winnie and the others; I haven't yet fig-ured out a way to get Peter and Dylan out of the Chateau. "As far as we can tell, the attack's in two days. If there's any chance at all that you have a lead, you need to share it now, while you still have the chance to change Diego's mind."

"I'm working on it," Harp mutters, returning to her typing.

"Harp—"

"Viv, I said I'm working on it! It's not like I don't get the stakes, okay?"

She doesn't quite yell, but her voice is hard, and I see some-thing entirely new in her eyes—a kind of grit. I don't know what she knows right now, what her informant has told her, but I know she'll turn it into a weapon if she can. I don't push her any fur-ther.

Late that afternoon, Frankie bursts into the command center, rushing to the shelf where she keeps the first-aid kit; Birdie trails behind, half carrying Kimberly, whose face is beaten and bloody. Harp and I rush to help, but Kimberly claims to be better than she looks. She tells us she was walking home from training with the others when she noticed a group of young Non-Believers breaking into an electronics store to loot it; when she tried to intervene, they pounced on her. Kimberly tries to laugh it off with us—"I'd have been dead if it hadn't been for Dragoslav over here," much to Birdie's vexation—but the incident unnerves everyone. It's hard to accept that it's no longer just the Believers that we ought to fear. We have to be on guard from every single person, no matter their ideology.

Thursday morning Diego informs me that I'll be joining him, Winnie, Elliott, and Robbie (filling in for the recovering Kimberly) later, on their final casing of the Chateau. I realize with a sinking heart that everything's settled: the attack will take place at noon tomorrow. Perhaps there was never any question whether it would or not.

"You're really going through with this, then."

Diego looks exhausted. "Don't start, Vivian."

"If you refused to attack the Chateau, Amanda would listen to you. She trusts you!"

"Vivian, please—"

"Don't do this to them." I gesture to the rest of the militia milling about the room, lacing up boots and polishing weapons, pretending not to eavesdrop. "We won't survive this—you know we won't. There has to be another way!"

"See, this is what I don't think you get," Diego snaps. "Amanda's not the only one who thinks this is a good idea—she and I planned it together, understand? You're seventeen, Vivian. I'm sorry, but it takes more than crossed fingers and daydreams to make real change happen."

I balk. "Don't act like that's what I'm doing! And don't pretend you're *actually* a soldier! I don't understand how you could possibly think this is the only solution—how you could think it's even a good one. Diego—you're not a murderer!"

He pauses then, and sounding truly curious, he asks, "Do you think it's that simple? Do you think it's a case of being a killer, or not being one? Because I think it's more complicated than that. We all have this monster inside us. For the most part we're able to keep it under control. But when things get dire—when the world keeps pushing you down, keeps pushing your family down, like it's trying to drown you—something snaps. And you realize: That ability is there. It's always been there. And it doesn't seem so inconceivable anymore, to take a life. Not if it means getting your head above water."

I'm silent, considering it. It's not that I don't understand him—I've felt it too, that monster. After Raj was killed, after I found out about my dad. When I thought the Angels were hurting Peter. When I thought Peter was one of them. I think at those moments I could have done it, if I'd had to. If it had come down to a choice between them or me, I think I could have killed the people who hurt me.

"Look," Diego says, "you and Harp tried the nonviolent tack. I respect that, I really do. But what good has it done you? You haven't found the information we need. You're still terrorists as far as the rest of the country is concerned. And it's not like you're even slowing the apocalypse down—things get worse out there by the minute. You tried, and you deserve credit for trying—but it's time to try something else."

"Harp has something," I insist, "something big. If you just gave her more time—"

"Enough." Diego's tone is rigid, and I snap my jaw shut—he's not listening to me. "We leave at nine tonight—it should only take an hour or two. I want to make sure the Church hasn't changed their security setup, that they don't see us coming. I figure you keep waltzing in and out of the place; I could use your eyes."

I'd like to refuse, but Diego has just provided me an opportunity I've desperately needed. "Fine. But while we're there, I'm breaking Peter Ivey and Dylan Marx out and taking them with us. I'm not going to let you kill them, so don't try and stop me."

He sighs. "Stop *you*, Vivian? If only I knew how."

| | | | |

You'd think by now I'd be so used to it I wouldn't blink, but I can't imagine sneaking into the Chateau again without feeling a sickening drop in my stomach. Maybe it's just the atmosphere of Amanda's command center: Kimberly's face still bruised from her attack, unhappy soldiers on the verge of snapping, the hours until tomorrow flying uneasily by. The only person who doesn't seem on the verge of a meltdown is Harp, who closes her laptop in the early afternoon for the first time in a long time. Shortly before I leave for the Chateau with Diego, Winnie, and the others, Harp gives me a hug.

"What is this?" I say, suspicious, pulling out of her embrace. "Are you sick or something? Are you dying?"

Harp laughs. "Oh, Viv. You act as if I never give you hugs randomly throughout a given day, simply out of my pure affection for you and the general goodness of my heart."

"Yeah. That's because you don't."

"Fine." She beams at me, then leans in to whisper, "I'm happy."

"Oh?" I feel a hopeful flicker. It's possible Harp's only talking about the secretive hours she keeps spending upstairs with Julian, but I know her well enough to sense traces of something bigger. "Do you think at some point you'd be willing to tell me why?"

"Very soon. By the time you get back, in fact, if all goes well. Trust me," she says, because I've made a face at her. "It will be very worth it."

Diego stands by the door, calling my name. It's time for us to go. On the way down to the car, Diego, Winnie, and Elliott walk ahead of me, deep in conversation, while Robbie trails behind. The mood between us has not yet quite thawed, but in the last few days, perhaps faced with the enormity of the act he's about to help commit, Robbie has slowly started to acknowledge my presence in the room again. This morning, he wordlessly passed me a carton of milk when I poured myself some cereal. I make a note to pull him aside when we get back to the command center, to try apologizing once more—I can't face the thought that tomorrow he'll march off to certain doom without having forgiven me. But for now we continue to the cars in our usual silence. The five of us traverse the familiar streets, so much emptier now of cars and people—it's the last day of August, which means the apocalypse is only three weeks away. People want to escape the cities and the coasts, to move away from earthquakes and tidal waves and nuclear attacks. We pull off Sunset, onto the lane leading past the Chateau, through the still side streets, till we reach the abandoned driveway I favor most. Diego explains that this will be a quick walk-through—he only wants the others to confirm the plans they already have in place. Elliott and Robbie will double-check the spots where they'll position the explosives and the sharpshooters. Winnie will make sure they haven't missed a single escape route. "And I'm going to help Vivian sneak in and usher her boyfriend to safety," he concludes with a hint of sarcasm.

"Wait." I turn to him. "Are you serious? I've done it before; I can do it again."

Diego regards me over his shoulder. "Yeah, you've done it before. But by your own account, your first two break-ins involved a whole lot of hiding in closets."

"But—"

"I don't doubt your abilities, Vivian. You shouldn't doubt mine. We'll move quicker if we do it together. You'll be safer."

Winnie looks down, avoiding my gaze, but I see her nod once. I know he's right, and I know he's doing it largely to put her mind at ease, so I don't argue further. Diego spends a few minutes running us quickly through stray details: confirmed safe spots on the route between the car and the Chateau, the time and location we'll meet when the job is done, what to do should any of us get spotted. I feel a vague unease thinking about how comparatively sloppy Harp and I have been on our trips here, how easily we might have lost each other. We leave the car in small groups— Winnie and Robbie first, followed after two minutes by Elliott. After he leaves, Diego and I are left in silence.

"You don't like me," he says casually after a moment.

"That's not true. Not totally true, anyway."

Diego stares out of the front windshield at the dark-windowed mansion above us; he taps his fingers on the steering wheel.

"I think," I continue, "if we weren't at war, I'd like you just fine. You're funny and smart and brave. You obviously care about my sister. And I know she cares about you, too."

"You just don't like the way I fight," he supplies when I lapse into silence.

"I don't like *having* to fight. If the Church didn't exist, I'd be getting ready for my senior year of high school right now. I'd be visiting colleges with my parents. I would—" I'm trying to keep the tremor out of my voice, and failing. "I would be normal. I'd be a person about to *enter* the world, instead of a person trying to hide from it."

Diego turns to look at me. For a moment, I expect him to return to continue his argument from earlier—to tell me that I'm young, that I don't know what I'm doing. I wait for the lecture, but instead he smiles.

"I get you. You know, back at the Good Book, you said I wasn't really a soldier? Well, I guess Winnie's never told you, but that's not true." He exhales deeply. "I enlisted two years back—after that explosion at Yankee Stadium? I like action; I like discipline. It was a good fit. And it was easy to do—automatic status as one of the good guys. Which, as you know, is appealing. There's no better club to be a member of, and I'd always felt like an outsider before. When Amanda recruited me, it felt like the same thing on a whole new level. You know I'm not a monster, Viv. Winnie wouldn't love me if I were. I want to do the right thing—I honestly believe Amanda wants that too—but I realize now as the clock winds down that you never actually know what the right thing is. No one ever takes you aside and says, 'Yep, that's foolproof. Go ahead.' It makes fighting a lot less appealing. Because I'm not sure if this attack is the right thing to do. But if it works the way Amanda wants it to—if it wipes out the Church leaders, if it makes a clean slate for the rest of us—doesn't it have to be *a* right thing?"

I don't know what to tell him. The problem is, I don't think it could possibly work the way Amanda thinks it will.

A blast splits the silence in half. Diego has already thrown open his door and leaped out of the car before I recognize the sound for what it was: a gunshot. "Stay here!" he shouts, disappearing down the lane. I'm so terrified I don't protest. But then I hear a woman's hysterical shrieking.

I scramble out of the back seat and into the sultry evening. I chase Winnie's screams, which I can hardly hear over the ringing in my ears, the sound of my panic. I run hard, catching up with Diego on the sidewalk, then overtaking him—"Viv, no!" he exclaims. I can't slow down, because I see her there at the foot of a driveway down the hill, and Elliott's with her; they're bent over a bump in the road, examining it. And then I get closer and recognize Robbie's shoes.

I drop to my knees. There's a wet black spot where Robbie's stomach should be, a liquid spreading like tar. His eyes are open. He's shivering but his eyes are open. I look into them; I say his name; I hear Winnie babbling to Diego, who has finally caught up—

"He doubled back. He went up that driveway. The house looked dark; we both thought it was abandoned. He said—he said he thought it would be a good spot for Kimberly to be stationed tomorrow. And then I heard a woman shouting, something like 'Get away!' She must have seen him coming and thought—I don't know! Maybe she saw his gun and thought—Diego, the Peacemakers at the Chateau will have heard that shot; we have to move—"

"Get the car, Elliott," Diego commands, and Elliott leaps to his feet and goes running.

Diego lowers himself next to me and touches Robbie's face.

Robbie looks up at him. "I'm sorry."

"Don't be stupid." Diego takes off his black jacket and presses it hard against Robbie's wound. "Nothing to apologize for."

"I shouldn't have gone up there. It was dumb. I didn't think anybody lived there."

"It's okay, Robbie," Winnie assures him in a trembling voice. "Really. Nobody is mad at you."

Robbie laughs weakly, and a thin trail of bloody spit pools in the corner of his mouth. "I feel really weird."

I wipe his mouth with the corner of my sleeve. "He needs to go to a hospital."

Nobody replies. We hear the car, racing toward us.

"This is really weird," Robbie tells us in a small voice, and his eyes fill with tears. "I'm sorry; I don't know why I'm crying. I just don't feel right."

Elliott screeches the car to a halt beside us and throws open the back door; Diego and Winnie lift Robbie carefully and quickly, placing him in the back seat. Winnie and I flank him; my hands replace Diego's on Robbie's wound. Diego takes the wheel and peels away down the lane and around a corner. Robbie isn't saying words anymore, just making low moaning noises through his chattering teeth.

"He needs to go to the hospital," I say again. "We need to get him to a hospital!"

"We can't risk it," Elliott insists. "The Church of America owns the hospitals. We'd be handing ourselves over."

Diego says nothing. He speeds down Sunset Boulevard, past lights and shops and billboards. It's like the real world, except it can't be anything but a nightmare, because Winnie holds two fingers to Robbie's neck; she shakes her head at me. Robbie is still breathing, but his breaths are shallow—his eyelids flutter and droop.

"He's going to die if you don't take him to a hospital." I can't tell if I'm whispering or shouting and I don't care. "Please! You don't have to stop—bring him to the emergency room entrance and we'll leave him there."

"But then the Church will have him!" Elliott protests.

"He'll be alive!" I shout. "Diego, please!"

Diego hesitates only a second, then he tells Elliott to pull up directions on his phone. Elliott complies, and for a moment I think it's going to be okay. There will be a hospital close by and we'll get there in time and maybe we'll never see Robbie again, but at least he'll be alive. But then on Robbie's other side, Winnie sits up and says his name softly — "Robbie?" — like she's trying to wake him up from a deep slumber, and I press harder on Diego's jacket and watch Robbie's pale face, and I listen as his breaths slow and slow and slow and then stop.

I can't stop screaming. I think, *Why can't I stop screaming? Why don't they tell me to shut up?* But then I understand it's just a noise in my head, a shrill white devastation, so loud it makes tears stream down my cheeks. I can't let go of Robbie. His blood is everywhere; I can taste it — hot and metallic. In front of me Elliott's shoulders are shaking. On the other side of Robbie, Winnie looks down at him with such love, like a mother, like my mother used to look at me — she hushes him though he makes no sound. She pushes his hair back from his face. So that if he were ever to open his eyes again, he could see.

We drive for minutes that feel like hours, and then we're in the parking lot behind the bookstore. We sit silently a moment before Diego glances up and whispers, "What's going on?"

I follow his gaze and see the back windows of the second floor bright with light. It's just after ten, but I understand his confusion. With the attack tomorrow, it was assumed Amanda's army would get as much sleep as possible — it's unclear when they'll next get the chance. But the lights are on, and as we watch, shadows pass in front of the window. Diego cuts the headlights.

"Something's wrong."

I wait for him to form a plan, to direct us where to go, but his hands still grip the wheel tightly. I see his eyes in the rearview mirror; he's terrified.

"I'll go," I offer. "I can see what's happening, and if everything's okay, I'll open the back window and give you the all clear. If something's wrong, I'll run."

Diego wordlessly shakes his head.

"I can handle it," I say. "I *want* to."

And I do—I have an irrational desire, an ache at the center of me, for something to be wrong up there. I'd settle for any faceless villain, the opportunity to destroy them. I take my hands off Robbie, trying to ignore his blood on my fingers, and reach for his rifle on the floor. "I'll bring this."

"Diego," Winnie says in a soft voice when he hesitates. "Viv's got this."

He turns in his seat to look at Robbie's face. I take a moment to look too. Here in the dark of the car, you can't see the blood soaking his center. Diego's expression twists, slashed through with anguish, and he nods.

I leave before he can change his mind. I make it around the building, through the front door, and halfway up the stairs before I begin to lose my nerve. I hear muffled voices, low and unintelligible and serious. I feel a nauseating plunge in my stomach. What if they're sitting there—Birdie and Kimberly and Colby and Harp—in calm anticipation of our return? What will it be like for them when I enter, gray-faced and alone, blood-soaked, clutching Robbie's rifle?

I open the door and the faces turn. Harp pushes through a crowd of people, bounds forward, her face alight with triumph, but time moves weirdly, like a film slowed down interminably, lingering on each excruciating frame. I see her take in the sight of me. Happiness into horror. People speak not in words but tones: confusion, alarm, panic. All of it slurred, incoherent. Somebody—Colby—pushes past, out the door. Faces in an awful flash: Amanda, Birdie, Frankie, Daisy, Gallifrey. Daisy and Gallifrey?

From the New Orphans? I'm dizzy, seeing things. Harp catches my arm. A figure moves through the crowd then—tall and curvy and determined, her black curls twisted on the top of her head in a tight bun, her lips pursed and frowning. She's at once familiar and completely wrong; my brain is broken, overlaying images of the present with what has happened in the past, putting her here in Los Angeles when she ought to be in South Dakota, still tearfully waving us goodbye. Across the figure's chest, wrapped in a soft blue blanket, is—of all things—a sleeping baby. I look up from the baby into the face of Edie Trammell, his mother, in a kind of helpless wonder.

"Oh my goodness, Vivian," she says in her warm voice, reaching out to help Harp support me. "Are you all right?"

CHAPTER SIXTEEN

O h, my God, Edie?"

Together Harp and Edie usher me to a chair, lowering me carefully into it. My throat is dry and her name comes out raspy. Edie smiles, apologetic and slightly bewildered, like the host of a surprise party gone horribly wrong.

"Is any of this blood yours?" Harp demands, examining my hands, my chest, everywhere Robbie's blood has soaked. I look down at my own body, hardly recognizing it.

"Robbie."

I don't have to explain further, because Diego walks through the door then, Robbie limp in his arms. He looks particularly small this way. At the sight of him, Kimberly shouts and someone starts crying; I hear Birdie say to herself in a quiet, horrified voice: "No." It is different from when Suzy and Karen were killed—I don't know why, exactly. Because he was thirteen, and because Suzy and Karen are already gone. Robbie's death is like an awful punctuation mark; it reminds us all that we were already grieving. Diego brings Robbie's body into one of the side bedrooms, while Winnie, who has followed him inside, explains in a hushed voice what happened. I bend forward, put my head between my knees—I can't listen to it.

I feel a hand on the back of my neck. Harp. She keeps it there the whole time, a warm presence on my skin that feels like home.

When I finally pull myself upright, the room is half empty—most of the militia has filtered into the room where Robbie lies. Of those who remain, I pick out faces I recognize from Keystone: Estefan, sharp cheekbones and shaved head, who'd promised Edie he'd help deliver her baby; Daisy, honey-colored hair pulled into a messy ponytail, eyes rimmed pink; Kanye, tall and broad-shouldered, bouncing a restless knee; Eleanor, with her pixie hair-cut, frowning in a corner. But there are others, too, people I've never seen before—a huddle of men and women by the kitchen window, older than the majority of us, all of them in identical pale gray uniforms. They look twitchy, uncomfortable. Gallifrey stands with them, murmuring things I can't hear.

"Who are they?"

"Well . . ." Harp sounds nervous. "I don't know how to do this now. But we have some good news. Some very good news." She pauses. "Actually, maybe Edie should tell you. I mean"—she catches herself—"Umaymah. She goes by Umaymah now."

"Oh, Harpreet!" exclaims the girl formerly known as Edie, beaming. "You remembered! But of course you and Vivian can call me whatever you like! We've known each other so long."

Harp has that frazzled look I know from our weeks on the road with Edie—our former classmate's open-hearted sincerity completely unnerves her. But I watch as she drags a chair over, and note something strange about her manner—something care-ful and formal. An awed respect I've never seen Harp extend to anyone. Edie bows to thank her, sinking into the chair with an almost regal grace. The New Orphans crowd around her, clustering by her feet like she's about to tell them a bedtime story. I glance at the strangers in the kitchen—they watch us with the same dazed expression. Edie pauses to gaze at the baby strapped to her chest, smiles sleepily at him, then looks up at me with wide, soft eyes.

"Six weeks old. I named him Naveen. Can you believe it?"

"He's beautiful," I tell her.

"Thank you. My heart breaks for that boy they brought in here. Robbie, you said? Do you think anyone would mind if I went in and said a prayer for him later on?"

I shake my head. Who is there to object? We're his only family, and as far as I'm concerned, the prayers of Edie Trammell are the only ones to which God, if such a thing exists, ought to listen. Edie turns, and says, "Would someone be so good as to bring up my prayer book?"

Eleanor's the first to her feet, though all the Orphans make an attempt. I glance at Harp, but she stares intently at the group in the kitchen.

"So much has happened these last two months!" Edie exclaims, and the Orphans nod, like this is sage wisdom. "I hardly know where to begin. The last time we saw you, you were driving to Salt Lake City. And, of course, we know what happened next, because we've been reading the blog. We love it, Harp—such an achievement. But you aren't the only busy ones. We've had quite a lot going on ourselves. I'm not sure if you saw, oh, about a month and a half ago now, our official 'truce' with the Church of America?"

Somewhere in the group of Orphans, there's a hiss, then giggles; Edie gives no sign that she's heard except a slight, indulgent smile—so maternal it gives me chills.

"We were . . . surprised by that. To put it lightly. We understood Goliath had no interest in violence, the way other branches of the Orphans did, but still we assumed he wished to be outside the influence of the Church. When we approached him with our concerns, he was patient at first—but he became snide: 'Where do you think money comes from? None of you have any idea how to get by in the real world!' And so on. Once we began to understand what he was really about, there seemed to be nothing left to do but . . ." Edie brings her palms together, as if in prayer, then pushes them apart. "Our differences were too fundamental to overcome. Goliath was furious to find we were not the docile followers he'd taken us for. He had no idea we were more than just faithful bodies."

"He kicked you out of Keystone," Harp says, disgusted.

But Edie looks surprised. "Kicked *us* out? Oh, no. As a group, we decided Goliath's needs were no longer being served by the New Orphans organization. We invited him to seek residence elsewhere. From what we can tell, he hasn't made it far—he comes to the gates every now and then, extremely addled, begging us to take him back. But actions," she says sadly, "have consequences. Goliath never understood that."

"What about the Church?" I ask in the silence that follows. "They didn't mind that you sent their youth leader packing?"

"They have no idea," Edie says sweetly. "I've been personally answering all Goliath's correspondence, as him, since he left us. I know it's dishonest, but . . . you know I still consider myself a Christian, Vivian? I really, truly do. And I think that's what gives me the energy to work as hard as I have against the Church of America. Because they stand for many things, but the last thing they stand for—the absolute last thing—is Christ."

Naveen makes a soft, mewling noise, and Edie busies herself rocking him back to sleep. Eleanor bursts through the door, clutching a large scrapbook to her chest like it's a precious relic; she pushes through the Orphans to take the spot directly at Edie's feet. I see Harp's eyebrows rise. Before we left her in South Dakota, I'd taken comfort in Edie's hold over the New Orphans; I knew their respect would keep her safe. Now, watching them huddle closer, I realize I underestimated their affection. I thought they found in her a warm, calming presence; I didn't anticipate they'd tap into some ancient store of strength in her, that she'd find it in herself to lead them.

I catch Gallifrey's eye and he smiles, almost as if he can read my thoughts. "Before Umaymah came to us, we thought we were free. We thought Goliath had given us a home outside the rule of the Church of America. We never realized what we truly lacked: Love. True liberty. Umaymah gives us all these things and more. She's unshackled us."

"Thank you, Umaymah," the Orphans exclaim in perfect unison.

"It was these two who brought me to you," Edie replies. "Without Vivian and Harp, our paths would have never crossed."

"Thank you, Vivian and Harp!"

In other circumstances, it would maybe be funny—all-knowing Edie, the Orphans clutching the hem of the long skirt she still wears from her Believer days. But I'm tired, and the nightmarish quality of Robbie's death has started to fade. It is starkly real now. Plus I'm still distracted by the strangers in the kitchen, keeping a disoriented distance from us.

"I still don't understand . . . what are you doing *here*? And who are they?" I gesture to the group and they shrink back from my gaze, like I've shone a blinding light upon them.

"Well, that's just it." Edie beckons brightly to them, and they inch forward slightly. "They're the whole point of everything, aren't they? They're the miracle, Viv. They're the ones who are going to change our world." She smiles at me encouragingly, like I'm a child on the verge of solving some elaborate math problem.

And then Harp says simply, "They were Raptured, Vivian."

| | | | |

As the others begin to drift back into the room, stunned and sniffling, Edie tells us a story. In another life, or told by another person, I might refuse to believe it. But Edie's the one telling the story—recent shifts in moral rectitude notwithstanding, she would not lie. She begins with the way they solved it.

Under her leadership and emboldened by Goliath's betrayal, the New Orphans committed themselves to actively undermining the Church of America however possible. They held a virtual conference with Orphans across the country and united each chapter under a common goal: ours. Edie knew from the blog that Harp wanted to find the missing Raptured; she used the money the Church corporation thought they were paying Goliath to send her Orphans to the twelve cities Harp's blog followers had cited. The local chapters assisted in the investigation. They had no idea what they were looking for or where they would find it. They only knew Edie wanted them to look. The New Orphans ingratiated themselves with Believers, listened to rumors, pursued every dead end. Even modest Edie doesn't hesitate to tell us it was hard work. The Believers insisted that the missing had been saved, that they were in heaven now. Non-Believers clung to a wide range of theories, as Harp and I already knew— alien abduction and spontaneous combustion. Loyal readers of Harp's blog were positive the missing three thousand had died like the faithful in Point Reyes, like my dad. Still the Orphans kept searching.

It was Kanye who found the link that brought this group of missing Raptured to us—these twelve men and women, whom Gallifrey dutifully ushers closer at Edie's command, all of them looking frightened and faintly embarrassed. In Santa Fe, Kanye listened sympathetically as a left-behind widow told him of her late husband—a devout Believer, he'd proudly held a job at the Church of America textile factory outside the city, down in the desert. It was a good job that paid well, but right before the Rapture there were massive layoffs. Redundancy, the Church of America said, and the widow admitted they must have been right, because even with the layoffs it seemed like the factory was as effective as ever—they were the number one source of Church of America brand women's clothing, one of the corporation's most profitable ventures. But the whole community was affected. Some were lucky enough to go quickly to their rewards with the Rapture, but others, like this woman's husband, couldn't bear the agony of being abandoned by both his Church and his God. He killed himself.

When Kanye reported back to Edie, Edie had them do a simple Internet search: the Church corporation proudly boasted their twelve flagship manufacturing plants across the nation—based in exactly the twelve cities Harp's blog followers had named. Edie had a feeling. A new mother of only a few weeks, she led the rest of the Orphans to Santa Fe. Through means that Edie is not quite clear on, and about which nobody pushes her to elaborate, the Orphans located the factory and made it past the Peacemakers. They found a large workforce there, but something was wrong. The workers were hungry, confused, dead on their feet. They skittered away in fear when Edie approached them. She tried to convince them to escape, to come with her; she promised she'd protect them, but only a handful—the group gathered with us—consented to go. Edie takes a long breath then and looks at them. As if she's been coached, a young woman steps out of the anonymity of the group and into our line of sight. Edie introduces her as Joanna.

"I don't know how to . . ." Joanna's voice is tentative, but strangely loud, like she's trying to speak over us. But we're silent, shocked, waiting for her to continue. "I'm from Rhode Island, originally. My family is not religious. That was never important to them. They were content not to know the how or the why, and that worked for them, but never for me. The last few years had been hard for me, and then . . . then I found Frick. Everything he said made sense, and I believed. And I pushed the Non-Believers in my life away—my parents, my friends. I thought it didn't matter, because my day was coming; I knew I'd be embraced by God; I knew I'd be saved.

"My pastor took me aside, three weeks before the Rapture. He said I'd been selected to be blessed by Frick himself at a secret Church compound in Santa Fe. I was beside myself with joy, with pride. I packed my bags and flew there, and I didn't tell anybody where I was going because there was nobody in my life to tell. They probably didn't notice I was gone until after the Rapture—that was maybe the first time they thought to look.

"A shuttle picked up a group of us—maybe nine or ten—at the airport. It brought us into the desert, to the factory. A woman gave us a tour. And I felt like I was part of this larger thing—like the Church and the corporation were a wonderful machine working for the glory of God, and I was a cog in it. So when at the end of the tour the woman told us they were short-staffed, and asked us if we would help for a while, lend a hand until the Rapture came, I said okay. We all said okay.

"And when after three weeks we were still there, the woman said not to worry. She showed us a video of Frick, one I'd never seen before, where he said that God cherishes the workers; he'll save them seats at the glorious banquet of heaven. The woman told us there was going to be a second boat, and we were sure to gain passage on it, giving back as much as we did. You have to understand: I thought nobody loved me except for Frick and God. I thought the harder I worked, the more they'd both love me. So I kept working. But there was never enough food, never enough water. They kept us in cramped rooms. About five hundred of us, I'd say, at that factory. All of us living right on top of one another. The dyes in the textiles made some people sick. The noise was so bad that I still hear it buzzing, even now. And at a certain point I guess it was like waking up from a dream—I realized I wasn't going anywhere. There was no heaven waiting, no life to return to, and I still believed with all my heart that the world beyond the walls of the factory was coming to an end. I knew a few who tried to escape—they never got far before the Peacekeepers found them, and we never saw them again. And others were just crazy—they thought we *were* in heaven; they looked for passages in the Book to prove it. After a while, I forced myself to agree. Because what else was I going to believe? That I'd been so stupid, so desperate, that I'd let them own me? That I was only there because I didn't have the courage to run away?

"It wasn't until Umaymah showed up," she says, turning with a rush of gratitude toward Edie, "that I even realized anyone was looking for us. So when she asked me if I wanted to leave, I said yes, of course. I would do anything she wanted me to."

Joanna stops speaking then, abruptly, as though there's more she wants to say but it would take more time than we have. Edie stands and makes her way through the New Orphans at her feet to slip an arm around the woman; she whispers comfort into the Believer's ear. The rest of us are still with astonishment. I see Winnie weeping across the room and realize that I'm crying too — I don't know how long I've been crying. I feel a wretched sorrow all over my body; every bit of me aches with longing for this story to not be true. But it is true — of course it's true. I don't know why it never occurred to me that the answer to everything would be as terrible and as mundane as this.

"Would you be willing," Amanda asks finally after a long silence, "to tell the world what you just told us?"

Joanna glances quickly at Edie, a terrified look on her face. But Edie doesn't meet her eyes. She dips her head forward to kiss Naveen's forehead softly and nods. I see Joanna straighten. Her eyes go hard with some effort as she turns to regard us all.

"Every word," she says.

CHAPTER SEVENTEEN

L isten up, everyone," Amanda calls. She wheels forward, taking a commanding place at the center of the room. "The arrival of these Believers changes everything. There'll be no coordinated assault on the Chateau Marmont tomorrow." There's a palpable release in the room, several relieved sighs, which Amanda ignores. *"For the time being,* anyway. What we're going to do is get these people"—she nods at Joanna and the others—"in the public eye as widely as possible. Harp: how long will it take you to write up Joanna's story?"

"We'll film her telling it." Harp reaches for Julian's nearby arm and checks the watch on his wrist. "It's quarter after one now—I can get it up by dawn if you get me a camera."

"We'll get you what you need," Amanda says. "But the blog won't be enough. Diego—wait until Harp's video goes live, but then we need to round up as many people as we can manage. Bring them to the Chateau Marmont at nine a.m.—I'll make sure a camera crew is waiting. We want a demonstration; we want Joanna to tell a crowd what she just told us."

Everyone seems to take a swift, collective intake of breath before they plunge into action. Edie nods to Harp and me, then glides with Naveen into the room where Robbie's body lies, Eleanor following with the prayer book and the rest of the New Orphans. Winnie and Frankie approach Joanna and the other Believers, offering food and water, assessing whether or not they need medical care. Harp throws open her laptop and begins to type. In the commotion, I make my way to her and say quietly, "I'm going to the Chateau."

"What?" Harp's head snaps up. She looks horrified. "Viv, you can't! Not tonight, not after what happened with Robbie."

"I need to tell Peter about this. I promised him I'd contact him once I knew for sure whether or not the attack was happening."

"He'll find out it isn't in the morning!" Harp exclaims.

I glance sharply at Winnie, afraid her attention will be caught, but she's still focused on the Raptured Believers. "I know it's dangerous, but I promise—I'm just going to tell him what's going on and then I'll come right back. This is important to me, Harp."

She takes a deep breath. "I'll cover for you as long as I can."

"Thanks. How are you?"

"Pretty fucking freaked out. You?"

"Yeah." I pause, not knowing quite how to ask her this question. "Harp. Do you realize this might mean your parents are alive?"

After a moment, Harp nods. "It occurred to me the first time Edie emailed. I need to talk to Amanda about organizing a rescue effort for the rest of the factories. There's a possibility they didn't make it, of course—they might have gotten sick; they might have tried to escape and been killed. But if they *are* alive, they're going to be so pissed when they realize I helped crack this case." She shakes her head and starts to laugh, but her eyes are bright with tears. "I can hear them now. 'Harpreet, why do you always have to *meddle?*' they'll say."

| | | | |

Back in Hollywood, I retrace the exact tracks of my sprint to Robbie earlier. I keep my eyes down, and when I see it, I pause. The stain of Robbie's blood on the sidewalk, copper in the glow of the streetlamp above. I can't stay here long. The woman who killed Robbie may still be watching, for all I know; Peacemakers might patrol the area. But I let myself take one deep breath, trying to gauge whether the air feels different here, whether something of Robbie lingers in the atmosphere. I want to feel his presence. I want him to give me strength to continue. But I feel nothing but fear, and the oppressive weight of having lost him. I walk on.

Down in the shadows behind the Chateau's garden wall, I remember the security camera. The kitchen entrance is out—I'll have to climb the fire escape, rickety as it is. I drag a recycling bin from the alcove out to the pavement and climb on top of it, pushing myself up on the thin fence behind the Chateau. I wobble slightly and pause to regain my balance. A few feet—that's the distance between me and the bottom rung of the fire escape. Not unmanageable for a being of unfathomable grace, but for a girl who only managed one chin-up in gym during the presidential fitness test two springs ago, maybe a bit of a stretch. I say a quick prayer to the universe (*Please don't let me fall and break my neck; that would be—above everything else—incredibly embarrassing at this juncture*) and leap.

My left arm catches, but my right fingertips are still stiff from the sprain. My grasp slips, and—heart racing, not knowing what else to do—I throw my leg up at an awkward angle, hooking my knee over the bottom rung. The ladder wobbles with my weight, making a trembling metallic sound. I hesitate—but no one seems to have heard. I pull myself up, rung by rung, until I've reached the steady platform at the base of the second floor windows.

On the sixth floor, I crouch by Peter's window and tap lightly on the glass. When nothing happens, I tap harder. Finally, I see a flash of movement behind the window. I hold my breath and brace my knees, ready to bolt if it's anyone but him. But when the window slides open, Peter's face looks out: pale in the moonlight, eyes wide and almost silver, an expression of astonishment on his face. He backs up so I can climb in.

"Christ, Viv," he whispers, "haven't you heard of texting?"

I shut the window behind me, and Peter lights a lamp on the bedside table. His sheets are tangled; the air in the room is heavy with sleep. He wears a pair of blue-striped pajama pants and no shirt—I avert my eyes from the curve of his hipbones. Peter watches me, waiting, but I can't speak. I am so happy and so miserable. I feel like I might start screaming.

"Viv?" He takes a step toward me. "Are you all right? You're trembling."

I look down and watch my body shiver. Peter moves swiftly to me, slipping one arm around my waist, the other hand holding tight to my elbow; he eases me onto the bed and sits me down. My mind is a whir of noise and light and fear. I don't know where to begin.

"What happened?" Peter urges when I don't answer. "Is Harp okay?"

I nod. "Peter. We found the missing Raptured."

209

For one uncomprehending moment, he just stares. But then he pulls away, quickly and forcefully, a look of surprise on his face like I've poked him with something sharp.

"What? How? Where?"

I tell him everything, keeping my voice low. I tell him about Edie and Joanna, about Amanda's plan for the demonstration. He reacts with uncharacteristic animation—leaping from the bed to pace in his bare feet, running his hands through his hair, making it stand on end. He opens his mouth to prompt me each time I pause; once or twice, he inhales sharply in anger. But he says nothing until I've finished, and then he waits only a moment before rushing to me, taking my face into his hands, and kissing me.

"What was that for?"

"Are you kidding?" He seems giddy. "We won. We won, Viv! There's no coming back from this for them. This is the end of the Church of America!"

I shudder. I don't want to hear him say it. Like making a wish on a birthday candle—if he says it out loud, it won't come true. He notices my discomfort and his grin fades. He sits beside me again, takes my hand into his.

"What is it, Viv? What's wrong?"

I shake my head. I don't want to say it. He just squeezes my hand, waiting.

"I don't know. I feel so empty. Like I should be happy that we know where these people went, that we'll be able to find some of them—most of them—alive. But . . ." My eyes spill over. "I just keep thinking—why did my dad get picked for Point Reyes? Why couldn't they have sent him somewhere else? Why do all these people get to be alive, but my dad doesn't? I mean, what's wrong with me?"

"That's a normal thing to feel, Viv," Peter says gently. "I felt that way all the time after my mother died. I still do. I'll see a mom out with her kids and I'll think—why *you?* What makes you so great? It's not pretty, but it's human."

I nod, unconvinced. "That's not the only thing that's bothering me. A friend of mine was killed tonight. Part of Winnie's group. We were on our way here, actually—only a few blocks away. He was shot. There was no saving him. I just . . . I've never seen someone die before. He was so scared. Even though we were right there with him—four of us, with our hands on him, talking to him, loving him—even with us there, he was alone. And my dad was alone too. There were other people there with him—but not us, not his family." I can hardly speak now, I'm crying so hard. "He had to do it alone."

I know if Peter pulls me to him, I'll stop talking; I'll simply cry. But he doesn't, and after a minute I'm so grateful. There's something about just sitting here, Peter's steady hold on my hand. It makes me feel like I'm getting stronger. After a few minutes, my eyes stop streaming; my voice no longer shakes. Only then, when I'm silent, does Peter move closer. He runs a hand through my hair.

"These things are awful, Viv. I'm sorry they happened."

"But that's just the thing, isn't it? It isn't happening. It's being *done*. It wasn't a mistake. The Church knew what they were doing. The woman who killed Robbie knew what would happen when she pulled the trigger, and she did it anyway. And who knows—she might not have even been a Believer!" I close my eyes. "What proof do we have that taking down the Church will change anything? What if it isn't the Church making people act like this? What if this is just the way people are?"

"I don't know," Peter admits. "There isn't proof. You just have to believe we're capable of better. Because the Church doesn't.

They count on us being scared and weak; they count on us turning on each other. And some *do*," he adds, seeing the protest in my face. "But there are millions and millions of people in this country, Viv. The people who scare you—Frick and my dad; the Angels; the Believers who killed Harp's brother; the woman who killed your friend—they're only the loudest. They've got access to screens and microphones, and they're counting on the rest of us keeping our heads low, because we're too afraid to fight back. But just because we're not as loud doesn't mean that we're alone."

I try to let Peter's words sink in. If it's a lie, it's a sweet one. If it's what he really believes, it makes me love him more. I don't think I believe it quite yet, but I want to, and that alone seems to fill this pit of despair in my stomach. I lean forward to kiss him.

"You give good speeches, Ivey," I tell him when I pull away. "It must be hereditary."

Peter can't help grinning—he pushes me onto the bed, pinning my hands above me, kissing me hard. I close my eyes, feel Peter trace a line of kisses down my throat to the hollow of my collarbone. The pleasure is like a tangible thing inside me, a tight line drawn from my head to my toes, a guitar string plucked and thrumming. He lets go to unzip my hoodie, and I touch the warm bare skin of his shoulders. I'm consumed with a weird urge to take a bite out of him.

He says: "Listen, don't take this as an insult—"

"Always a promising start to a sentence."

"I thought you were pretty before and everything. But this dressed-in-black, traipsing-around-enemy-territory-in-a-bonnet, climbing-up-fire-escapes Vivian is really doing it for me."

I push him off me; he laughs and rolls onto his back. Hesitating a second at my still-new boldness, I climb on top of him.

"You realize, of course, that us bringing down the Church

means I won't be climbing up many fire escapes after tonight, right?" I say. "Once I lose fugitive status, I'll probably revert to wearing bright colors and using doors."

Peter's eyes grow wide. "Maybe we should postpone this demonstration a while. I'm not ready to say goodbye to Ninja Viv."

We lose nearly an hour this way, kissing, pausing only to try and make each other laugh. It's the most alone I've ever been with him, and I feel a slippery, tumbling feeling, the unasked question: Are we doing this? Right now? But I decide to relax. It's enough to be here with him; it's enough to know that after tomorrow we'll have who knows how many secluded hours to spend together. Finally he pauses and opens a drawer on the bedside table. He pulls the sledgehammer pendant out from within and folds my hand around it. "Keep it," he says. "You'll need it even when Ninja Viv retires." I slip it into my pocket.

"I should go," I say.

"I'll see you tomorrow, though." Peter leans back and blinks sleepily, smiling at me. "In public, even. The sun will be up!"

The crook of his shoulder looks so inviting that even though I know I have to leave, I crawl into it, laying my head on his chest. I hear the steady, comforting thump of his heart. "Do you realize that after tomorrow, we could go on dates? Theoretically, we could eat a meal together. We could sit down in public with each other and actually eat a meal."

"Oh man." Peter yawns. "I'd enjoy that so much. We should go to movies. You like movies, right?"

"Who doesn't like movies, Peter?" I hear him laugh. I feel my eyelids grow heavy; I try to force myself up. *Five more minutes.*

"You'd be surprised, Viv. Anyway, that's what we'll do. After tomorrow."

And his chest starts to rise and fall, slow and steady. I feel

213

temporarily drained of my sadness and fear—there's a pleasant, numb sleepiness in my limbs. *I'm just going to close my eyes for one second*, I tell myself, and warm and comfortable, with Peter's arm around me, I drift into sleep.

| | | | |

When I snap awake, I know instantly it's much later. I still hold the last image of the nightmare I had in my head: Robbie's blood-ied face, his mouth open and screaming. The ceiling is bright with sun, and I realize with an awful plummeting sensation that the thing that woke me was a sharp noise—the smacking of skin on skin, a burst of angry muttering. I push myself up in bed and there they are at the foot of it, smiling curiously down at me: Ted Blackmore and Michelle Mulvey. Their expressions are a perfect blend of malevolence and genuine pleasure, like I'm a delicious meal they're eager to dig into. I stare back at them, reaching be-side me to where Peter lies, to wake him. But he's not there: the bed is empty. I feel a flare of horror at the sight of the empty sheets, but then Mulvey shifts, revealing the scene behind her. Peter is on his knees by the window; two Peacemakers hold his arms at a painful angle behind his back. His mouth drips blood. I nearly scream, but Peter shakes his head. We're long past the point of screaming.

"Vivian Apple!" Mulvey delights in drawing out each syllable. Her blond hair is pulled into a bun so tight I can see the outline of her skull. "You look *positively* angelic when you sleep! Doesn't she look like an angel, Ted?"

"Frick bless her," Blackmore agrees, starting to laugh. "She re-ally does. Like an absolute angel."

CHAPTER EIGHTEEN

I don't speak. I don't move. I sit there in bed and wait for the Angels to stop laughing at the joke. When they finally do, Mulvey wraps a strong hand around my forearm, digging her nails—painted a pale pink but filed sharp, like talons—into my skin. She yanks me out of bed. *Don't fight; don't cry out.* I catch the time on the clock as I fall to the floor: just after seven. Harp will have posted Joanna's story by now, and soon she'll be here. Maybe Peter and I can escape during the chaos, but only if we give them no reason to hurt us. Mulvey kicks the pointed tip of her shoe into a tender spot below my rib cage.

"Up," she demands.

I get to my feet. Two more Peacemakers have arrived. One is older, with an eager, friendly face; the other is Derrick, the huge Peacemaker usually stationed outside the kitchens. Under Blackmore's orders, Derrick pins my arms back; he and the other Peacemaker escort me into the hall. Peter is dragged out behind us. "Don't hurt her!" he calls out—an unconvincing warning that makes all the Peacemakers laugh.

Doors open by inches as we struggle down the hall, and I see the eyes of nervous Church employees peer through the cracks, only to disappear when they see Mulvey and Blackmore bringing up the rear. The Angels get into the elevator, but the Peacemakers drag Peter and me down the stairwell. I feel Derrick slow down slightly, and I realize with a crushing panic that he's letting Peter and the others pass. "What are you doing?" Peter shouts, struggling against the arms holding him. "Viv!" But they just pull him screaming down the steps. My composure cracks when Derrick pushes me against the wall of the narrow stairwell; I lose my footing and slip a bit, crying out, but he presses himself firmly against me.

"Come on now, son," warns the older Peacemaker, sounding nervous.

"Tempted the blessed Taggart's son into falling? Is that what you did?" Derrick's voice is a hot wet slick in my ear. "Do you know what happens to whores, little girl?"

"Derrick, let's not—"

"Shut up, Wilkins!" Derrick snaps at the other Peacemaker. He returns his mouth to the side of my face. "They shall be burnt with fire, little girl. That's what's going to happen to you, when the Day of Judgment comes."

"Come on." Wilkins sounds firm now; he pulls Derrick back. "They're waiting. You can have your fun later on."

A pause, then he relents. Wilkins takes my arms now, but if I thought he'd be gentler, I'm wrong—he yanks me down to the lobby with even more force, drags me through the ornate, oak-paneled foyer where I once surreptitiously served champagne, and down another short set of steps through a door I recognize as the main entrance. Two sleek cars wait in the drive. I glance hopefully at the gates where Harp and the others will gather—maybe they're here already? Maybe they came to look for me? But in the brief moment before I'm pushed into the nearest car, I see no one. The gate is open, anticipating our exit; the spot where Harp will stand shimmers in the excruciating heat. But it's empty.

Inside the car is icy air conditioning and Michelle Mulvey typing on a smartphone. "Okay," she calls to the driver, and we trail the other black car into the hills of Los Angeles.

We weave through a maze of wide commercial boulevards lined by tall palms and dotted with signs of impending doom: the smashed glass of storefronts; starved-looking families pushing their belongings in shopping carts; huge signs reading NO WATER in front of the scorched façades of restaurants; more than a few motionless heaps by the side of the road I realize after a moment to be bodies; a red pickup truck straddling an intersection, on fire. I glance up to read a Church billboard above—THE ROAD TO HEAVEN IS NARROW, AND OVERCROWDED WITH THE DAMNED—and notice the foreboding heaviness of the clouds, the sepia-toned sky.

The wide boulevards soon give way to narrow residential streets lined by hauntingly empty mansions. Mulvey finally slips her phone into her attaché case and turns to me, folding her hands primly over one knee.

"So, Vivian." She has a bright, expectant look on her face. "You know, it'll sound funny, considering the position we're in, but I do admire you, in a way. It takes a bold young lady to stand up to something capable of squashing her like a bug. That's what I think you are, Vivian—a bold young lady, I mean. But in these times, you might find it a safer course to put the emphasis on the *lady* rather than the *bold*.

"If you could stand a little advice, I think you should consider . . . *redirecting* your prodigious energies," Mulvey continues.

"You're smart. Surely you can appreciate that the situation is not as simple as your friend's blog makes it out to be. For instance, I notice Harp never once mentioned all the Church of America's charitable works. Just last year, we gave over ten million dollars to inner-city food banks!" She raises an eyebrow at me as she pauses to let this sink in. "And even if—theoretically—we told a lie or two, can't you appreciate that such lies give sense to the senseless? Do you understand how much chaos would reign if people didn't understand what was happening, or why?"

"It seems pretty chaotic even *with* the lies," I say, thinking of the bodies on the sidewalk, but Mulvey shakes her head.

"Trust me, Vivian. It would be worse. Any idiot can see the planet is dying. Can you imagine what would happen if we told ourselves it was all our fault, rather than the righteous course of an angry God? The guilt would be unbearable, Vivian. As a nation, we'd fall apart. The government would shut down. Mass suicide. Mass murder. It'd be the collapse of civilization as we know it."

"But . . . it *is* our fault!" I protest. "And those things *are* happening now, because you've convinced everyone there's no time to stop it!"

Mulvey makes a disappointed, tsking sound at me. "Here's some more advice: I think you really need to work on how you get your message across. You sound *very* negative right now. It might interest you to know that we did some internal polling? And about sixty-seven percent of Believers said they didn't believe your story because you and Harp both came across as, quote, 'angry shrews.' You should think more about the image you project into the world."

I'm amazed. I can tell she's no fool—some part of her genuinely believes what she's telling me, wants me to believe as well—but her lack of self-awareness makes me furious.

"It must be really nice," I say, turning to the window, "to have this story to tell yourself when you're up late at night, thinking of all the people you've killed."

Pain, stinging and sharp across the left side of my face. Then a dull roar in my head. Mulvey has hit me hard, the force of it smashing my head against the window. I touch my jawline and come away with bloody fingers; her nails have sliced me.

"You're a child." She speaks calmly now, but I sense the quivering undercurrent of rage, and I make a point to remember: *sore subject.* "It was optimistic to hope you'd be capable of understanding things far beyond your maturity level."

Coolly then, as though only pleasantries have passed between us, Mulvey takes her phone from her bag and types furiously upon it. When she looks up again, she has a cruel smile on her face. "By the way—though of course you'll say it's none of my business—but even a secular society considers it pretty déclassé to give it up to boys you barely know in hotel rooms. Not a good look, Vivian. Have some self-respect."

| | | | |

The car enters a wooded area, climbing higher through the rolling hills. I press my face to the window, trying to memorize our route. I catch snatches of a breathtaking vista through the trees: the city before us, thick tendrils of smoke rising up disconcertingly from more than one neighborhood. How far are we now from the Chateau Marmont? Soon my friends will descend upon it with the supposed Raptured. When that happens, will Mulvey and Blackmore be called away to deal with them? Will Peter and I be able to overtake the Peacemakers? I remember Derrick's breath on my face and try to still the queasy flutter in my chest.

Finally a structure appears in front of us—white brick with a large gold domed roof. An expanse of green lawn in front of it has been turned into a parking lot; our car rolls up to the front steps of the building, and I watch an alarming number of Peacemakers burst through the front doors. The group splits in two, and one marches to my door—before I can react, they've flung it open and pulled me from the car.

"Beautiful, isn't it?"

I look across and see Peter being handled in the same way. His mouth falls open at the sight of my bleeding face. Blackmore, following at a short distance, continues speaking as if we're in the middle of a casual conversation.

"It used to be an observatory, until we bought it last year." He walks alongside the guards pushing me up the steps and inside. "I have to say, I feel a twinge of guilt when I think how we've denied the public this place. But it's just too rich a metaphor, don't you think? This open view up to the heavens? Makes you want to cry."

The Peacemakers deposit us inside, and I have a moment to take in the large, marbled rotunda—above us, inside the dome, are painted stars and moons and gods and goddesses. Mulvey pushes me to our immediate left, through heavy doors under the words HALL OF THE EYE; Blackmore shoves Peter behind us. It's an old exhibit, suffused with blue light, one wall lit with images of the cosmos, and I scan corners, seeking possible exits. Then I feel Peter's touch, his warm fingertips on my forearm. When I turn to him, I see his stare fixed on the center of the room.

Pierce Masterson stands there behind a long oak table; when

he sees us, a smile spreads across his face. Beside him, looking tired and thin, lost behind a pile of papers and what appear to be several open copies of his own incoherent tract, is the Prophet Beaton Frick.

"Come closer," Masterson commands genially. "We're not going to bite."

Mulvey and Blackmore urge us forward, pushing us into the empty chairs across from Frick. The last time I saw him, he was unkempt, unwashed, and unmedicated. Today he seems peaceful and calm, though still far from the imposing figure I first glimpsed in YouTube videos. He has a straggly gray-black beard; his eyes are rheumy red. I glance quickly at the papers scattered across the table and read distinctly the words *New Apocalypse Edition*. When I look up, I see Masterson watching.

"We're working on a new version of the Book to release in the days after the apocalypse," Masterson explains, his tone perfectly relaxed. I'm reminded again of a cat, this time stretching lazily in a pocket of sun. "Correcting some mistakes and omissions in the original draft. No offense intended, Miss Apple, but I was actually hoping we'd get hold of Miss Janda first—it seems to me she's the brains of your operation. Sharp writer. I'd love to get her working on recording some of the Prophet's newest visions." He gestures to Frick as he says it, and to my surprise the old man blushes under his beard, like he doesn't want the attention.

"Well, if she's anything like her friend here," Mulvey mutters, picking up a stack of the papers and glancing through them, "she's going to take an annoying amount of convincing. Pierce, you remembered to include the bit about the new lifestyle brands at the megastore, right? 'The Lord blesses us with designer goods at low prices' or whatever it was?"

Masterson ignores her. Mulvey falls into a chastened silence and sits at the table beside Blackmore, who scrolls through a tablet. I begin to sense what Peter meant when he told me that Masterson made him nervous. There's nothing particularly threatening about him: he's tall and slim, dressed elegantly in a linen suit with a flower in his lapel; his smile remains fixed firmly in place. But somehow he seems to exude power over the entire room.

"Convincing?" He smiles at me. "I like a challenge. But I admit I'm always surprised by how many reject Beaton's story. Don't misunderstand me—the man is obviously insane." He pats Frick's shoulder patronizingly. "And yet I've always found his vision of the world quite beautiful in its way. It's simple. Everyone has a role to play, and all God asks is that each person play it. Men are men and women are women. The rich thrive; the poor starve. Good triumphs over evil. Sacrifices are made for the welfare of us all. No shades of gray. I find it quite moving.

"I do think, though, that this new edition will improve upon it slightly. It seems shocking to me that Beaton would leave out a messiah. A messiah is the best part! A suspenseful buildup and then—a miraculous savior appears. So *satisfying*, don't you think?"

I stare into his amused eyes. "Sacrifices," he said—is that what my father was to him? Just a part of Frick's story? Something that had to disappear to make it seem true?

"Tell me why you don't like the Church of America, Vivian."

All eyes are on me now, even Frick's. I hesitate—the last time I spoke, Mulvey hit me in the face. This ought to be a trap, but Masterson's tone is curious. I take a breath and try to sound as calm as possible.

"I don't like that you think you can decide—you think you get to choose who's allowed to live a reasonable life, and who isn't.

I think you're careless with people. You only let a small fraction consider themselves human."

Masterson nods thoughtfully. "That's very well put. I take your point—to be entirely honest, I don't think you're wrong in the slightest. And yet I think you'll find these are tenets that can be found in plenty of religions and plenty of cultures throughout the whole of human history! The Church of America didn't invent the idea."

"But you're the ones making a profit off it," I reply.

He has a funny look on his face—surprised, but not displeased, like he's enjoying the debate. He touches a finger against his nose, points to me. "Sharp. Very sharp. Although extremely naive, of course. I see what you mean, Michelle—hard to convince. Still, maybe we'll have better luck with Miss Janda. Ted, can you check her blog to see if there's been any update today?"

"I just did," Blackmore replies, not looking up from his tablet. "Nothing."

"What time is it?" I blurt.

I want to take it back the second it's out of my mouth—it sounded too eager, too anticipatory. All three of Frick's Angels turn their watchful eyes on me. Beside me, Peter goes very still. Masterson flicks his wrist to check his watch.

"Quarter to eight. Whatever made you ask?"

"I don't know! No reason!" But my voice trembles. Everyone is right—I'm truly the worst liar of all time. I make an effort to let my expression go blank, to look as I ought to at this moment: confused and frightened. But inwardly, my thoughts are spinning—why isn't Joanna's story posted? Harp said it would be up by dawn. The demonstration should start gathering outside the Chateau at any moment. Perhaps it already has. So why have none

223

of these three highly placed people—the core of the Church of America—received so much as a phone call?

"Vivian, honey." Mulvey's voice has gone syrupy again, as though she hasn't recently gouged my face with her fingernails. "Is there something you want to tell us? Is Harp in trouble? We can help," she assures me when I glance away, "but only if you tell us what's going on. You'll be in absolutely no trouble whatsoever, I promise you."

I stare across the table. Frick flips through the pages of his own Book with a mild expression, as though he's trying to pretend he doesn't hear the conversation.

"You know what I think?" Blackmore says after a long pause, putting down his tablet and circling the table to stand behind me. He claps a meaty hand on my shoulder. "I think Vivian might have some idea of what Amanda Yee has planned."

I must look startled, because Masterson smiles and says, "Oh, Vivian. Did you really think we didn't know about Miss Yee? You must think we're so *stupid*. No one else has the resources to hide you so well; no one else could have cloaked your online presence so thoroughly. Who did you suppose we thought whisked you away from San Francisco the night we finally found you? If there's one thing Miss Yee is good at—and, sadly, I'm afraid there really is only the one thing—it's hiding. She and her associates have made a number of sloppy attempts on the Church over the years—I remember in Florida, she hired a young man to do away with poor Beaton here, only the assassin burst into the wrong office and frightened Phyllis in accounting half to death." The three Angels chuckle at the memory. "Amanda Yee has grit, certainly, but no sense of execution."

I catch Peter's glance out of the corner of my eye. Is any of this true? Was Amanda's plan for the demonstration less foolproof than it seemed early this morning? Has something gone wrong to keep it from happening? All at once and far too late, I realize that I have never trusted Amanda's judgment before — what made me think it was right last night? Across the table, Masterson frowns.

"Please don't tell me you've put all your faith into Amanda Yee. I know you're smarter than that. Listen," he says, leaning forward, his tone becoming conspiratorial, "I'm serious now. I know what you think of us, but you have to understand — we're trying to do what's best for *you*. For the whole country. Miss Yee has strong convictions, but she's dangerous. I'm afraid if anyone you care about plays any part in her plan — I'm thinking of poor Harp, of course — they're in trouble. Amanda doesn't care if innocent people get hurt, by accident or design, if it means making a statement."

I remember what Amanda told Winnie a month ago: *When you're gone, they're not my problem.* Like she expected my sister to die filling her desires — like she wanted her to. Masterson is not wrong about her. And yet — giving her up would mean giving up Harp and Winnie, too; Diego and the soldiers; Edie and the Orphans; just about everyone I care about in this imploding world. I take a breath and look Masterson in the eye.

"You'd know all about hurting innocent people, though — wouldn't you? You pompous, *evil*, unrepentant douchebag."

Despite his attempts to go unnoticed, Frick starts at this. Peter bursts out laughing, but he stops when Blackmore grabs my shoulder and throws me to the floor. Peter charges Blackmore; he lands a blow directly on the Angel's jaw, but Blackmore is quick and hits him back, sending him stumbling toward Mulvey, who leaps on his back to hold him down. Masterson comes around to crouch beside me; Blackmore places a heavy foot on my chest. I notice now a gun that Masterson has removed from some unseen holster; he holds it casually against his knee and asks, "Do you know what the Book of Frick says about young ladies with sharp tongues?"

I remember the Believer mother and daughter in Dylan's crowd at the Grove. "'*The voices of young girls give Satan much pleasure and Jesus untold grief,*'" I quote, trying not to sound too sarcastic.

His eyebrows rise. "Very good! Chapter twenty-three, verse seven. Do you know the next line of the proverb?" When I don't answer, he continues: "'*If a girl insists on saying wicked things, better cut out her tongue than hear the devil's laughter.*' Is that what you'd like me to do, Vivian?"

I shake my head, my eyes fixed on the gun.

"I didn't think so. So let's work with each other now. You don't have to give us all the details of Amanda's plan. I ask only for an address. Simple, right? Just the address of where she's been hiding you, and we'll consider ourselves friends. I'd take an intersection, even."

I move my eyes from the gun to Peter on the floor, Mulvey's knee digging into his back. I don't want to die. If I manage to live through this moment, there's still a chance I could have any number of precious hours to spend with him and Harp and Winnie. I don't know how or when or where, but they could still happen. When I think about it like that, it seems so simple. The name of the bookstore is there on the tip of my tongue. But then I have a flash of memory: Robbie. Not the nightmare of his screaming face, from which I awoke this morning; it's the thought of him dancing last week, banging his head around, kicking wildly, all that glorious energy gone.

"Fuck off," I say, as politely as I can manage.

Blackmore puts more weight on his leg on my chest. Masterson stands, looking disappointed.

"You, my dear, lack proper appreciation for your own tongue. But maybe that's the trouble." He strolls to where Peter is held and points the gun at his head.

I'm screaming senseless noise, words like "no" and "please," and then I realize I'm not the only one. Mulvey has laid herself flat upon Peter to shield him, and Blackmore leaps forward. "Pierce, don't!" he exclaims, seemingly horrified.

Masterson looks impatient. "If the boy dies, you get promoted, Ted. Be sensible here."

"The public loves him!" Mulvey insists. "We'll need him after the apocalypse to ease the transition! Pierce, don't be rash!"

"This is ridiculous!" Masterson lowers the gun. "He is as much use to us as his father. Neither of them will be necessary once the Messiah rises alongside Frick on Judgment Day! And I don't remember these hysterics when I killed Taggart!"

There's a long, heavy silence. I see Peter raise his head to look up at Masterson, the words wielding their slow and awful effect. Blackmore no longer holds me down, so I rise to my knees—I start to cross the distance between us, wanting to pull Peter close to me. I think the Angels will stop me, but I realize none of them are watching. They're all focused on Frick, who stands trembling at the table, his eyes wide and streaming tears, his hands tearing at his long, tangled hair.

"Adam?" he moans, low and animal. "You sacrificed Adam?"

He collapses on the table, weeping, and now Mulvey and Blackmore rush to his side, petting at him ineffectively, trying their best to comfort him. "Why did you have to break it to him like that?" Mulvey hisses at Masterson. "He's so sensitive, Pierce; you might have sent him into a terrible tailspin!"

"This is *embarrassing.*" Masterson gazes at his colleagues, then strides past me and to the door of the exhibit. He calls to the Peacemakers stationed outside, "Can we get these two out of here while Michelle and Ted pull themselves together? Jesus, what a display."

I rush for Peter now, but the Peacemakers are quick. They stream into the room and charge me before I'm steady.

"Peter!"

And I see him glance up at me as the Peacemakers pull him to his feet—he looks as though he doesn't know what's happening, as though he doesn't recognize me. I say his name again, but my voice dies in my throat when I feel something slam hard across the back of my head. My vision goes fuzzy around the edges and then it fades to black.

CHAPTER NINETEEN

I wake much later in a small windowless room. I hear the echo of footsteps above. My head throbs painfully, but when I touch the cut on my face, I note the blood there is dry. I push myself off the mattress they've left me on and pause, feeling the room tilt. I try the door in the wall opposite—locked, obviously. I throw myself against it, again and again, screaming until my voice goes hoarse. Where is Peter? Is he close enough to hear me? Have they taken him back to the Chateau? Or . . . has Masterson convinced the others that the Church no longer has use for him? The possibility makes me literally sick with fear—I drop to my knees and throw up on the concrete floor. *He's alive*, I tell myself. I try to believe it's a fact, and not a prayer. *Peter's alive. He's okay. You didn't come this far only to lose him.*

I assume the Angels will arrive shortly, to push for more information on Amanda. I try to think of a detail I can give them— small enough to keep Harp safe, big enough that they'll tell me what they've done with Peter. But hours go by and they never arrive. I don't know what time it is. The only light comes from a single overhead fluorescent. Could Amanda have gone ahead with the plan—has she confronted the Church with Joanna and the others? That would explain the absence of the Angels, but it also means my friends are out there putting themselves in danger.

I lie on the floor in a space somewhere between sleep and waking, and after a long time, I hear the turning of the lock. I wait for the door to open. When it does, I barrel ahead, slamming past the Peacemaker who stands there and into the wide, white hallway. I hesitate for half a second, trying to decide in which direction to run, but something heavy sweeps under me, tripping me, and I tumble to the floor.

"Why are you doing this?" asks a familiar voice, and when I look up I see Wilkins, the slightly less sadistic of my Chateau Marmont escorts, dragging me by my foot back into the room. "You're only going to make it harder on yourself when the time comes."

"I don't give a shit," I hiss, embarrassed at how easily I was stopped. "Masterson can do whatever he wants with me."

Wilkins shakes his head, depositing me back on the cot; on his way out, he kicks in a metal tray with a small plate of peas, a couple of pieces of sandwich bread, a cup of water. He closes and locks the door, but I can still hear his muffled voice. "That's not what I'm talking about, child. I mean Judgment Day. Don't you *want* to be saved?"

| | | | |

Time passes this way—days, and then weeks. Every twelve hours, they open the door to slip me my pathetic meals, and every twelve hours, I try to escape. None of the Peacemakers are as sympathetic as Wilkins, and I begin to collect bruises all over my arms and ribs. After ten such attempts, the Peacemakers finally notice the pattern and enlist multiple guards to block the door, but not before one, enraged at having been made to chase me, gives me my first black eye. Still I keep trying. It's not as though I actually expect to make it past them. I'm weak, and every day I grow weaker. But I'm going crazy shut up in this room, cut off from Harp's voice and Peter's face and Winnie's faith in me. The longer I go without seeing them, the more they begin to feel like good dreams I'm trying hard not to forget.

Still, I know they're alive. At least once a day, one of the Angels appears to interrogate me. This is how I know they've yet to find Amanda's militia. And Mulvey lets it slip early on that Peter's okay, too—she shows me a video on her phone of his most recent press conference in front of the Chateau, in which he triumphantly announces my capture.

"Blessed be the Peacemakers for neutralizing the threat of this spiritual terrorist! May Believers worldwide no longer fear her wanton desires and shameless harlotry!"

His strain is obvious to me—his voice is shaky and the hair at his temples is dark and flat with sweat—but the gathered crowd cheers. In the video, Mulvey and Blackmore stand beside him, watching him carefully; they usher him away the second he finishes speaking. Mulvey gazes at her phone with satisfaction.

"See, Viv," she says warmly, "your boyfriend is a team player. So why aren't you?"

I say nothing. I have a pretty good idea of how they manage to continue pulling Peter's strings—so long as I'm locked up here, he'll do what they tell him.

"If you could give us even the tiniest clue as to what Amanda

Yee has planned," she continues, "it would be such a help. Think of the lives you could save. Think of Harp! Masterson has big plans for her—he wants to put her talents on the national stage! Don't you want to support her in this amazing opportunity?"

"If I suggested to Harp that writing the new Book of Frick would be an amazing opportunity," I say thoughtfully after a moment, "she'd projectile vomit in my face."

Blackmore, meanwhile, seems convinced that I'm a secret Believer holding out for a guaranteed shot at eternal splendor. "Let's say you absolutely, without a doubt, have a place on the second boat—would you give us the address then? Okay, let's say you, your mom, your dad, any pets if you have them, Harp, Peter—the whole gang—how about now? These are very coveted spots, you know," he says sternly when I don't reply, as if he's not talking entirely within the realm of make-believe. "The least you could do is say thank you."

These two question me a half dozen times each, but I never see Masterson. Then one day when the door to my room opens, and I brace myself for my usual sprint into a sea of Peacemakers, he stands there alone. Masterson holds a vase full of bright yellow daisies and a plastic jug of water. I'm so shocked I can't move. He hands me the water and I sink onto my bed, gulping deeply from the jug. I watch Masterson set the flowers on the floor, fussing with them slightly, to best display the arrangement. Satisfied, he pulls over a chair from the corner and sits so we're knee to knee.

"How are you, Vivian? It's been a while. Do you know how long?"

I lower the jug of water and shake my head slowly, afraid of the answer.

"Three weeks."

Masterson glances at his sleeve and picks at an invisible bit of lint, as though he doesn't want to see my horror. I had no idea I'd been locked in this room for three weeks. I pass a shaking hand in front of my eyes and wipe away the tears that pool there.

"I want to apologize for my colleagues," he continues. "I know they've grilled you endlessly. Both seem baffled by their lack of success: 'She's given us nothing! She's got a death wish!'" He shakes his head. "They can't make heads or tails of you. Mulvey doesn't understand why you reject the protection of the corporation, and Blackmore's too thick to recognize a true Non-Believer when he sees one. How insulted you must feel by them. I, on the other hand, think I understand you quite well. Your beliefs are impenetrable—not in a higher power, necessarily, but in the good of your friends and your cause. You're convinced of it. I doubt we could offer you anything that would move you to sell them out. I admire this quality, Vivian. I've no interest in pressing you for information any longer. To be honest," he says, taking out his phone, "I've rather lost interest in the information itself."

It takes me a moment to understand. "Sorry?"

Masterson looks up. "I have no interest in pursuing Miss Yee anymore. You're clearly unwilling to help, and there's no point in wasting time. Why should we? When they've shown themselves so willing—practically *eager*—to back down?"

"What are you talking about?" I ask, trying to keep my voice steady.

"Oh! That's right." Masterson waves his hand around to indicate the bleak room. "No Internet! You haven't seen Miss Janda's latest post!"

He busies himself with his phone again, and I wait with teeth clenched. When he hands it to me, the browser is open on Harp's blog.

233

TRUTH TIME, MOTHERFUCKERS!

Well, I was going to have to come clean sooner or later, and with the second boat chugging merrily along to my door, I thought I might as well clear this up before things got out of hand:

THIS BLOG IS A WORK OF FICTION.

Your mind is blown, right? That's because of my deft story-weaving skills. Truth be told, I've always been a regular William Shakespeare or, like, the lady equivalent of Billy Shakes (who would that be? Beatrix Potter? Guys, I need to read more). Anyway, all of this — our madcap cross-country travels, Viv Apple and Peter Taggart's scintillating will-they-won't-they tension, and MOST IMPORTANTLY the claim that the Church of America faked the Rapture and killed/kidnapped thousands — is made up. I'm sorry! I have a wild imagination and a lot of free time now that the world is about to end. My BFF Vivian always told me it would backfire. "Harp," she used to say, "don't you think the blessed Church won't take kindly to your EXTREMELY FICTIONAL TALES? Like the Book of Frick says, *'Thou shalt not lie.'*" Being a lot stupider and way more of a heathen than Vivian, I was like, "Surely they'll accept this wacky romp for the elaborate fantasy it is!" But now that I have more readers than ever before — two million hits just yesterday, you guys, wow! — it strikes me that maybe God's not looking too kindly upon my considerable storytelling skills. In fact, he's probably all, "Harp, give it a rest or I'll hit you with a lightning bolt."

So this, dear reader, is my final post. Thanks for

tolerating my tall tales, and I wish you luck and peace as the apocalypse draws near. Let's go indulge in a can of Christ Loops in penance for consuming these lies as entertainment. Most importantly of all: Vivian Harriet Apple, you were right! I should never have started this blog all on my own without any of your help. I hope before our days on earth end, you can find it in your heart to forgive me.

Frick bless you all,

Harp Janda, Liar

Confidential to VHA: Winnie says tell them whatever you need to tell them. No matter what, we love you and we choose you.

I wish the post said anything other than what it says. But as long as I stare at it, the words don't change, and soon they swim as my eyes fill with tears. I don't try to hide them from Masterson this time.

"It's a bit obvious, as far as bluffs go," Masterson says delicately. "But I admire the effort. I suppose she thought if she publicly declared it to be a lie, we'd see no reason to keep you here. Her optimism is inspiring, but of course too little, too late. All I really take from it is that Amanda's army is afraid to make their next move if it means getting you hurt. Oh, don't cry, Vivian." Masterson pulls a handkerchief from his pocket and holds it out, but I don't take it. When I look up, I see an expression of true pity on his face. "The revolution is dead, but look on the bright side—your friends are willing to lose the war to save you."

He gets to his feet then, politely returning the chair to its spot against the wall. Before he reaches the door, I wipe my face with my sleeve.

"When are you going to kill me?" I ask. I can't take not knowing it any longer. "If I'm no use to you, if you've won already—
why don't you just kill me?"

Masterson gives me a small, bracing smile before he leaves.
"Patience, Vivian. In time, all good things will come." He locks
the door behind him.

| | | | |

I cry all night, screaming into the mattress; I cry until my eyes
are red with heat. I'm scared for Peter. I miss Harp—I remember
the way she squeezed my sprained hand on a hill in San Francisco,
the promise she made to pull me out of the pain that threatened
to swallow me. I cry because she's dug herself into a hole now,
and I'm not there to take her hand. I think of Winnie. I think of
my mother and my father, Wambaugh, Raj, Robbie—all of them
lost to me in one way or another. I cry because it took me so long
to become the person I've been these last few months—bold and
angry and trying, despite the costs, to be truly good. I cry because
I'm proud of this person, and look at how she ends: locked in
the basement of an observatory in Los Angeles, never to see her
friends or her family again.

The next morning, my head is splitting with a grief hangover
when Wilkins arrives at my door. But he doesn't have a tray of
food with him. He holds a pair of handcuffs.

"Come on," he says, in his nervous way. "You have a visitor."

I stand and let him cuff me, too tired and confused to question
him. The Angels have never met me anywhere except this room
before, but they're the only visitors I can imagine. I briefly indulge
in a fantasy of someone, anyone, else—Harp in an absurd costume or Winnie with a gun; Peter in character as Church spokes-

man—but swat it away. It's physically painful to raise my own hopes this way. Wilkins leads me up a dark stairwell, through an open door leading to a stone deck outside, overlooking the city. I squint at the light, but the sun's not actually out—the sky is still the same dusty brown it was the day they brought me here. There's a faint, acrid smell of smoke in the air. Michelle Mulvey stands there, grinning at me.

"Vivian! You're looking so well!" She dismisses Wilkins and leads me to a long table laden with breakfast foods: green apples and plump grapes, croissants with three kinds of jam and a stick of butter, a plate of golden sausages still steaming. I'm so dazzled by the breakfast, by the aching brightness of the sky, by Mulvey's oddly friendly reception, that it takes me a moment to realize we're not alone. At the end of the table, a boy stands from his chair and shakes his curls out of his eyes. He smiles his brilliant white smile at me.

Dylan Marx reaches out to shake my cuffed hand. "So nice to meet you—Vivian, was it? Michelle's told me a lot about you."

I glance at Mulvey and she beams encouragingly.

"Hi . . . ?" I hope my confusion will be interpreted as shyness. I stare at him. My heart pounds violently in my excitement—*I'm going to get out of here; I'm going to be okay!* Dylan just smiles. After a long moment, he looks at Mulvey.

"Oh!" she exclaims. "I'm going to run inside—lots to do, lots to do. But why don't you two make yourselves comfortable? I'll be back in a bit."

She skips to the door. In a loud, false voice, Dylan says, "So I hear you're from Pittsburgh? That's so funny—I am too! What neighborhood?"

We hear the door slam behind her. Dylan's grin fades. "Shhhh!" he hisses before I can speak. He pauses by the door Mulvey has just left through, scanning the windows. Satisfied, he returns to the table and pulls out a chair for me. "Jesus, Apple, you look like *shit*. Are they not feeding you? Eat something; I don't know how long we have. Is that a black eye?"

Dylan sits beside me; he throws sausages and croissants on my plate; he slices me an apple. I touch the puffy skin around my eye—I'd almost forgotten about the bruises on my face. I take a voracious bite of sausage and feel warmed to my toes.

"What's your plan? How did you convince them to let you in?"

Dylan laughs darkly. "Michelle Mulvey is extremely confident in my powers of persuasion. I saw her at the Chateau last night and she told me all about this enemy of salvation she was dealing with—young girl, very stubborn, one of those deceitful bloggers who's been causing so much trouble? I wondered if there was anything I could do, if she thought I could use my array of talents to entice you over. She *loved* the idea. She's a snake, but I think she likes you. It seemed to really break her up, the idea that you were going to waste away in the Griffith Observatory. Anyway, she set this up, told me to turn the charm to eleven. 'She has a boyfriend,' she told me, 'but he's not as cute as you!' The woman is nuts."

"Okay," I say. "Did you drive here? Maybe you can tell them you want to take me for a walk—like, you want to show me the glory of God in nature. They trust you, right?"

"Yeah," Dylan replies, buttering a croissant. "Maybe. Vivian, eat something. They made this whole spread just for the two of us."

There's a hesitation in his tone that makes me uneasy. I struggle to swallow my bite. I push my plate away.

"You're not here to help me."

"Yes, I am!" Dylan's voice gets squeaky in his insistence. "When we're done here, I'm going to tell Mulvey what a great kid you are, how I think you're turning around for the better. You have to play along, though—tell them you're starting to change your mind. Ask for a Book of Frick to study. And for God's sake, stop doing whatever it is you're doing that landed you these bruises!" Dylan reaches out to touch my face, a brotherly gesture at once loving and completely exasperated, but I pull away. He sighs. "You don't need me to save you. You could easily save yourself, if you would just make a goddamn effort."

"By lying."

"By lying, yes. Christ, Viv, for such a hardened Non-Believer, you have a very rigid concept of the Ten Commandments. You're allowed to lie to save your own skin."

"Like you do?" I keep my voice low—for all I know, Mulvey is pressed up to the door, eavesdropping—but I'm furious with myself for thinking Dylan was here to rescue me. "How's that going, by the way? Sleeping soundly? You never wake up gasping in the night, wondering what Raj would think of you now?"

"Please"—Dylan clenches his teeth—"stop using him against me. Stop thinking you knew him better than I did. I know perfectly well what Raj would think of me, and I know what he would do. He'd usher you to freedom. He'd be the hero—he wouldn't think twice about it. He'd also get himself killed in the process. I loved him, okay? But part of the reason he's gone is he could never for a second put his own life first."

He seems on the verge of tears. I don't want Mulvey to come out and see him worked up this way, and I feel a pang of guilt. I remember the Rapture's Eve party in the abandoned mansion, Dylan and Raj swaying on the dance floor, whispering and laughing together.

"I'm sorry." I lay my hands on top of his. "You're right. I got my hopes up when I saw you; that's all. It's not your responsibility to save me."

"I would!" Dylan assures me. "I'm not evil, Viv! If I didn't have Molly to worry about, if I wasn't trying to get the fuck out of this city, I'd do it in a heartbeat."

"You're leaving?"

Dylan nods. "That's why I came. I wanted to say goodbye. It's not safe here anymore. There's a huge wildfire at the edge of LA—it started in San Bernardino last week, and it's spreading fast. Seventeen thousand acres destroyed already. They don't think they can stop it before it hits the city." He frowns at my blank expression. "You didn't know? Viv, look."

We stand and he leads me to the edge of the deck. We're high above Los Angeles, and I realize now why the air is so thick, why I thought I smelled smoke when I first stepped outside. Far in the distance, but not far enough for comfort, a black cloud hovers over a hot orange glow. I feel as though I can actually see it moving closer. Beside me, Dylan shudders.

"I can't get stuck here. And anyway, I have to get out before tomorrow. When I leave in a few minutes, I'm getting in my car and driving straight to Colorado. I'm picking up Molly, and we're finding a place to hide, somewhere the Church will never track us down. I'm not interested in getting caught in the next great sleight-of-hand."

I'm trying to follow the thread, but the fire and my hunger have turned my brain fuzzy. I don't understand. "What happens tomorrow?"

Dylan looks shocked. "Jesus, Viv, how long have they had you here? The second boat. Tomorrow is the next predicted Rapture."

The solid ground beneath me seems to slip away. Masterson told me I'd been here three weeks, but somehow it hadn't quite sunk in—the second Rapture is tomorrow. That means the so-called apocalypse—the rise of the Church's Messiah—is only two days away.

"Blackmore's made it *very* clear all Church employees are guaranteed passage on the second boat. I can't honestly believe he'd kill us—what would be the point? What good is a church without Believers? But I'm not going to risk it. It's the end of the world. I want to die on *my* terms—and that means protecting Molly until I can't protect her any longer."

I keep my eyes on the faraway flames. The Angels obviously know about the fire; they won't put themselves in harm's way much longer. Sometime in the next twenty-four hours, they'll vanish from Los Angeles. They'll reappear late on the day after tomorrow, September 24, on television screens everywhere with Frick and their Messiah, and the Church of America will live on—possibly forever, although who knows how long forever will be. If the Angels succeed in making their employees disappear tomorrow—whether they hide them or kill them—that means they'll take Peter, too . . . And it means that I have run out of time. "Patience," Masterson told me, when I asked him when I was going to die. He knew then they were going to let me burn.

"Dylan," I say. "Unless they've moved, Harp's in an apartment above a bookstore called the Good Book. I don't know the address, but it can't be too hard to find."

"Wait." Dylan shakes his head; he covers his ears. "Don't tell me this. I don't want to know this. If the Church stops me—I can't know this, Viv!"

"I need you to go there before you leave," I continue, as if I haven't heard him. "Tell her where I am. Dylan, grow up!" He's plugged his ears with his fingers, like a child; I lift my cuffed hands and wrench one arm away. "This is important! Tell her she needs to post Joanna's story. Now. As soon as possible. Tell her to post the story and come for me, if she can. If the fire spreads here before she's able . . ." I shake my head. "Tell her to run."

There's a creaking sound behind me. "Everything okay out here?" Mulvey calls from the doorway in her honeyed voice.

Dylan grins at her beyond my shoulder. "So great!" He drops his voice to a whisper, keeping the smile plastered on his face. "Viv, I don't have time; it's too dangerous—"

"Please, Dylan, help me!" I hear the click of Mulvey's heels and shut up; I try to look happy and appropriately dazzled by Dylan's attention.

"What do you think, Mr. Marx?" Mulvey gives me a bright, assessing look when she reaches my side; she links her arm with mine. Her sickly sweet perfume fills my nostrils but I force myself not to pull away. "Can our girl reform her wicked ways?"

Dylan beams, puts a hand on my left shoulder. In the moment before he takes my other arm to help Mulvey usher me back into the observatory, I take one last look over my shoulder at the vast, smoggy city, the creeping flashes of fire in the distance. *Please, Dylan,* I think. *Please.*

"Personally, I think," he says, his voice nearly catching, "that Vivian Apple has an extremely bright future ahead of her."

| | | | |

After Dylan leaves, I try to keep track of the hours. I count to sixty; I count to three hundred sixty; I lose track and start again. I try to imagine Dylan's path. *Now he's getting in his car,* I think. *Now he's heading to the Good Book.* After what feels like a long time, the door opens—Wilkins again, sliding the tray across the floor: Church of America brand beef jerky (A SNACK FOR A SAMSON, reads its slogan on the wrapper, NOT A DELILAH), three apple slices gone very brown, another small cup of water. I could kick myself for not stuffing my face this morning when I had the chance. I watch Wilkins move to shut the door, and before I totally understand my own motives, I speak.

"Big day tomorrow."

Wilkins gives me a suspicious look. When I don't charge at him, when instead I reach for the jerky and take a sad, salty bite, he relaxes slightly. He smiles.

"Yes, indeed! I only pray that God and Frick see fit to save me." I watch as he narrows his eyes, assessing me. "You could pray too, you know. I'm not saying it's a guarantee, but if they saw you repent, if they knew you were at least *trying* to be holy . . ."

"It's okay, Wilkins." I try not to look too amused—I'm weirdly touched by his last-ditch effort to convert me. "I think I'm a lost cause, but it's nice of you to make an attempt."

He nods, but doesn't move from the doorway. I wonder if he's trying to come up with some kind of pep talk. "Do you have any kids, Wilkins?"

His neutral expression fades. "Why?"

"Dude." I take another bite of jerky. "I'm not going to hex them. Just trying to make a little conversation before you ascend. Once you're gone, I'll be waiting for the apocalypse in total silence, so I might as well get my casual chitchat in while I have the chance."

"No kids," he says, after a long pause. "Never been married. If it weren't for the Church of America, I'd be all alone in this world."

There's a longing in his voice that makes me feel a twinge of sympathy.

"Wilkins," I say after a long moment, "can I ask you for a favor?"

243

"What?"

"I really like your watch." I nod to his wrist, the chunky fake gold. "Can I have it?"

"Are you serious?"

"You won't need it up there!" I coax him. "They don't have *time* up there."

He pauses, and I see the play of emotions on his face—skepticism fading into confusion. He glances at the watch, runs a fond finger over its face. He says, "I'm . . . I'm not sure what Mr. Masterson would think of that."

"I don't think he'd mind." I'm careful—Wilkins seems about to fold. After a long pause, I say gently, "Come on, Wilkins. Think of Frick. What would Frick do?"

He ponders this. Then his face goes hard. "Frick would probably tell you to buy your own damn watch."

I scowl, but he's right. I shouldn't have used Frick's name to appeal to his sense of goodwill and charity, because Frick's writings have no notions of anything like that. The person I'm thinking of is Jesus. Still, it's a blow—I'd hoped to be able to watch these next hours, possibly my last, as they pass. I lie across the cot, turn my back on Wilkins. For a moment I feel him hover behind me, and I nearly shout at him to leave me alone. But then I hear a heavy clinking sound. I don't dare to look until he's closed the door. He's left the watch on my tray, gleaming next to the rotten apple slices. I slip it on my wrist and check the time: 7:36 p.m., on the eve of the second Rapture.

| | | | |

Sometime during the night, I wake and listen.

I know I'm inside, locked in a room underground, just about

as far away from other human beings as I could be here in Los Angeles. But still I'm sure I feel a shift. Something has happened—the second Rapture. Everything is different now. The quality of the air feels different. I almost feel like I should be able to hear the anguished howl of the city outside: By now they know they're stuck here. They think they have less than forty-eight hours left until the apocalypse. I feel every atom in my body poised in anticipation of the end: the end of this fake apocalypse, the end of me. Right now I'm not sure which will come first.

In the morning, no one comes—not that I expected them to. The Peacemakers have to be the most loyal members of the Church's devoted following; it makes sense they'd be spirited away wherever the Angels went. There's still a chance that Dylan got to Harp in time, that my friends will come and rescue me. An hour goes by, then two, then several. But in the evening, I spiral into panic. I begin my assault against the locked door all over again, hurling myself against it—I use my right shoulder, as my left is still sore from the first attempt.

"Is there anybody out there?" I scream. "Please, somebody help me!"

All night it goes on like this, well into the next morning. I thought Wilkins's watch would give me comfort, that seeing the hours pass would give them form, make them feel solid. But instead, the time slipping away underscores how alone I am in this building, how closely death must hover. With no sensation left in my shoulder, I kneel in front of the door and pry at the knob with my fingers, tearing my nails into shreds. My hands are bloody from the effort. It's no use. I retch but there's nothing left in my stomach. I lie on the concrete floor, weak and exhausted. I'm going to die here. I must have known it since they locked me up, but it's as though I finally understand. I'm never going to see Harp or

Peter or Winnie again. I'm going to die here, and it won't happen quickly. It's only a question of what will kill me first: hunger, thirst, or fire. I slip my injured hand into my pocket and snake out the sledgehammer pendant Peter gave me. It was enough to make me feel strong once. I press it against my heart and wait for its magic to work once more.

I fall into an uneasy half sleep, unable to relax my rigid limbs, unable to ignore the pain in my arms, my throat, my fingers. After a while I become aware of a figure in the chair by the wall, gazing down at me. I can't focus on him, but I know who he is. I recognize the way he sits—his ankle crossed over his knee. I want him to go. Not because I don't miss him—just because I don't want him to see me like this. I wish he could have seen me those few months I was strong. When I speak to him, my voice comes out a croak.

"Daddy."

"You know what to do if your clothes catch fire, right, honey?" he asks, his voice an echo in my head. "You stop, drop, and roll."

"I know. That's what I'll do."

"Good. And careful not to touch the doorknob, okay? If there's a fire in the hall, it'll burn the skin right off of your hand."

I try to push myself up to see him better, but my hands sink through the floor. I have a feeling he's smiling at me; he's waiting for me to figure it out; he'll be so proud of me once I manage to sit up straight. I feel a sharp pang then. I've just remembered a terrible secret about him, a secret I know I have to tell him but don't want to.

"Dad." I will my eyes to focus on him. "You shouldn't be here. You're dead."

And at that moment I can really see him for the first time: the freckles on his cheeks and his messy brows, the tiny scar on his upper lip I don't know the cause of and never will. I watch the grin slip off his face, and I watch him frown, confused and sorry.

"Oh, that's right," he says, and disappears.

Then I dream that the lock is turning. Someone is at the door to my room, and somehow they have a key. I try to get to my feet; I say, "I'm here!" but I'm dizzy with sleep and pain and hunger. The room swirls around me, and I have to lower myself on the bed, heart racing.

The door pushes open. Derrick, Wilkins's Peacemaker partner from the Chateau Marmont, sticks his head in. When he sees me, he starts to laugh.

Not a dream, then—a nightmare. I think to pinch myself, but when I glance down, I see my scratched and bloody hands and know it's really happening. I struggle to stand as Derrick steps inside.

"What are you doing here?"

"This city is on *fire*, little girl." He's menacing and huge under the flickering fluorescent. I notice his glazed eyes and a sharp, whiskey smell. He's drunk. "Didn't you know? Judgment Day has arrived, and thanks to you, every last one of us feels the flames of hell lick our backs. Even me. You couldn't just let it be true. You *had* to defile the Prophet Taggart's son. You *had* to step in and spread your disgusting story."

I don't understand, but I feel a surge of anger, stronger than fear, stronger than hunger, a simple annoyance that he tracked me down just to pin all the Church's atrocities on me. If I ever had patience for Believers who wanted to convince me of my own wickedness, I've officially run out of it.

"It's so odd," I say, "that God didn't want you around up there in His kingdom. What a *catch* you are. He must really be kicking Himself right now."

Everything goes white. Derrick has smacked me, and before I can shake the spots from my eyes, he hits me across the other cheek. I feel the sting of the cut on my jaw breaking open. He's going to hurt me worse than I've ever been hurt before. Derrick takes me by the throat, pushes me against the concrete wall. I scream, kicking fiercely, trying to land my foot hard in his groin. But his grip only gets tighter; with his other arm, he digs an elbow in my gut. I feel my breath leaving me, my legs going weak, a dark shadow at the edge of my sight. I'm going to pass out, I realize. I have a kind of vision then. I see the three of us—Harp, Peter, and me—in Point Reyes, at the moment we found the trail to Frick's compound. We came together to link our arms around one another's shoulders, tired and triumphant. We made a triangle. I hold on to it, this image, this last thread of consciousness. I would die like this a thousand times, as long as I still got to live in that moment.

But then there's a sickening crack, and Derrick stumbles forward, his weight pressing me against the wall. He's heavy, but my body seizes in relief; I gasp for breath, my eyes streaming. Someone pulls Derrick off me, and when I'm able to focus, I'm sure for a moment that I *am* dead. Because there's no logical explanation for what I see: the woman who stands before me, the butt of the rifle she holds still poised in the air, reared back from when she slammed it against Derrick's skull, her red-blond hair long and swinging down her back, eyes burning with a fury like I've never seen, until she glances at my face.

My mother.

CHAPTER TWENTY

M om?"

My body trembles in pain and shock and I realize when I say it that I'm sobbing. My mother leans forward and puts a soft hand on my forehead. It's a gesture I recognize from any number of childhood sick days—for some reason she's checking me for fever. Her eyes well up.

"He was going to *kill* you!" she exclaims, like she can't believe it. She glances down at Derrick's body, motionless on the floor, and I see for the first time that Winnie and Kimberly are with her, both of them unbelievably intimidating with their rifles strapped across their backs and belts of ammo. Winnie checks Derrick's pulse, and my mother raises a hand to her mouth. "Oh my God, Winnie, is he . . . ? Tell me I didn't . . . ?"

"He's alive, Mara." Winnie looks up and catches my eye; her worried face breaks into a grin. "If anything, I'd say you went a little too easy on him."

Mom sighs. She turns back and wraps her arms around me, holding me too tight against her. My body aches, and I can't stop crying. It's a release like I've never known, more powerful even than the moment I discovered her alive in Winnie's apartment. Because this time, she came to me. She looked for me, she found me, and she saved me.

"What are you doing here?" I manage to croak.

Mom doesn't get the chance to answer before I hear new footsteps and peer over her shoulder. Harp stands in the doorway, backpack on her shoulders, clucking her tongue.

"Vivian Harriet Motherfucking Apple," she says, taking in the scene around her with a skeptical eye. "You never call, you never write—you're always bleeding from the face in the basements of observatories with weird men lying unconscious on your floor. Seriously, dude—you've changed."

I tear myself away from my mother and throw my arms around Harp's neck. "I thought I was going to die here," I murmur into her shoulder. "I thought I was going to die."

Harp hugs me back tightly. "Trust me, we'd have gotten here a lot sooner if we'd had any idea where you were. Especially if we'd known you were locked in a room, looking like you'd just crawled your way out of a fucking grave or something. Jesus, Viv." She holds me at arm's length to get a better look. "They really did a number on you."

"I'm fine. Really!" I insist, looking at all of their dubious expressions. The open door, Harp, my warrior big sister, even the wonderful, confusing presence of my mother—they've made my face stop throbbing, the ache of hunger fade. "How did you know where to find me?"

Harp gives me an exaggerated eye roll—a telltale sign of a great story to come—but Winnie steps forward, lays a hand on my shoulder. "We'll tell you on the way."

"Oh shit—that's right." Harp gently slaps her forehead and

looks at me. "We have to hustle if we want to save your boyfriend from certain doom."

"Why?" My knees buckle under me, and Harp and my mother have to take me by the elbows to hold me up straight. "Where's Peter? What have they done to him?"

"We'll explain," says Winnie. She leads us into the hallway and heads for the exit at a jog with Kimberly, Harp, and me right behind. Mom hesitates, maybe to check on Derrick, who I can hear moaning quietly now, but after a moment she catches up.

Everything hurts. My legs are achy with disuse and my lungs sear with pain. The dark observatory seems to have been abandoned all at once, in a panic—doors thrown open, papers scattered across the floor, guns and batons and pocket-size Books of Frick left behind, dropped wherever their owners stood. If I didn't know better, I'd believe the second Rapture had happened the way Frick said it would: one moment the Believers were here, the next they were gone. But outside, we spill onto the steps leading down to the lawn and into the light of the setting sun, and I see the tread of car tires across the grass, scorched from the speed at which they flew—the Church left Griffith Observatory in a hurry, but they left of their own accord.

Winnie leads us to a car. I've only just gotten in—Harp and my mother flanking me in the back seat—when Winnie turns the ignition and peels down the long curving road. My mother has to scramble to shut her door, which still hangs open as we move.

"Okay, so," Harp begins eagerly, "we had no idea where you were. We figured the Church had taken you—to be honest, we kind of hoped. The worst case was you'd been attacked in the street, that you were . . ." She trails off. I know what she's thinking: Robbie. "I was scared. Winnie wasn't exactly keeping it cool herself."

"Understatement of the motherfucking century," Kimberly interjects.

My mother roots around in the bag strapped across her shoulders and starts to pull out random food items: a spotted banana, a granola bar, a plastic bag full of nuts. My stomach growls and I give her a grateful look, gorging on them as the others continue the story.

"I should have known you would go to see Peter that night." Winnie drives way above the speed limit, but her voice is as steady as her hands on the wheel. "I should have made you take me with you."

"And I'd always assumed that if you were going to die, I'd be there. That we'd do it together, in a cinematic blaze of glory." Harp's voice is light, but I know how serious she is. "So we were quite the barrel of laughs for a while there. Right after you disappeared, Peter shows up on TV and gives this rousing speech saying they've caught you. I figured he'd sold you out. I almost told Amanda to go ahead and blow up the Chateau then and there — but of course, for all we knew, you were inside. They talked about you on the news every day. They kept calling you a witch. They said you were being kept in a secret location, that they were interrogating you to find out Satan's plans for America on the day of the apocalypse. They said at one point you opened your mouth and a python crawled out of it, spitting venom at your interrogators—" Harp breaks here, unable to keep from laughing; when she sees the grim look on my face, she laughs even harder, doubling over, literally slapping one knee. "Oh God, I'm sorry; it was just so good. I can't even—Oh God. Anyway. We were so desperate I went on the blog and told them the whole thing was a lie, that I'd made it up—"

"Masterson showed me."

"He did?" Harp can't keep a little note of pride out of her voice.

"He called it an obvious bluff."

She scoffs at this. "Well, of course it was. But we had to give it a shot. We hoped they'd show mercy—maybe release you, or at the very least go easy on you. Anyway, *clearly* it didn't work. And Amanda was not exactly thrilled we'd done it without her go-ahead—"

Kimberly laughs. "I take it back. *That's* the understatement of the century."

Winnie takes over. "Amanda had wanted to go ahead with the demonstration, to make Joanna public. But we'd asked her to wait—we worried if we went public with the missing Raptured while the Church still had you in custody, they'd kill you in retaliation. That wasn't exactly a deterrent for Amanda, of course. But Diego took my side, and so did the rest of the militia—and obviously, Umaymah wasn't about to let you die. She left with Joanna and the rest of the Believers and she only told Harp where they were going."

Harp grins. "They were still in LA, but Amanda didn't know where. Plus I gave Edie the video of Joanna's story on a flash drive, and destroyed the copy on my laptop. Amanda couldn't get her hands on it, and she couldn't move forward without the Raptured Believers."

"They'd stepped up Peacemaker presence at the Chateau by a lot," Winnie continues, "so we couldn't search it without mounting a full-scale attack. We decided to wait for the second boat before we looked for you—we figured they'd clear out of the Chateau and the city, and we could launch a proper rescue mission. We counted on you being alive, and them leaving you behind. And then, two days ago, pretty much all hell broke loose."

"Dylan showed up," Harp interjects. "The night before the

Rapture. He was jumpy as fuck, but he told us they were keeping you in the observatory."

"Harp and I are ready to jump in the car and go at that point," Winnie continues, "but then a special Church broadcast comes on—they're playing it on all the networks."

"Blackmore speaks, leads a Hail Frick, encourages everyone to stay calm no matter what happens. But then Peter gets up and . . . oh, Viv." Moved, Harp presses a hand to her chest at the memory. "He was incredible. He starts with his notes—and he's all hell and damnation this and secular morals that—then he looks up, right into the camera, and says: 'They're lying to you. They lied about the first Rapture and they're lying about this one. They're going to kill you if they take you, so don't let them take you.' Then the feed cuts out. The newscasters come back all confused, telling us that Taggart's son has been possessed by Satan, Frick have mercy on his soul—"

"Which was exactly the wrong thing to say," Winnie notes. "Because even if you still believe, the demonic possession of the face of the Church of America on the eve of the second Rapture is not exactly going to inspire confidence. Everyone panicked. Harp gets in touch with Umaymah; they post the story about Joanna then and there, while we figure the Church would be preoccupied, and the response was—"

"A thousand comments in the first *five minutes!*" Harp exclaims. "The site kept going down, so many people looked at it! But they shared the video. They kept on sharing the video."

"And now everything's a mess, basically. *All* the major Church of America dioceses are getting mobbed today. New York, Boston, Chicago, DC, Minneapolis, Seattle. Because guess what? In the chaos, the Church wasn't able to pull off a second Rapture. Not a single reported disappearance. The Believers feel betrayed—they don't understand why the Church would promise a second Rapture in the first place, and they're demanding answers. The Church News Network—what's left of it, anyway, because it seems like half the anchors headed for the hills after Peter went rogue—is taking the line that Believers didn't try hard enough; they let their minds be swayed by lies and secular temptations. But that's only gotten Believers more riled!"

"Plus the Non-Believers have heard Joanna's story," Kimberly adds with a grin, "and they're *pissed*. Thirteen Church of America megastores set on fire across the Midwest."

"And the New Orphans across the country are mounting full-scale attacks against the factories where the rest of the Raptured are hidden. The Church has got its back to the fucking wall." Harp sounds unbelievably satisfied.

I try to feel the pleasure she does, but it's so much information, too quickly, and my head still pounds. I stare ahead, trying to focus on the blur of the city as we race to its heart. Harp and Winnie have glossed over an important detail, the most important, and I'm struggling not to throw up.

"What did they do to Peter?" My voice is hoarse. "They wouldn't have kept him alive after that. How do you know we can still save him?"

For the first time since we got into the car: silence. It's a horrible weight in my stomach, a sinking stone. I press my bloodied hands to my throat.

"We don't. There was nothing after that initial report, after they said he was possessed," Harp says. "All we know is that if he's alive, he'll be at the Chateau. That's where the Angels are holed up, and that's where we're headed. Diego and Edie are waiting for us there. But I guess we should prepare for the possibility—"

"He *could* still be alive," Winnie interrupts. "The Church has had their hands full these last twenty-four hours. There's a huge riot surrounding the Chateau right now. Believers, Non-Believers—everyone wants answers. The Peacemakers have been holding them back, but they've opened fire twice already, and the mob's only getting bigger. It's stupid, really—any reasonable person would be hightailing it out of the city right now. There's a fire closing in on West Hollywood, and these people are going to burn if they don't get out soon."

For the first time, I manage to focus on the scene outside the car. The other lane of the highway is jammed, and as we pass I see people abandoning their cars, cradling children to their chests, weaving their way through traffic. More than once, a car comes barreling toward us, heading the wrong way down the highway in their desperation to get out; Winnie pulls us deftly out of the way each time. The winds are still hot and powerful, rattling a storm of dust and sand and broken glass across the windshield. The power's out on every other block, whole neighborhoods shrouded in menacing darkness. Somewhere out there, massive flames inch toward us. But still we head for the Chateau. We aren't reasonable people. If Peter is alive, we will find him. If he isn't, I will kill the people who killed him. Diego is right: I have in me that monster he told me about, that single splinter of madness that makes destruction possible. Right now it's bigger than shock, bigger than sorrow. It transforms me into something less than human, just a pillar of righteous flame, ready to consume Masterson and the Angels, wanting to spit out their fleshless bones.

"Vivian?" says a soft voice to my left, and I start. I've nearly forgotten that my mother is in the car. "Are you thirsty?"

She holds out a plastic water bottle. I gulp it down, and even lukewarm, even with an aftertaste of plastic, it's the most delicious thing I've ever tasted. When I'm done, I watch my mother stare eagerly out the window, like a tourist trying to spot celebrity homes.

"Mom. What are you doing here?"

She glances at me and quickly away, looking sheepish. "After . . . after you left, I felt terrible. I thought you were dead. I would just sit there, refreshing the feed, searching your name. 'Vivian Apple captured.' 'Vivian Apple dead.' Or sometimes 'Harp Janda captured,' 'Harp Janda dead.' I had no idea Winnie knew where you were, that you were alive. After she moved me and left, it was like I was in a daze. I started to get angry at the Church. What right did they have to hunt girls as young as you? To turn you into fugitives? I started to realize: If they got you, it would be all my fault. If they got you, I'd never forgive them.

"Then one day I search your name and up pops Harp's blog. At first I think—she's seriously bad news. I figure she's disturbed or something. It's a terrible story. An awful, ugly lie. I read it and I had to walk away. And then I came back and read it again. I couldn't stop reading it. It took time—too much time, probably. But then something clicked. Because what did I really think had happened? I tried to imagine Ned, shooting up into heaven like he said we would, and suddenly it seemed crazy. Like . . . science fiction. And then it was different: The lie was the terrible story. And the truth was just the truth.

"They were still looking for you, but I knew you were okay so long as Harp kept posting. I was depressed, though. Couldn't sleep. I just read the blog all day. Until I read Harp's story, I hadn't thought of Ned as dead. I hadn't thought about what we'd done to you—the both of us." She hesitates. "Finally, one day I search 'Vivian Apple captured' and it turns out you had been. I knew it was inevitable, so at first I thought there was nothing I could do. I cried and cried. I couldn't get out of bed in the morning. I got sick. But then, just a few days ago: it was like I woke up. I knew you needed me. They said Los Angeles, so I got a car and came here—I mean, technically," she corrects herself, sounding embarrassed, "I *stole* a car and came here . . . I drove to LA, and the only time I stopped was to call Winnie. I didn't think I'd reach her; she'd told me she was leaving the country. But she picked up. I said, 'Vivian needs our help.'"

"No," Winnie corrects her, deadpan, "you said, 'I'm going to save Vivian and you better be willing to lend a hand.'"

Mom smiles wryly. "Okay, yeah. That sounds right. She gave me the address where I could find her. I got here this afternoon and discovered, to my surprise, that I gave birth to not one, but two complete badasses. I know what you must think of me"— this comes out in a rush and her eyes spill over with tears—"I know how badly I've let you down, and I'm sorry. And maybe it means nothing coming from me, but you have to know—I'm proud of you, Vivian. I'm so proud of you, and if your dad could see you now, he would be too. You are like nothing we ever imagined."

I feel the car begin to slow, and dare to glance out the window. Ahead of us, strikingly white against the flame-colored sky, the Chateau Marmont sits. Flooding Sunset Boulevard is a writhing mass of people, restless bodies surging forward and falling back, like a furious ocean wave. They surge up the lane leading to the Chateau; they scramble to climb the trees blocking the bungalows from sight. At the periphery of the crowd are the casualties of the Peacemakers' gunfire, limp bodies slick with blood, abandoned by the protestors who push insistently forward. Helicopters swarm overhead, casting spotlights on the crowd; reporters pour out of news vans parked nearby, jostling to get closer. Beyond the Chateau, miles away but still close enough to strike cold fear in me, a thick black cloud of smoke rolls in.

"This is as far as we're going to get." Winnie parks the car and opens her door, and all at once I can smell the blood and fire and sweat; I feel the crackle of electric anger in the air, and my heart starts to pound because it's so terrible but so beautiful all at once. We're going to push through this crowd. We're going to get inside this building. And then we're going to put a stop to the apocalypse.

I follow my mother as she steps into the bright hot evening, but then I hear Harp call, "Viv, wait!" And when I turn she's crouched in the back seat, picking an object up from the floor of the car. She holds it out to me with a fabulous, terrified grin on her face. My sledgehammer.

"I think you'll be wanting this," she says.

CHAPTER TWENTY-ONE

The four of us maneuver our way to the edge of the crowd—Winnie and Kimberly stride ahead confidently, while Harp, my mother, and I trail behind. As we get nearer, Winnie raises a hand, and I see Diego a dozen yards away, waving back. With him are all the surviving members of Amanda's militia, plus Edie and the Orphans beside them. Edie is arm in arm with Joanna, who looks different from the last time I saw her: steadier, more determined, the color returned to her cheeks. The rest of the rescued Raptured are intermingled throughout the group. They hold weapons and seem frightened but ready. I scan my friends' faces, registering their astonishment at the sight of my own. And then I cry out in surprise—because standing behind Diego, in plain sight and yet so unexpected my gaze passed right over him, is Dylan.

He steps forward, smiling awkwardly, to accept my arms thrown round his neck.

"Dylan. Thank you. You saved my life. Harp said you told her where I was, but I didn't realize you were still here—I thought you were leaving!"

"Yeah, well," Dylan drawls. "Like I said—you have a way with guilt, Apple. Anyway, I figured the Church has enough going on that they won't go after Molly right away. I talked to her this morning—the school has a bomb shelter they'll hide out in for the next few hours. She'll be fine without me, I'm sure."

I keep my hand on his arm, to comfort him. "She will be, Dylan. We're here to fix things for her. Everything will be different tomorrow."

"Yeah. I know." He tries to seem cool, but his eyes flick nervously around us; he raises a trembling hand to push the hair out of his eyes. I can't say anything else, because Diego steps forward and stares at me, then pulls me into an enveloping hug.

"I'm happy you're okay," he murmurs. "I wish we'd gotten to you sooner. If we'd had any idea where you were—"

"It's fine," I tell him. "Really, I'm fine."

He squeezes me so hard it hurts. But over his shoulder I see Winnie beaming at the sight of us, one hand pressed to her chest in her joy, and though I roll my eyes at her, I can't help but feel a brief flash of perfect peace. Diego is part of my family now. All of these people are part of my family. The only thing missing is Peter.

"What's the plan?"

Diego turns to Edie, who reaches out to touch my cheek. "We were waiting for you before we made one. Oh, Viv, look at you!" I worry she's about to cry, but instead Edie's face splits into an incredulous grin. "You look like Joan of fucking Arc!"

Beside me, Harp's mouth and eyes turn into giddy, disbelieving saucers—we've never heard Edie swear before. I laugh at them both. "Is Naveen okay?"

Edie nods. "Eleanor was so good as to stay behind with him. We didn't know what to expect," she explains, gesturing to the riot between us and the Chateau.

"And what about Amanda?" I ask, looking for her. "What does she want us to do?"

Diego inclines his head toward the crowd. "She's in there somewhere, but she's given up on us all. We're in charge of ourselves now."

It's a thought that should bring comfort, but doesn't—I have no idea what we're supposed to do next. At a loss, I turn to Harp, who stands on tiptoe, seemingly trying to assess the size of the crowd. When she turns to us, she has a determined look on her face, and everyone—soldiers, Orphans, Believers—closes in to form a huddle. I feel a wild spark of pride that this girl, this girl who always has a plan, is my best friend in the entire dying world.

"We're no good out here," she says. "We have to get inside; we have to confront Masterson with Joanna, and catch it on a live stream. We have to get the Angels on camera so no one has any doubt. What time is it?"

Nearby, Julian dutifully checks his watch. "Quarter past ten."

"Quarter past ten?" I echo in disbelief. I look up—the sky is the electric color of a tangerine.

"Oh," Winnie says, grimacing. "We forgot to mention that— the sun has been setting later and later over the last few weeks. The scientists think it's probably dying."

Horrified, I open my mouth to press for more information, but Harp interrupts.

"Let's worry about that later, okay? The Church will have to introduce the Messiah soon—before midnight. It seems stupid, though, to push it this long with this mob outside. It's already well into tomorrow on the other side of the world. What are they waiting for?"

I'm starting to feel stronger now, surrounded by these people and this crowd; my thoughts flow more easily. "Masterson will push it to the last possible moment," I say. "If it's still September twenty-fourth in the United States, the story still works. He wants to wait until the Believers here have lost all hope. But you're right—we have to get into the Chateau and find him and the new Messiah before he gets the chance. Let's move."

Diego and Winnie lead the push into the crowd. From the outside, the mob seemed like a solid mass, moving in a kind of frenzied harmony, but inside, they're unwieldy. Believers cling to one another, singing "Jesus (Thank You for Making Me American)" in a high spooky warble. Various sects of Non-Believers are scattered throughout. Some seem to be here just to feed off the chaos, drunks and junkies and the apparently insane. These are the hardest to get past: they jostle at us with sharp elbows, scream in our faces; when we try to push past them, they push us back. I stick close to Harp. The crowd is sweaty and noisy and I feel claustrophobic; my ears buzz and I have to close my eyes. A hand grasps at the back of my hoodie and I cry out in alarm, but when I turn I see it's just my mother, looking pale, trying not to lose me in the chaos.

I hear a scuffle to my left—a fight breaking out between two kids in tattered jeans and one huge Believer. "You're so gullible, old man!" one of the Non-Believers taunts. "We wouldn't be in this shit if it weren't for people like you!"

The man laughs a hollow laugh and says, "People like *me*? It's because of *you* Frick has forsaken us."

I turn back to Edie and Joanna, everyone trailing behind me, and call out, "Hurry!" I don't want to get stuck in this. Dylan is some yards away with his arms in the air, a cluster of teenage girls clinging to him. I see a flash of silver—a knife in the hands of one of the Non-Believers. The Believer he threatens is quicker; he slams the kid to the ground. The other Non-Believer lunges forward and the man pushes back; then the crowd around them starts screaming, and someone with a baseball bat swings it back, and I watch in horror as it collides with Gallifrey's face. There's an awful snapping sound. He slips to the ground; beside me Harp shouts his name. The crowd presses in on the fight. In one swift movement, Elliott reaches down and plucks Gallifrey off the ground; he throws the Orphan over one shoulder. "Keep moving!" he calls.

With a couple hundred yards between us and the Chateau Marmont, a human chain of singing Believers blocks our progress. Diego tries to move past, but the women and men are arm in arm, screaming, weeping. He's unable to break them apart. I look beyond them, to seek a better route, but suddenly a low, harsh voice in my ear squawks, "God damn you!"

I try to ignore it, clinging tighter to Harp. Diego takes a tentative step around the singing Believers. But then I hear the voice, louder this time—"God *damn* you!"—so loud it makes my ears ring, and now a hand is on my arm, turning me roughly around, forcing me to face him.

He's a Believer only a few years older than me, sweating madly. He shoves me hard, and I tumble back into Harp. I move to block him with my sledgehammer, but Diego and Winnie have already stepped in front of me, and even the sight of their guns does little to subdue him. He stands his ground, glaring at us from over Diego's shoulder.

"It's *their* fault!" he shouts. "If they hadn't gone and spread that stupid story, we wouldn't be in this mess. We'd have been saved! But Frick's left us to die here, and it's all because of *them!*"

I'm uncomfortably aware of the people closest to us turning at the commotion. The singing Believers hush midchorus, and there's no mistaking the wave of murmurs spreading farther and farther. They know who we are. We're smack in the middle of a desperate mob, and this is the moment we've finally been spotted. It's like every nightmare I've had for the last two months coming true at the most inopportune of moments.

"Keep going," I cry to Winnie, who's trying her best to shield me. "Just keep moving!"

But then an odd thing starts to happen. The chain of Believers breaks, opening to us like a gate, and as neighbor whispers to neighbor, the crowd parts—reluctantly at first, but then more and more rapidly, until there's a nearly open path between us and the Chateau. Diego and Winnie flank Harp and me so no one can touch us. As we pass I hear scattered furious outbursts ("You had to go and open your big whore's mouth!" screams a Believer woman who throws herself in our path; Harp just waves as Diego pushes her away), but most gaze with a sort of wonder. Right at the front of the crowd, I see a group of kids our age applauding wildly. "Fuck yeah!" a girl screams out. "You guys are my heroes!"

At the front of the crowd, we're faced with a resolute line of Peacemakers in riot gear, bulletproof shields and automatic rifles in their hands, guarding the entrance. I pause to catch my breath. Their expressions stay neutral as they watch us approach, which only makes them scarier: inhuman, mechanical. Diego sighs.

"I was really hoping not to shoot anybody today," he mutters. Then, over his shoulder, "Cliff House? You with me?"

They push to the front, guns in hand, forming a protective half circle around us; Kimberly blocks me with her body. "Get down," she instructs. "Start pushing your way to the side." Harp crouches obediently but I panic—nobody in Amanda's militia wears bullet-proof gear. If they open fire on the Peacemakers, they'll be taken out in an instant. There has to be another way. And then just like that, I see it.

"Wilkins!" I call.

He's barely recognizable behind his reflective sunglasses, but he jumps at the sound of his name. His perplexed colleagues turn to look at him. I push past Kimberly and Diego.

"Wilkins!" I wave. "Hey, Wilkins, it's me!"

"Viv, what is this?" asks Diego's voice in my ear, but I just keep waving.

After a pause, the Peacemaker reluctantly moves toward me. I step forward to meet him, ignoring my mother's gasp and Winnie's attempt to grab my arm. Wilkins lowers his gun. He stares at me, his expression unreadable; then he takes off his sunglasses.

"Vivian, what are you doing?" He sounds worried.

"Just sayin' hi. I missed you the last few days. Did you take some personal time, or . . . ?"

He takes another step, this one slightly more aggressive. I hear a shift behind me as Winnie and Diego assess this threat. But I hold up my hand to calm them. I trust him.

"I came here late the other night," he explains in a low voice. "We all did. They told us we were guaranteed a place on the second boat. I sat out there, by the *pool*, waiting to be Raptured. Nothing happens. Then yesterday morning, they wake us up; they say there's a riot outside and we better take care of it. No explanation for why we're still here. That's a little rich, I think, considering I haven't even gotten a paycheck in the last two months."

"They're lying to you, Wilkins. They've been lying the whole time."

He still looks dubious. "Maybe. I'm not gonna pretend there aren't things that don't add up. Like—they said you were a witch, right? But wouldn't a witch break herself out of a jail cell?" He shakes his head, pondering this. "But how do *you* explain the sky, okay? How do you explain the fires and the winds and all that stuff? Someone's angry up there, Vivian. You have to admit that someone's angry."

"Maybe someone is," I say, feeling desperate. "But I don't think that someone is on the Church of America's side at all. Do you?"

Wilkins sucks on his front teeth. I can tell I'm getting to him, but he seems determined not to answer.

"Listen." I hear footsteps and see that Harp has come to stand by my side. "We need to get in. We're not going to hurt anyone, but we need to look for Masterson, Mulvey, and Blackmore. If they're still here, we can make them explain."

Wilkins stares at me for too long of a moment, and I'm sure he's about to refuse. But then he nods to his right, drawing my attention to the Peacemakers behind him, watching us. "Okay. But what am I supposed to tell these guys?"

I shrug. "Whatever you think they need to hear."

Wilkins considers this, then beckons us to follow. He leads us to a Peacemaker at the center of the line, who straightens as we approach and spits.

"Listen, Beau," Wilkins explains. "I know this is unusual, but these two girls—you recognize them, right?—they want to turn themselves in. They've admitted to being enemies to salvation, and they want to make things right by the Church."

"I thought this one was *already* turned in." Beau frowns at me.

"I was," I tell him. "But then I broke out. I want to turn myself in for that, too."

He narrows his eyes, and I prepare myself for something terrible. But then Beau shrugs. I start to get the feeling that Wilkins is not the only one losing patience with the Three Angels of the Church of America.

"Whatever. I'd say to take them to Masterson, but there's no telling where *he* is. Maybe bring them to the cottage where they're holding the Taggart kid?" I grab Harp's arm to steady myself. "Oliver's on guard over there; he'll know what to do."

I see Beau stiffen then. He lifts his rifle to aim at something behind us, and when I turn, panicked, I see Winnie and my mom approaching with hands raised.

"They want to turn themselves in too!" I cry, moving quickly to block them.

Winnie hears this. She nods deeply, immediately understanding. "We broke her out of Church jail and it was wrong. Please— we just want to make amends in our final hours."

I can tell Beau is not entirely convinced, but he just shakes his head at us. "Get them out of here," he snaps at Wilkins. Wilkins begins to lead us through the open gate, but we hear a shout of "Hey!" We turn. Beau gestures to the sledgehammer still in my hands, the rifles across the shoulders of my mother and sister. "Strip them of their weapons first, idiot! Do you want to get us all killed?"

Wilkins silently takes them, though I see his face flush red at the insult. Our weapons in arm, he ushers us down the long drive. I move carefully, afraid Beau will change his mind. Wilkins nods to the Peacemaker standing at attention in the entryway to the adjacent garden, and then he leads us past the garden wall.

When the other Peacemaker can no longer see us, Wilkins gives a rifle back to my mother and a rifle back to Winnie. With a slight, confused frown, he places the sledgehammer into my outstretched hands. He leads us through the garden, turned brittle and brown during LA's eternal summer, past a pool that must once have looked inviting but is now half-empty and spotted with dead birds. Ahead of us, a row of picturesque cottages is all commotion. Doors are thrown open, and panicked Church employees dart in and out. I glance in as we pass and see scenes of chaos: an arguing couple throwing towels into a sloppily packed suitcase; two women sitting on the floor by the bed, one weeping and the other trying to comfort her ("Of *course* they won't kill us—we're very low-level!"); a man slumped against the door frame in the midst of a wrenching phone call ("Just tell her Daddy loves her and he'll be home as soon as he can—no, I have no idea when that will be, Judith; it's the goddamn apocalypse!"). There are couples rolling together on the lawn, clinched in one last romantic embrace as the final moments approach; drunks stepping over them, sobbing, clutching bottles of champagne in their fists. With a shudder, I notice a body floating face-down in the other pool.

Finally, at the end of the row of bungalows, we see a Peacemaker stationed at a front door that remains closed. There are black iron bars over this building's windows. He glances warily at us as we approach, noticing our weapons and then our famous faces. His grip tightens on his gun. Winnie puts a hand on my arm, gives me a look as if to say *I've got this*, then bounds confidently up to the Peacemaker guarding the door, surprising him so much she's able to knock him out cold with one punch.

Wilkins gasps. "Oh, sweet Jesus!" he cries, as Oliver the Peacemaker goes tumbling. Wilkins looks at us with a new fear in his eyes and then goes running in the direction we came.

"We have to stop him." Winnie doesn't sound happy about it. She lifts her rifle to her shoulder but I put my hand on it, push it down.

"Leave it," I say.

"Viv—"

"He won't tell anyone," I promise her. I don't know that it's true, but I want to believe it. I still wear his watch around my wrist. Winnie seems dubious, but she lowers her weapon.

I turn and assess the door. The knob is locked. We don't have long until everything falls apart. I throw myself against the door, pounding on it. "Peter! Peter! Are you in here?"

There's nothing at first, just the distant dull clamor of the mob behind us. But then I hear his voice behind the door:

"Viv?"

"Get back!" I shout. I take a step away from the door and raise the sledgehammer high over my head, and as Winnie, Harp, and my mother realize what I'm about to do, they stumble backwards onto the lawn. I bring the hammer down hard in the general vicinity of the doorknob, but miss, removing a significant chunk of the frame. I try again, and dent the door itself.

"You know this guy probably has keys on him, right?" Harp points out, kicking lightly at Oliver's unconscious body.

I ignore her, slamming the sledgehammer down once more, and this time I hit my target; the knob shudders in place like a loose tooth. I try again and again. My arms still ache from my own escape attempt, and it's not like I've ever been physically strong, but there's something about this act, born of love and the clock ticking down, that feels within my grasp. At last the knob gives with a metallic pop, and I step forward. I see Peter's fingers graze the hole the knob has left behind. He opens the door, peers out cautiously at the four of us. When his gaze drifts to me, sweating and panting and shaking and bruised, his eyes widen in appreciation.

"Damn," he says, nearly breathless.

It's the best compliment I've gotten in a while. Peter comes to me, kisses me softly. He takes my chin into his fingers and gently tilts my face up so he can see it better under the still-bright sky. He turns it from side to side.

"It looks worse than it feels," I tell him. In truth, I can't feel any pain at all right now; I'm drunk with pleasure. "Are you all right?"

Peter nods. Other than the dark shadows under his eyes, he looks more or less like he always does: handsome and kind, a little bit like he just woke up. "They left my face alone—Mulvey's orders. She sees a future in me—a redemption narrative, she says. I'm sure Masterson would have killed me after the stunt I pulled on TV . . . did you hear about that?" I just grin at him, and Peter grins back. "Yeah, well. I can't imagine that thrilled him. But Mulvey and Blackmore hid me here—I think they still feel guilty about my dad—and I haven't seen Masterson since."

I stand on tiptoe to kiss him again. When he pulls away, he glances at Winnie and Mom, who gaze back politely. And suddenly, even though we're standing in the middle of Hollywood with a fake apocalypse hurtling toward us at full speed, my life feels unbelievably normal.

"Oh." Under my bruises my cheeks go pink, and nearby Harp glances up at the sky in a nonchalant way, whistling. "Peter, this is my sister, Winnie Conroy, and my mom. Mom, Winnie, this is Peter Ivey. My boyfriend."

Peter shakes their hands shyly—"Nice to meet you, Mrs. Apple"—while Harp giggles to herself. Winnie nudges at her with an elbow, but her mouth is twitching. My mother seems nervous; her eyes are oddly bright.

"Well!" she says in a too-loud voice. "Isn't this weird? I always thought when I met Viv's first boyfriend, we'd be sitting down before her prom and looking at her baby pictures!"

I cover my face, hoping this will render me invisible. "Oh God, Mom, please. No."

"I'd really like to see those someday, Mrs. Apple." Peter grins.

"Hopefully Pittsburgh is on fire right now," I say, "and our house burns with it."

"You think I didn't upload those to the cloud?" Mom laughs, and she sounds so like herself I can't help but join in. "Come on, Viv. Have a little appreciation for the savvy of your dear old mom."

"Actually"—Harp gestures toward her backpack with her thumb—"I happen to have a laptop right here on my person. I could fire it up pretty easily! We could create that perfect family moment as we speak."

I lunge at her and Harp cackles, trying to unzip the bag with one hand and fight me off with the other; Peter and Mom laugh together, watching us, and it's a perfect moment: my best friend, my boyfriend, my mother, and me. But then Winnie clears her throat, and I snap out of it. I feel at once a grasping panic—there is too much left to do, and the hold I have on these people I love is tenuous at best.

"I'm sorry," Winnie says when we fall silent. "But we can't slow down. As far as we know, the Angels still plan to broadcast the rising of their Messiah. We'll need to confront them before they get the chance. Except—oh, shit!"

I understand at the same moment Harp does. "Joanna!" she groans.

The Raptured Believers, the linchpin of our whole plan, are still behind the gate with the rest of the riot. Without Joanna to confront the Angels on camera, Harp's live stream will be nothing more than the accusations of three terrorists and a boy possessed by Satan, a dull series of denials from the Three Angels—assuming we can find them—most likely followed by our own gruesome deaths.

"We need one of the Raptured Believers for any of this to work," I say. "Look, I'll head back out and get Joanna." I start to move in the direction of the gate, but Winnie grabs my arm.

"The guards won't let you," she insists. "And for all we know, Wilkins has already told them we assaulted a Peacemaker. They could be on their way here as we speak."

"What if," Peter thinks out loud, "we found Frick? If we could get him on camera before they broadcast the Messiah—that would work, right? If he said anything like what he told us in Point Reyes that night—"

"If we could get Frick to say the Rapture was faked," I realize, "that would be enough."

"Frick?" my mother echoes, sounding mildly panicked. "*Beaton* Frick?"

"But where do you think he'd be?" I ask Peter.

"No idea. They'd probably give him a nice room, as a show of respect . . ." He trails off, absent-mindedly examining the nearby cottages.

"He's probably inside the Chateau," Winnie points out. "They'd want to keep him close—as far from the crowds as possible."

Peter nods. "Look, let's try the sixth floor and work our way down. We have no time to waste."

We race back through the garden and past the guard at the stone wall; Winnie slams her rifle into his temple to ensure he doesn't follow. As a cluster, we move in through the entrance and make our way to the main staircase, racing up, pushing against a tide of escaping Church employees. One or two glance at me and I see the frightened glimmer of recognition, but nobody tries to stop us. The employees know better than the Believers outside the various sins of the Church of America, and they're attempting to get out while they can. As we climb up to the top of the Chateau, the sounds of the remaining Believers' panic floats up with us—howling and unintelligible shouting, and, on the fourth floor, a single, alarming gunshot. The sixth floor is quieter than the others, its doors all closed. The employees here are higher up. Either they know about the Messiah, or they're more inclined to trust Masterson to get them out of this mess. I check Wilkins's watch: ten to eleven.

"What do we do?" my mother whispers. "Bang on the doors, screaming Frick's name?"

Harp and Peter and I exchange a look.

"Mrs. Apple," Harp replies, "that is *exactly* what we're about to do."

I take one side and Peter the other; Harp rushes ahead. Winnie has her gun at the ready should Masterson or the others appear. I bang on each door with my sledgehammer. "FRICK!" I shout. "BEATON FRICK!" Peter's voice goes scratchy echoing mine. Doors open and the rooms' occupants peer out in alarm—I see them exchange dark glances, and I know they know where he is. But no one points us in his direction.

Then, from around the corner, Harp's voice: "Hey!"

Peter glances at me and together we run; we see her at the very last room at the end of the hall. She's got her foot stuck between the door and its frame, her hands pressed against it; Harp pushes madly, but someone inside is determined to shut her out. Peter reaches her and throws his shoulder against the door. We hear a cry as the person behind it falls back—the door swings open easily. Winnie and my mother have caught up to us, and together we enter the room.

Inside is Beaton Frick. The sight of him makes my mom gasp and drop to her knees. He's far better groomed than the last times I saw him: clean-shaven, hair cut. There's something of the old Frick in him—confident and businesslike—but then he gives me a small wave of recognition, his eyes simultaneously delighted and alarmed, and I know his mind is still a mess. On any other occasion, his presence would be the most notable thing about a room. But tonight our attention is drawn to the other person in it.

He's sprawled on the floor, kicking wildly in an effort to get to his feet, but he's too tangled in his long, linen robes. He's young—Winnie's age, maybe—with shoulder-length auburn hair and a beard of the same color. He resembles Jesus to a degree that's at once incredible and deeply hilarious. And he glares at us all, propping himself up on one elbow, chattering darkly into the phone he holds to his ear.

"Thanks for your concern, Jeremy, but I'm fine. No, it's not them; it's a bunch of insane-looking teenagers. Yes, I remember what the contract said. Thank you so much for that. Well, what am I supposed to do? They just burst in here! Ask them what? Okay. Hang on."

The Messiah fixes his scowl on me. "Are you here to kill me?"

We're all too startled to answer. Then the Messiah snaps at us with his fingers, like he thinks we're maybe deaf. I shake my head at him.

"They say no, Jeremy." He pushes himself to his feet and continues speaking as if we haven't interrupted. "Anyway, my point is, you *told* me this was prime time. You told me I'd be in capable hands. But the fact is, five hours ago they stuck me in a room with a"—his voice lowers briefly to a theatrical whisper—

"*lunatic,* and told me I couldn't be seen. I haven't heard from them since!" A brief pause, then the Messiah starts shouting. "Yeah, I know about the riot! Talk about your unsafe working conditions! I want you to call Masterson now and remind him I belong to the guild!"

Behind him, Frick sits patiently on the bed, giving us a mild, polite smile, like the Messiah is a badly behaved grandson he cannot bring himself to rebuke.

"Is that really the tone you want to take with me, Jeremy? Maybe you've forgotten—you work for me. That new vacation home in Boca Raton—that's thanks to *me!*"

Winnie pushes past me then, marching up to the Messiah. She snatches the phone from his hand and shouts, "He'll call you back!" into it. She hangs up and turns to the actor, who is cowering a little now. "What's your name?"

Though his eyes are still frightened, the Messiah seems to remember himself. He pulls himself up to his full height, folding his hands peacefully across his chest. "Why," he says, in a very different voice, softer and vaguely British, "you know my name, child."

"Guy's *good,*" Harp deadpans after a pause. "You've got to give him that."

Winnie looks disgusted, and though she's a full head shorter than the Messiah, he shrinks when she begins to speak again, her voice quiet and deadly. "I hope they're paying you a lot of money for this. I hope you were able to buy a big house you'll never live in, and a shiny car you'll never drive. I hope knowing those things are out there is satisfying to you, because the Church *owns* you now. Do you understand? Do you know what happens when they don't require the people they own anymore? Do you know what happened to the Raptured Believers?"

The Messiah cringes, like he'd rather she didn't bring it up. Winnie turns to Frick.

"And you. Do you understand who this is? Do you get who the Angels will claim he is?"

"I think so." Frick speaks in a quiet voice. "I think I do."

"And that's okay with you?"

Frick shakes his head and Winnie looks satisfied. But then he abruptly thunders, "Because there's no rescue from the eternal torment America faces! God has damned us all to a world born into fire, and he'll laugh without mercy as we burn! This man is an impostor, and we shall feed him to the hounds when they bound up from the mouth of hell!"

Behind me, my mother murmurs a shocked "Oh my."

Winnie catches my eye and grins. "Yeah, okay," she says. "I think this will work."

| | | | |

My sister leaves first, scoping out the hallway. Harp and I follow with Frick. My mother is behind us, and Peter brings up the rear, half dragging the struggling Messiah. "Listen, if something happens to the costume, it isn't coming out of my wages," we hear him mutter. Harp leans forward to catch my eye and the two of us stifle laughter.

This is how it happens. With my face turned forward and my mouth a wide grin. A Peacemaker appears at the end of the hall, his gun already aimed at us. It takes a moment for me to understand—because how can it happen when I'm laughing, when we've won? But then I hear the blast shatter the easy silence of the sixth floor, then another, then a third—this last from Winnie, who hits her target. People are screaming—my mother and the Messiah, but also the Church employees around us, who come pouring out of their rooms now against all logic. They see the body at one end of the hall and Winnie at the other, rifle still poised, and they run, shouting, as if chased. One man lunges at Winnie, tries to pin her down; she throws him off, but not easily. She glances at me over her shoulder.

"Run, Viv!" Winnie shouts. "Get them downstairs!"

Frick has gone rigid with shock, and I tug hard on his arm to pull him forward, past Winnie, who has stumbled to the floor. The hall is full of people. The man who lunged for Winnie grabs at Harp's ankles; my best friend trips. I see the Messiah dart past me; Peter runs after him. Finally Frick moves and we push through the crowd; I glance back quickly to make sure Harp's on her feet, and she is. But that's when I realize my mother hasn't stopped screaming. Not since the second shot rang out. I stop in my tracks. I look back at her, through the mess of people streaming away from the scene. She's on her knees in the middle of the hallway, screaming, and I'm trying to see: Where was she hit? Where is the blood? But then I see Winnie.

She lies on her back on the floor in front of my mother, a massive dark stain spreading across her chest. She blinks, dazed, at the ceiling. Mom crawls forward and lifts her head to cradle it, and I let go of Frick's arm—*Stay here!* I shout, or mean to shout— and slip my hoodie off my shoulders and go running, stumbling to my knees. I press the sweatshirt down hard on her chest. Winnie lowers her eyes to me, smiling weakly.

"Tell Mara she's got to pull it together," Winnie says.

And I watch her eyelids quiver a few long seconds, then close.

CHAPTER TWENTY-TWO

It happens so quickly that it hasn't happened. Time is still in flux. All it would take to reverse it would be the careful retracing of footsteps, a throwaway gesture done slightly differently. Where do we begin?

Winnie's head rests against my mother's knees; Mom wails at the ceiling. I watch a rust-colored stain spread against my sweatshirt. Harp sinks to the other side of Winnie, places a hand on her arm. From below comes a mighty din—scuffling and shouts, a series of piercing, heart-lurching screams—and I dimly understand that the mob outside has broken through the gates and into the Chateau. I want to curl beside the body of my sister, let the chaos swallow me up. But instead I think of Winnie: at once so strong and vulnerable, impossibly adult. I try to channel her.

"Mom. You have to calm down. Look: she's still breathing."

My mother takes a breath and watches Winnie's chest rise and fall unevenly. Tears stream down her face, but she manages to stop howling. Harp watches me, waiting for my next move. We need a doctor. I feel a presence loom over my shoulder, and after a moment, Frick kneels beside Harp on Winnie's other side.

He takes my sister's hand into his. My mother watches with an expression I can't decipher; Harp inches slightly away.

Frick begins to pray.

"Dear Lord—"

"No!" Horrified, I grab Winnie's wrist and tug her hand free from his grasp. I may have only known her a few short months, I may have known about her for not much longer, but I'm positive the last thing Winnie would want in her final moments is a false prophet muttering empty words over her body.

My mother reaches over to touch my face. "Please, Viv. Just let him finish." Her eyes are red and wild with grief. I think then of my father. Maybe Mom is thinking of him too.

And then it no longer seems like the time to make a stand. Frick's prayer is not for Winnie. It's for my mother, who despite everything must cling to some small hope that Frick or someone like him will be able to tell her a story that brings her some peace.

I bow my head, and Frick, after a pause, continues.

"Dear Lord, please watch over your daughter in these moments. If it's your intention to call her home tonight, guide her with wisdom and peace. Thank you for sending her to protect us this day. Amen."

"Amen," my mother says, and Harp and I say it too.

The roar from downstairs swells then, frenzied and alarming. Soon they'll breach the upper floors and the bedlam will be upon us. We have to face it now—it's what Winnie would want, what she *does* want—but the thought of leaving her terrifies me. So long as she takes these shallow breaths, I don't see how I can go.

"I'll stay," my mother tells me. "Do what you came to do. I'll watch over Winnie."

"Are you sure?" I have a quick, surprising pang of jealousy—it isn't the old fear I had in San Francisco, that my mother secretly prefers my sister. It's the fact that Winnie belongs to *me* too now—that we chose each other and she is mine.

"She'd never forgive herself if she was the one who kept you from bringing down the Angels." Mom smiles sadly. "She'd be absolutely furious."

I nod. Harp stands and tugs at Frick's arm; he gets up dutifully. My mother lowers Winnie's head to the floor; she moves to where I kneel. Her hands replace mine on the hoodie.

"We'll send help," I tell her.

My mother just nods, her gaze fixed on Winnie's face. I stand, picking up my sledgehammer, which I dropped on my way to Winnie's side. I look at Harp.

"Viv, old bean."

Her voice sounds strangled and uncertain, but my best friend puts out her hand and I take it. She squeezes once, and then again, as if to say, *I won't let it wreck you.* I squeeze back, remembering that she knows exactly how I feel, remembering that before anyone else, I chose Harp for my sister. Her eyes ask a question I don't know how to answer, so I just say, "Stay close."

I take Frick's other arm, and together we rush down the hall. My thoughts are a blur, but I know that despite the pandemonium, we need to make our way downstairs, as close to the lobby as we can get. We need to find three things: help for Winnie; Peter; and the Angels. I hum it like a chorus as we race down the stairwell. *Help for Winnie; Peter; the Angels.* The crowd gets louder with each flight we descend, but we don't see physical signs of the melee until we reach the fourth floor. There, we fight our way through a thrashing mass of bodies. I hazard a glance down the hall, anxiously seeking Peter's face, but all I see is violence: Non-

Believers busting down the doors of the hotel rooms, dragging Church employees out by their hair; Peacemakers wielding black batons, bringing them down hard on the heads of the rioters; desperate Believers clinging to one another, screaming for answers. I watch this last group take in the sight of Frick with shocked expressions and then call out his name, pushing toward us with their arms outstretched.

"We need to move!" I shout to Harp, and we maneuver Frick forward.

Halfway down the steps to the third floor, we meet Diego. Behind him are the people I most want to see: Estefan, the New Orphans' nurse; and Frankie, with her first-aid kit strapped to her back.

"Diego! The sixth floor—Winnie—"

"Peter told us." He's already moving past me, his face pale, deftly shouldering his way through the throng on the stairs. Estefan and Frankie chase after him. "Viv, do you know what you need to do?"

"No!" I shout after him, but he's gone.

The crowd gets thicker the closer we get to the lobby. I am finding it harder and harder to breathe. I try to keep an eye out for anyone familiar—for Peter especially—but all I can see in my head is the stain of Winnie's blood on my sweatshirt. Before I realize it, we've reached the lobby, where all is chaos. Frick stays steady, a buoy in a wild ocean for us to cling to, but his face is clouded over with panic, and I worry he'll melt down in the face of this sheer anarchy. There are too many people, all of them screaming and fighting and pushing their way forward—we will never find any of our friends in this mob, let alone the Angels. The only way Masterson would enter this mess is at the side of the Messiah. Across the room is an empty platform. The crowd in front of it is an unrelenting knot, but if we could get past them, if we could get Frick up there, where the whole room could see him—that would be the end of it. We would win.

From the other side of Frick, I hear a sound that makes my blood go cold: Harp screaming. I wheel around. Two scrabbling men have crashed into her, their hands around each other's throats. Harp goes tumbling to the floor and I move to help her, but something slams hard against my injured right shoulder and the pain makes my vision go black—I wobble on my feet, holding on to Frick's arm to keep from falling. When I pull my head up, disoriented, my best friend is nowhere in sight.

"Harp!"

I drop Frick's arm and knock people aside using the sledge-hammer, not caring whether or not I hurt them. My eyes are on the floor. If Harp has fallen, she'll be trampled. I push a woman out of my way, but she only bobs in place, eerily still. Her out-stretched arm points at something. I don't give it thought until I notice the man beside her has frozen as well. I realize then that they're looking at Frick. He stares back at them, bewildered. I thrust myself forward to get to his side.

"Frick!" cries out a Believer in a hoarse voice. "Beaton Frick!"

A ripple of awareness rushes through the crowd in our im-mediate vicinity—the melee continues on all sides except this one pocket of shocked silence. A woman collapses against me, sobbing, "Oh, hallelujah, sweet Jesus, we are saved!"

"That's not Frick," snarls a voice in my ear, and I see one of the young Non-Believers who started the knife fight outside. He as-sesses Frick with skepticism. "It's a fucking hologram."

As if to prove his point, he reaches over and shoves Frick hard, sending him stumbling backwards. The nearby Believers gasp. I push myself closer and block Frick's body with my own, my eyes still scanning the room for Harp. An elderly woman presses in to grab Frick's hand.

"Your Holiness." She trembles with excitement. "Don't let me die among these animals. I've tried so hard to be good. Won't you please save me?"

"Our baby!" calls another voice, a man. He pushes his wife forward, and I see a screaming baby wrapped in a sling around her chest. They're pressed so close against me I can smell the milky sweetness of the baby's skin. "We've failed you, but please, he's just a newborn. God will save him, if you tell Him to! God will listen to you!"

Behind me, I hear Frick stutter; he's confused. "I'm sorry— I—it's too late!"

"Not a hologram," the Non-Believer kid is now saying, "but definitely an impersonator—"

"Why did you forsake us, Frick?"

"We did everything you asked. We bought everything you told us to buy. Everything!"

More and more Believers push toward us now, reaching to touch Frick's clothes, his skin, begging for answers. The baby screams piteously, squashed against my shoulder; his mother yelps in panic as the crowd closes in. Non-Believers also attempt to force their way forward; I see furious eyes and weapons brandished overhead.

"Why are you protecting him?" A Non-Believer woman tugs hard on my arm, trying to get to Frick. "He deserves everything he's gonna get—stand *aside!*"

But I can't move; I can't let him die before he speaks, before they understand. It's not enough for the Believers to feel abandoned—they need to know they've been lied to. Otherwise someone down the line will try again.

I clasp Frick's hand tightly, but the circle squeezes tighter around us. I'm shouting now—"Please! Please back up!"—aware of the woman with the baby panicking at my shoulder. From behind me a heavy hand comes down hard on my head; it pushes me down. I'm so surprised I stumble. Someone kicks me hard in the small of my back and I go sprawling forward, knocking over another person, a Non-Believer boy who instinctively elbows me in my mouth as we go tumbling down. My sledgehammer flies from my hands and I lose sight of it in the sea of legs ahead. I taste the blood on my teeth and the crowd surges forward again, trampling me; someone steps on my ankle, twisting it; someone else uses my shoulder to give them height. I scream, trying to grab on to someone, but each time, I'm pushed back down. It's like drowning: the limbs and screams of the people closing above my head like waves, the frantic desperate scrabbling to pull myself up to the surface, and finally, awfully, my body slipping into weakness, going slack, losing the will or ability to fight back, knowing that once I do, it's all over, that this will be the end for me.

"My children, why do you fight one another?"

The voice booms through the Chateau, amplified so loud it shivers in my teeth. Everyone stills—the teeming mass above me, the mob closing in on all sides. In the curious silence, the slow search for the source of the sound, I feel a hand clasp around my arm and pull. I look up to see who's helping me and find a middle-aged Believer in a bonnet. "Are you all right?" she whispers, when I'm on my feet.

I nod, dizzy, and wipe my mouth with the back of my hand; it comes away slick with blood. When I follow the crowd's gaze I see the Messiah on the platform where I'd hoped to bring Frick, bathed in golden light. He looks surprisingly convincing. An uncomprehending murmur travels across the crowd, and then individual Believers begin to lose it: they fall to their knees, gasping, screaming, swaying. Most of the crowd seems too stunned to fight this wave of instantaneous faith. I see a Non-Believer woman cross herself, then gaze down at her hand with an expression of immense puzzlement.

"Come closer, my children," booms the Messiah.

The crowd moves tentatively, as if approaching something wild. They can only get so far—a barrier of Peacemakers has formed in front of the actor, keeping everyone at a safe distance. Behind it, I see Masterson, Blackmore, and Mulvey. They make exaggerated faces of surprise and gratitude, grasping one another's hands. I can hear Masterson's incredulous exclamation: "We're saved! We're saved!" Here and there, I see men positioned with news cameras; they turn to capture the sight.

"You have been so faithful," the Messiah continues, "so good and true in your belief, in so uncertain a time. Your strength appears superhuman to my Father in heaven. He wishes to reward you for your unwavering belief."

"Praise Him!" a voice in the crowd exclaims, and others echo in a chorus. "Praise Him! Praise Him!" Under that, there's an unintelligible, hopeful murmuring. I watch the arms of the faithful rise in a staggered wave, phones in hands to record the scene. Up ahead, I catch sight of Julian. He stoops down, and when he straightens—my heart swells—I see Harp sitting on his shoulders, a camera in her hand.

It's time. I push my way to Frick. He stands in the middle of the mob that pressed in on him—some of their hands still grasp the sleeves of his jacket. He watches the Messiah with a look of stunned outrage on his face.

"My children," the Messiah continues over the grateful voices of the faithful, "you shall not die tonight."

The Believers in the mob cheer and surge, hands outstretched, wanting to touch him. I take Frick's arm and drag him forward.

"Bless the Church," says the Messiah, "for opening your eyes to the error of your ways. Bless the Prophet Frick in heaven, for leading you into the kingdom of glory. Bless him"—the Messiah raises a shiny copy of the New Apocalypse Edition of the Book of Frick—"for leaving us this miraculous book, this new edition of his Holy Word, available for only nineteen ninety-nine at Church of America megastores worldwide."

"Look!" a voice at my shoulder calls. "Praise God! The Prophet Frick has returned to us! Amen!"

We elbow our way through the crowd. When they see us, Believers gasp and cheer. I see the Messiah falter at the uproar Frick's presence has inspired. He hasn't noticed the prophet yet, but I watch Masterson focus on the circle of joyous frenzy surrounding Frick and me. His brow furrows and my heart leaps, because I know we have him now: he was only going to bring Frick to the fore if they could control him, keep him quiet. They had no idea how furious Frick would be with this display. The Messiah spots Frick and—apparently improvising—beckons him forward. I give Frick a push, and the Peacemakers break apart, their faces dumb with amazement, to let him pass through.

"Ah," the Messiah says, his grin uneasy, "let us together rejoice in this miracle! Your prophet is risen, and stands before you to lead you again in faith!"

Masterson helps Frick onto the stage, and I see him whisper furiously into the old man's ear. But Frick gives no indication he's listening. He glares at the cheering crowd, raising a hand to silence them, and though Masterson pulls at him, trying to get him out of the range of the Messiah's microphone, Frick won't move.

"You," says Frick, gazing murderously upon his faithful followers. "You accept this false idol without hesitation, without question?"

The exultant mob wilts. The Messiah flinches and tries to speak over him ("Oh, good prophet, we are so—we rejoice at your resurrection—we—") but Frick has more practice addressing large crowds, and he booms over the Messiah with ease.

"You believe the fairy story he tells you? You refuse to accept your imminent destruction, the swallowing of this world into hell? You disgust me with your treachery, your simple-minded acceptance of this lie. You doomed, luckless heathens! The time of your annihilation is nigh!"

Masterson snaps at nearby Peacemakers, and a gang of them ascends the platform to take Frick, though they seem as perplexed and distressed as the rest of the crowd. Frick struggles against them, screaming bloodily. I hear a current of alarm spread behind me; someone cries out, "Let him speak!"

"Fellow Believers—" Masterson takes a step forward, adjusting the flower on his lapel. He speaks in the cool, intelligent voice he uses on talk shows. "Resurrection is an extremely disorienting process, and the Prophet Frick is simply tired. Forgive him his puzzling remarks. Dear Lord, won't you say a prayer for those collected here?"

But the Messiah seems nervous, aware of the shift in the murmuring crowd; he doesn't hear Masterson's plea. The Angel calls again, sharply, "Lord!"—and only then does the actor realize he's being addressed. He again summons the beatific look of the savior, spreading his arms wide.

"Dear Father," he intones, "bless these faithful few, and may they always have the courage to align themselves with the Church of goodness and rightness. Keep watch over your prophet, Frick; may he return quickly to his senses."

But then the Messiah ducks, and there's a crashing sound—someone has hurled a glass from the bar; it explodes against the wall behind him. The sight of the savior ducking for cover is not inspiring, and the crowd begins to boo. My body trembles at the sound, as if it's music—beautiful, swelling music. I feel a calm, happy warmth spread from the center of me. The jeers grow louder and louder, as Frick tries to wrestle his way out of the Peacemakers' grip, and I watch giddily as Ted Blackmore makes a break for it. He darts off the side of the platform, into the waiting arms of the crowd. Masterson doesn't notice; he holds a fistful of the Messiah's robes and spits unintelligible words into the actor's ear. But the Messiah's face is sharp with fear; he shakes his head.

"I'm sorry," he says, the mike picking up every word. "This is too much for me. I just don't have the training."

Michelle Mulvey lets out an anguished cry, and she too goes running—but the Peacemakers, their allegiance shifting with every passing second, are ready for her; they catch and hold her in place. I turn my head to seek Harp, aloft on Julian's shoulders—she doesn't see me; she's beaming at the scene her camera records. There's a violent push then that knocks me forward. The Messiah is backed against the wall, looking frightened, and Frick continues to shout incoherently. The Believers struggle toward the platform; I realize with a cold panic that a stampede is about to break out, that I'm standing right at the head of it.

The world is watching, and if we're going to win, we need to do it with as little bloodshed as possible. But how to calm them? I search the crowd around me for my friends—Elliott or Birdie or Colby, even one of the New Orphans, anyone who can help me hold back this tide.

Then I feel a tap on my shoulder: Edie Trammell stands beside me. I don't understand how she made her way through the crowd without injury. I'm half convinced she just materialized here, feeling her presence needed. Beside Edie stands Joanna. Their hands are entwined.

"Edie!" I cry over the thunder of outrage behind me. "We need to hold them back!"

But Edie just turns to me, winks. Then she bounds up the platform, pulling Joanna with her. She plants herself in front of the cowering Messiah and stares expectantly at the crowd, waiting for them to silence themselves, and astonishingly—as if they've been shamed into harmony by Edie's watchful eye—they do.

"Brothers and sisters," Edie says when she's sure the room is listening. "I know your confusion and your anger. We have put our faith—among the most precious of our human abilities, our capacity for believing without seeing—into a cruel lie. The Church of America is a lie. The deluded, hateful beliefs of a maniac, monetized and profited from by this man"—she waves dismissively at Pierce Masterson—"and his associates. We've lost our families. Some of us have lost our freedom. We're here to tell you what happened to the so-called saved Believers of the first Rapture." Edie nods to Joanna. "But before we do—"

I hear a scream and the pop of a gunshot. The crowd erupts once more. I cry out and leap forward, my eyes on Edie, but she stands unhurt, looking surprised. She glances over at Masterson with mild interest, and when I follow her gaze, I see his right shoulder horribly dark with blood. He drops the pistol he'd taken from his holster, clapping a hand over his wound. Masterson turns a pale glance to someone at the front of the crowd. Kimberly stands there, giving him a cheerful wave, Dragoslav perched on her shoulder. Masterson begins to wail.

Edie watches him sympathetically, then glances down at the

Peacemakers. "Would one of you be so good as to take him out of here? Thank you *so* much," she says, when two hustle forward to comply. "You're *so* helpful. God bless you. If there are any doctors in the house, could we get Mr. Masterson some medical attention? It would be a shame if he were to pass away before he's prosecuted for his crimes."

The hush of the crowd seems to have taken on a new tone, a watchful stillness—they're transfixed by Edie's calm warmth, her control, her apparent disinterest in the fact that she has just narrowly escaped an assassination attempt.

"What I wanted to say," she continues, "was this: The world is dark, and frightening. This country is huge and unknown. Some lie in wait, wanting to manipulate us, to turn us against one another—for money, or for power. It doesn't matter. All I know is they will not be able to do it if we hold tight to one another. If we find in ourselves the capacity to love without fear or condition, to accept the humanity of others as simple, irrefutable fact. I believe we are capable of this. I believe we're each of us good enough to work toward this. Who knows how much longer we have? Who knows when and why we'll eventually vanish into oblivion? It's easy to hide ourselves away from one another, to cloak ourselves in distrust, to extend our love to only a few, and privilege our own welfare over the fate of people we've never met. But I believe the business of being human is so much bigger, and so much better, than that."

I feel a warm hand slip into mine. Peter stands beside me, looking exhausted. His right eye is shiny with a burgeoning bruise, and he has a deep gash across one cheek. With a frown, he touches the corner of my bloody lips. He inclines his head to the side, and together we turn away from Edie to make our way through the crowd. They're listening to her, faces open and calm, some crying. I can't help but wonder—if the first charismatic speaker to stand up in front of the nation following the fall of the Church had preached a message of violence and doubt, would the people of America have clung to that just as quickly?

Peter glances back to make sure I'm still with him, and I smile, happy he can't hear my cynical thoughts at this moment. Slowly we make our way to Harp, who films Edie's speech from her perch on Julian's shoulders with an expression of deep amusement. When she sees us, she taps Julian's head; he crouches to let her dismount. Harp hands him her camera and kisses his cheek; I watch his face flush as he straightens. My best friend skips over to us and leaps onto me, folding her legs around my waist. I laugh in my surprise, and a nearby Believer, attentive to Edie's words, hushes us with a prim frown.

"Ugh." Harp sticks her tongue out at the woman when her back is turned. "Let's get out of here. I need some *air.*"

She drops to her feet. Together we move in the direction of the door, but I stop when we reach the staircase.

My mother descends, red-eyed, her whole front soaked with blood. The sight of her brings it back like a bad dream: Winnie. I break away from Harp and Peter and maneuver through a cluster of entranced Believers. My mother sees me then and she stops on the last step, her whole body shuddering as she weeps.

I rush to her and pull her close, smelling her sweat and the tang of my sister's blood; she folds her arms around me and cries into my hair. My eyes well up too, but I try to hold it together. There will come a day when I'll have to really feel Winnie's loss, when I'll think of everything she did for me, the oasis she provided in a country that wanted me dead. I'll have to imagine then all the sunny future days we will not spend together. But for now, I have to hold it in. My work isn't done yet—we still need to flee the hotel and the city before the wildfire destroys it all. One day, I'll let myself think of the sisters Winnie and I could have been—the sisters we haltingly, happily were. But not today. My mom pulls away and reaches into her bag. She pulls out a set of keys and hands them to me: Winnie's.

"Diego told me to give you these," she whispers. "He said he'll be down soon and he'll bring—he'll bring her with him." She begins to cry all over again. "I'm sorry . . . it's just—I thought we were going to be a family. Earlier, when we were all together—I was so happy. I thought we would be able to take care of one another."

"We're still a family," I tell her. "You and I. And Winnie and Dad, too. Just because they're gone doesn't mean we're not a family."

My mother glances across the crowd at the platform on which Edie stands; then she turns back to me. She wipes her eyes with her sleeve. "I know you're right. I just—I don't want to let you down, Vivian. I want to be a good mother to you. I want to be the *right* kind of mother."

"There's no right kind. Just be yourself, Mom. Just be yourself and be there for me, and seriously—that will be enough."

"Okay," Mom says, but she's distracted now. Her attention has been caught by Edie's warm, thunderous voice, and I look at my old classmate with her. Edie leans in to the Messiah to speak clearly into his microphone; she talks passionately of her belief in a God with a plan for us, a God who won't let us die alone. I glance at my mother. Her mouth opens slightly in her absorption.

"Mom? We need to leave soon—the fire is getting close. I'm

going to go out and bring Winnie's car closer to the front gate, okay?"

"Mmm?" Her arms slip from around me and she begins to drift toward the back of Edie's rapt audience. "Okay, sweetie. I'll be here. Just let me know . . ."

I gaze for a moment at the back of her head, her long curly hair I love so much. Harp edges over, a careful expression on her face, waiting for me to react. Maybe she thinks my heart is breaking. Even I'm surprised that it's not. I know now that my mother will always be searching. I can't divert her from her quest for herself; I can't insist that I alone should be enough for her. She is more than just my mother—she's a person all her own, and she has a right to seek answers. She's just not satisfied yet. I realize that a part of me loves that about her, even as it hurts. I make a pact with myself at this moment: Even if my mother never finds the thing that turns her life into the story she wants to tell, I'll always be there for her. I'll always care.

But that doesn't mean I won't go searching too.

Harp takes my arm, and together with Peter we walk down the short set of steps and out into the night. The sun hangs lower in the sky now, and for the first time since we came to Los Angeles, I feel a slight, shivery breeze. We make our way down the long drive, past the people who still mill outside on the winding lanes, tending to the wounded and discussing the evening's events in low, outraged tones. On Sunset Boulevard, Winnie's car still sits where she parked it, all the doors flung wide open. I see it sparkling in the sun. The smell of smoke is stronger now, and when I look up, I see the black cloud hanging ominously over the hotel. It's time for us to move.

"Edie needs to get everybody out of there," Peter observes.

"Let's give her a few more seconds," I say. "It's a nice speech."

"Besides," Harp adds, a little sarcastically, "she's laying important groundwork for the up-and-coming Church of Umaymah."

Peter's eyes widen. "You don't really think that's what she's trying to do, do you?"

"*Trying?*" Harp echoes. "Probably not. *Accomplishing?* Almost definitely. But I'm not complaining. Life is long and dumb and devastating. People should believe whatever they need to believe to get by. And let's face it—whatever's in Edie's head is probably better than most. Still, I wish she'd wrap up." Harp puts a hand to her stomach, frowning. "If we don't burn to death first, I'm definitely going to die of hunger. Aren't they supposed to have good Mexican food here? I'd sell my soul to Beaton Frick for a motherfucking burrito."

I laugh. Then I glance at Wilkins's watch, and what I see there makes me shiver with a loose, giddy surge of pleasure. I hold my wrist out so Harp and Peter can see.

"Look."

Both the minute and the hour hand are solidly on the twelve, but as we watch, the second hand swings past. 12:00, Pacific Time: the first minute into the day after the apocalypse.

Harp starts to laugh; racing away from us, she throws herself into an awkward cartwheel in the middle of the abandoned road. Peter seems unable to speak. He slips his arm across my shoulders and kisses me on my bruised head. We have to go back inside, find my mother and our friends, get everyone out of the city before it turns to ash. After that—who knows? We have no real idea how much time we have left. I only know I'm capable of facing it so long as I have these two people by my side. I drink in the sight of Winnie's abandoned car waiting for us. I think of wind in my hair, the salt of ocean in my mouth, the radio blasting—Peter in the passenger seat, tapping the beat on his knees, and Harp in the back, singing at the top of her lungs. The keys are in my pocket. There is still so much work to be done. The horizon ahead is unreachable, but on the way, there are so many possibilities.

For the first time in I can't remember how long, I have a question on the tip of my tongue for which there is no definite answer. It is all fear and all promise, as wide open as the highways that wait for us. When Harp stands upright, and Peter turns to me, his eyes bright with anticipation, I try to hold my laughter at bay long enough to ask it:

"Where do you want to go now?"

ACKNOWLEDGMENTS

I am so grateful to my fantastic agent, Sarah Burnes; my wise editor, Margaret Raymo, my thoughtful copyeditor, Karen Sherman, my tireless publicist, Rachel Wasdyke, and everyone at Houghton Mifflin Harcourt; Emily Thomas, Jenny Jacoby, Jan Bielecki, Ruth Logan, and my friends at Hot Key Books; Salvatore Pane and Manjula Martin for reading the first draft with such intelligence and care; the rest of my indispensable San Francisco writing group—Melissa Chandler, Kate Garklavs, Melissa Graeber, Brandon Petry, Arianna Stern, plus members emeritus Phillip Britton and Denise Morrow—for weekly smarts, jokes, encouragement, and inspirational devotion to the blood moon; my Harp, Alice Yorke, and the rest of my friends and family for their support, free promotion, and use of their names—especially Kimberly Townsend, Lizz Tooher, Corinne Brenner, Caitlin Landuyt, and Rachel Fershleiser, Queen of the Booternet.

Thank you to my husband, Kevin Tassini, who makes all things possible and lets me steal his ideas. And most of all, thank you to my parents, the kindest and most supportive people in the world, who are absolutely nothing like Vivian Apple's parents.

ACTON
PUBLIC LIBRARY
60 OLD BOSTON POST RD.
OLD SAYBROOK
CT 06475
860/395-3184